HARLEQUIN
HEARTWARMING

Rancher to the Rescue

USA TODAY BESTSELLING AUTHOR
Patricia Forsythe

LARGER PRINT

"You can't sell off any part of Eaglecrest, Brady," she said, lifting a stricken face.

He leaned forward and gently asked, "Do you have a better solution?"

"I don't know," she choked out. "But there has to be one."

"What is it you're so afraid of?"

Tears ran down her face as she said, "You're putting everything at risk. It's all I have left of my mother and you're going to give it away to strangers, people who didn't even know her—"

"No, Zannah."

Full of pity and sorrow, he tried to pull her into his arms, to comfort her.

She jerked away. "You don't understand. You've never been rooted in a place the way I am. This ranch is my security."

"And it still will be, Zannah."

She surged to her feet and stood facing him, hands clenched at her sides. "You lied to me. You said you weren't a corporate raider, but that's what you are."

Dear Reader,

Writing a book set on a ranch is always a joy and a challenge. Many of my relatives have been ranchers who often talked about changes in the market, the best kinds of grass to plant to fatten up their cattle and the mistakes they'd made over the years, as well as the triumphs. As I write and create characters and their situations, I try to recall those conversations and make the problems and solutions as real as possible.

In *Rancher to the Rescue*, Zannah Worth and Brady Gallagher enter into an unexpected partnership engineered by her father, who has decided he's ready to retire and pursue a new interest. Zannah doesn't like change and doesn't want a partner. Brady is all about new ideas and changing things up, so getting together on any issue is quite a ride—especially the falling-in-love part.

I hope you enjoy this visit to the Eaglecrest Ranch and cowboy college.

Happy reading,

Patricia Forsythe

HEARTWARMING

Rancher to the Rescue

—

Patricia Forsythe

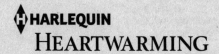

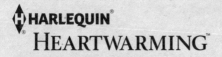

HARLEQUIN®

HEARTWARMING™

ISBN-13: 978-1-335-88963-8

Rancher to the Rescue

Copyright © 2020 by Patricia Knoll

Recycling programs
for this product may
not exist in your area.

This edition published by arrangement with Harlequin Books S.A.

For questions and comments about the quality of this book,
please contact us at CustomerService@Harlequin.com.

Harlequin Enterprises ULC
22 Adelaide St. West, 40th Floor
Toronto, Ontario M5H 4E3, Canada
www.Harlequin.com

Printed in U.S.A.

Patricia Forsythe is the author of many romance novels and is proud to have received her twenty-five-book pin from Harlequin. She hopes there are many more books to come. A native Arizonan, Patricia loves setting books in areas where she has spent time, like the beautiful Kiamichi Mountains of Oklahoma. She has held a number of jobs, including teaching school, working as a librarian and as a secretary and operating a care home for children with developmental disabilities. Her favorite occupation, though, is writing novels in which the characters get into challenging situations and then work their way out. Each situation and set of characters is different, so sometimes the finished book is as much of a surprise to her as it is to readers.

Books by Patricia Forsythe

Harlequin Heartwarming

Oklahoma Girls

His Twin Baby Surprise
The Husband She Can't Forget
At Odds with the Midwife

Her Lone Cowboy

Visit the Author Profile page
at Harlequin.com for more titles.

This book is dedicated to my dear friend Roz Denny Fox, a wonderful writer who has been a constant source of inspiration and encouragement over the years.

CHAPTER ONE

"Do you think we should be taking bets on whether that guy is more likely to injure himself or someone else?"

"What?" Zannah Worth looked up from the pile of unpaid bills she'd found in her father's desk. She glanced at Sharlene Wahl, longtime head housekeeper at Eaglecrest Ranch and Cowboy College. Joining Sharlene at the window, she looked out at the dozen new students who were starting the week-long course to learn horsemanship and the cattle business. "Who are you talking about?"

Sharlene pointed. "That guy in the black hat that looks like it should still have the price tag dangling from the brim. Sits a horse like he's wearing iron underpants. Did you ask him if he'd ever been on a horse before?"

Zannah looked where Sharlene was pointing. "Oh, Brady Gallagher. Yes, he said he had."

Sharlene shook her head. "Did he mention if it was recently, maybe on a merry-go-round?"

Zannah snickered at the mental image of the tall, solemn-faced man sitting atop a carousel pony, then forced herself to look stern. "He did say it was a while ago." She gave Sharlene a pained look. "And you've got to quit making snarky comments about the guests."

"And you've got to quit laughing when I do. Besides, snarkiness is my superpower."

Zannah raised an eyebrow at her.

"I'm too old to change," Sharlene teased. All innocence, she glanced away and fluffed the short, outrageously blond hairdo that made her look far younger than her sixty-five years. Her lifetime of physical work on ranches and in the hospitality industry had made her strong of body and determined of mind. She had two young women working for her on the housekeeping staff and had advertisements up to hire another. Zannah knew that even with more help, Sharlene would still outwork any of them.

"It's never too late to change, or so I've heard you say," Zannah pointed out.

"Hmm. I hate it when you quote me back to me."

Zannah laughed then returned to the window to study the rider. He sat leaning forward in the saddle as if he expected his horse to bolt and he was trying to get ready for it. However, the mare was bighearted, laid-back and eager to please. She wouldn't be going anywhere without her rider's direction, but the rider didn't seem to know what that direction should be. "Mr. Gallagher does seem a little tense."

"And he's got a death grip on the reins."

"Maybe he's scared."

"Zannah, honey, take another look at him. I doubt he's ever been afraid of anything in his life. No, something else is going on with him. You talked with him last night. Do you think he's fearful? Or shy?"

Frowning, Zannah peered more closely at the man she had met at last night's barbecue along with all the other new arrivals. The group seemed to be a lively bunch, including three families with small children, but Gallagher had been quiet, observing those around him, listening to the ongoing conversations, though not initiating any, and responding politely whenever anyone spoke to him. Thinking about it now, Zannah realized he hadn't answered any questions about himself but had redirected interest onto whoever he was talking to at the time. He had asked a couple of people who were returning guests what they liked about the experience at Eaglecrest. She thought it was probably because he wasn't sure how he was going to like the place. She had seen that before, but most often, unsure guests ended up loving not only the ranch but the full experience.

She had exchanged a few words with him, so she knew he was here alone. That wasn't uncommon, but their most frequent guests were family groups or a collection of friends, usually men, who wanted an out-of-the-ordinary story to tell the guys in their offices back home.

Most of their guests were only here for fun, but this one-week course taught the basics of ranching and often served to pique the interest of some of the guests who would return later for the longer course. Zannah doubted that Mr. Gallagher would be one of those returning.

As for his horsemanship, Sharlene was right. From what she could see, he wasn't afraid of his horse, but he wasn't taking command, either.

After last week's group of hard-drinking men, she was glad to have one who was as quiet as Gallagher seemed to be. He had listened carefully as she explained that Eaglecrest was a working ranch and they would be participating in real ranch work, including riding, vaccinating, herding cattle and camping out.

"No, I don't think he's fearful or shy," she finally said in answer to Sharlene's question. "I thought he seemed...solid."

"Do you mean stodgy?"

"No, I mean genuine, or stable." She paused. "Although I'm not quite sure what I'm basing that on, since I only spoke to him for a minute. The impression I got from him, I suppose."

"First impressions are very telling."

"Or they can be completely wrong." Zannah gave a small shrug as she tried to sort through the numerous impressions from last night's barbecue. "This week we've got the Bardle family—mom, dad, three kids—all eager to be here..."

"I know." Sharlene grinned. "Their little

boy was ready to get started at six this morning, running around outside in nothing but boots and underwear. Fortunately, his dad got him back inside."

Zannah laughed. "Then we have two couples who are best friends, a single dad and his two daughters. They all seem like they want to learn and have fun, but Mr. Gallagher is all business."

She glanced at the papers she had dug out of the desk. "I can't find any paperwork on him."

"And you might not if Gus was in charge of it."

"I know," Zannah answered on a sigh.

"He's never liked doing paperwork, or keeping the books."

"I know, but it's still necessary." Zannah waved the papers in the air. "This is no way to run a business. He's lived and breathed this ranch almost his whole life, and now it's as if he's lost focus."

Sharlene gave her a searching look. "He has. I'm glad you're here to take over." She smiled sympathetically at Zannah's dismay. "And it will probably help to have Joelle and Emma here for the summer. His granddaughters will remind him why he's worked so hard to maintain Eaglecrest."

Zannah smiled. "I hope so," she said.

Sharlene returned her attention to Gallagher. "Maybe he's one of those people who can't relax." The housekeeper stepped away and picked up the trash can beside the desk. As she emptied it into a large plastic bag, she went on. "Still, I think you need to watch that one."

"I will," Zannah answered as Sharlene left the office to continue her trash pickup. Even though she teased the housekeeper for her comments about the guests, Sharlene was always spot-on with her observations, which usually helped the staff when working with newcomers.

She was probably right that something else was going on with Gallagher. Zannah watched as he glanced around to see what everyone in the group was doing. He picked up the reins and gave them a slight shake to get Belinda moving. The mare took a couple of steps and stopped, ears twitching uncertainly because she didn't know what was expected of her.

Zannah shook her head. She knew that her

cousin Phoebe had carefully matched each rider to a horse. One of the reasons for the get-to-know-you barbecue was so Phoebe could study the clients and choose a mount for them. It never paid to put a rider and a horse together who had opposite dispositions. Which meant Phoebe had given the easygoing mare to Gallagher because she thought they would make a good match.

In addition, Phoebe demonstrated the standard riding techniques step-by-step. She was an excellent teacher and certainly had the experience to back up her lessons. She had ridden since infancy and had been Arizona state barrel-racing champion three years running. And she had taught riding at Eaglecrest for six years. Maybe this guy only needed more time and individual attention.

Phoebe's usual assistant, Juan Flores, was off for several days, taking his mother to doctors' appointments in Tucson. Since Phoebe was busy with other students, she probably hadn't noticed Gallagher's struggles.

Zannah gave a despairing look at the papers she'd found. She was glad to leave the mess in the office behind. Although she'd been back on Eaglecrest for six months, it had only been in the past few weeks that her dad had let her take over the bookkeeping for the ranch. She'd been shocked at the financial state of the business and even more shocked at how little she truly understood about the complexity of the ranch's operations.

She tried to smooth back the stray curls that relentlessly escaped her ponytail, then clapped on the Stetson her brother, Casey, had given her as she hurried outside.

As she whirled out the door, she stumbled against someone and was caught by two rough hands, which gripped her shoulders. She looked up to face her father.

"Hey, girl, where you going in such a hurry?" August Worth asked. He released her and rocked back slightly on his heels as he looked her over, then met her eyes. He was nearing seventy, and his hair was turning white. But except for some joint stiffening, he was still strong and healthy, his focused gaze as clear and blue as ever. They were the same height now that time and arthritis had taken its toll on his body. "I thought you were going over the books today, planning to balance the accounts on that fancy computer program of yours."

"I'm going to help Phoebe. Juan is off for several days, remember?" She nodded toward the corral. "Mr. Gallagher seems to be having some trouble." She gave him a steady look. "And I would happily balance the accounts today if I could find all the receipts. There was a big stack of them crammed into your desk."

He glanced away. "Oh, yeah, I forgot about those. I meant to give them to you."

Zannah closed her eyes briefly, reaching for patience. "I can't believe that in all this time, I didn't give a minute's thought to checking your desk. Dad, you never used to cram important papers away like that. What are you thinking? What's going on?"

Gus tilted his head and looked up, not meeting her gaze as he hedged. "I didn't cram them away, honey. I left them where I could find them when I got around to them."

"It seemed like you were hiding them."

"I needed the desktop for something more important."

Zannah glanced back. Now that she thought about it, it was true that the desk was unusually neat.

Her dad made a restless move. "Nothing is going on. Nothing."

She narrowed her eyes at him. "I know you fought tooth and nail against me taking over the bookkeeping, but we've got to modernize…"

"Yeah, yeah, I know. It's an old argument, and you won."

Zannah stared at him in dismay. "I thought you were okay with it. This way, you're freed up to do other things. We talked about this for a year before I moved back home."

"I am. I am." He held his hands up as if he was trying to ward off her questions. "Gotta go."

"You've always been busy, but lately I hardly ever see you."

Gus gave a small shrug but didn't answer. He had never been one to share his deepest thoughts, but he'd never been so reluctant to answer her questions, either, which only made her transition to managing the ranch that much harder.

"I can't run this place if you don't help me get everything I need." She tried to sound reasonable, not let her frustration seep into her voice, because that only seemed to fuel his stubbornness.

"Ah, you can figure it out. I didn't have any

training in bookkeeping when we started the cowboy college, and we did fine."

"That's because Mom did the books. And after you took over, you were audited twice," Zannah pointed out, looking at him with a mixture of annoyance and loving exasperation. "It's really important that we account for every penny. From what I can tell, our profit margin is thinner than a knife blade, and I had to request an extension on our taxes."

"Well, then I guess it's a good thing that you're here to save the day." He nodded as if it was all settled. "Yup, I have full confidence that you're going to take care of everything in case I need to be gone for a little while."

"Gone?" Zannah stared at him. "Where are you planning to go? This is the first I've heard of you being gone."

"A little vacation." He waved a hand in the air. "Only taking a little vacation."

"When have you *ever* taken a vacation? Or even a day off?" Memories of ten years ago flashed through her mind. It had been the worst months of their lives, with him working every day, chasing stray cattle and daydreams, disappearing into the mountains for hours at a time. He hadn't been vacationing, though. He'd been avoiding her mother's sickroom, leaving the burden of care on his twenty-year-old daughter's shoulders.

Zannah stuffed those mental pictures down. She couldn't face them right now.

"Everyone deserves a little vacation once in a while, right?"

"Of course, but…"

"Gallagher, huh?" Gus broke in, nodding toward the corral. "Be nice to him."

"Who? Gallagher?" It took her a moment to redirect her thoughts back to the guest she'd been on her way to help. "I'm always nice to our guests."

"Yeah, well, sometimes you're a little prickly."

"Prickly?"

"Yeah, and this guy's important."

Zannah studied him for a second, then stepped around so he'd have to look her in the eye. "Important, how?" she asked.

"Just…important, so don't be mule-headed like you get sometimes."

"I'm not mule-headed. I'm focused and… single-minded, but if I ever *am* stubborn, I learned it from you."

Gus brushed that statement aside. "I'm only trying to tell you to be nice to Gallagher."

Hands on her hips, Zannah eyed him suspiciously. "Dad, what's going on?"

"Uh, nothing." Gus turned and hurried away. "I've got work to do," he said over his shoulder.

"Fine, but get me the rest of those receipts— and Mr. Gallagher's record of payment. I can't find it."

He waved a hand. "Sure, sure. See you later." He zipped around the corner.

"For a man who's always complaining about his arthritis, he can haul his behind when he needs to," she muttered, continuing to the corral.

As she walked, she glanced up at the sandstone cliffs, striped in hues of tan, white, brown and deep red. Eaglecrest was nestled in a beautiful little valley, bisected by the San Ramon River. It backed up to the cliffs, and farther to the west, the property spread out into rangeland. In the distance, she could see the foothills of the White Mountains. The view always made her happy. She had missed it so much during the years she had lived in

Las Vegas that she never failed to appreciate it now.

Eaglecrest Ranch had belonged to her mother's family, the Graingers, since the 1920s and had gone through many financial ups and downs along with the price of beef. Matters had improved when her father had started the cowboy training college. He had fully focused on it, and the running of the ranch, ever since her mother died.

Now, though, Zannah didn't know what was happening with him. He'd never been a big reader, but lately, he'd been studying topographical maps. When she'd asked about them, he'd whisked them away and said he was doing some research.

She knew that over the past few years, she had become wary and suspicious, questioning people's motives. She didn't want to be like that, and certainly not with her dad. Still, she knew there was something going on.

She glanced around to see that all their other guests were following Phoebe's instructions and getting to know their horses. Mr. Bardle had his excitable six-year-old boy, Liam, on the saddle in front of him, carefully showing him how to use the reins to flex the animal's head smoothly from side to side. Some of the guests were on horseback, walking their mounts around the corral, and the others were almost there.

She caught Phoebe's attention and pointed to herself and then Gallagher, indicating she was on her way to help him. Her cousin gave her a nod and a grateful smile.

As she approached, she saw that Gallagher was still sitting stiffly in the saddle and had an expression on his face that said he would like to be almost anywhere else.

He didn't look scared, though. More resolute, as if he was going to get through this no matter what. Again, she thought of the previous evening and the watchful attitude he had shown. There was something about him that felt odd to her. She shook it off, reminding herself he was a paying guest who deserved the best experience possible at Eaglecrest.

"Good morning, Mr. Gallagher," she called out as she approached him. "How are you and Belinda getting along?"

Gallagher pulled back on the reins to stop Belinda, who had been taking uncertain steps. He looked down at Zannah as she strolled up to Belinda's head and looped her arm under the mare's neck. She stroked the silky hair and black mane as she smiled up at him.

"Not sure," he answered, resting his hands on the saddle horn. "Call me Brady. And I don't know much about this."

"Well, that's why you're here, so you can learn. What seems to be the problem?"

"This horse…"

"Belinda," Zannah supplied.

"Belinda doesn't seem to understand what I want her to do." His expression was serious, and his head cocked slightly as he waited for her answer.

Zannah continued to smile, trying to lighten the mood. "You only need to relax. She's a smart girl. She can tell that you're tense, but don't worry, she's taken care of newbies before." Zannah looked down to see that his shiny new boots were in the stirrups at an awkward angle. His calves weren't snug against Belinda's flanks so he could easily give her direction.

"Oh, here's part of the problem," she said, placing her hand on his knee. He jerked, causing Belinda to move back. Gallagher took the reins in one hand and reached down with the other to soothe the horse.

"Oh, I'm sorry, Mr. Gallagher—uh, Brady," Zannah said. "I didn't mean to startle you."

"It's okay. Like I said, I don't know much about this."

She paused and blinked as she processed how he'd gone from awkwardly holding the reins to expertly quieting the mare. In an instant, he was back to looking unsure of himself. She refocused, wondering if she had imagined it.

"Sit straight, but easy in the saddle. Your job is to let her know who's boss. Keep your calves tight against her ribs. That's how you'll give her directions. Horses are a lot like little kids. They need to know someone's in charge. Don't worry. You two will get used to each other, and she'll be your partner the whole time you're here at Eaglecrest."

"Oh, yeah? I can't change horses if I need to?" Brady asked.

"You can, but I don't think it will be necessary," she answered, trying to understand the weird vibe she was getting from him. "You and Belinda need to become friends and partners."

"Maybe we got off to a bad start," he said.

"I'll dismount and you can show me how to get going with her."

"Didn't Phoebe do that?" Zannah asked, glancing to where her cousin was speaking earnestly to a nervous young girl on the back of a placid pinto.

"Yeah, but I guess I missed something." Brady stepped down and stood beside her.

Zannah looked up at him, taking in his solemn expression and the watchfulness in his deep brown eyes. He was tall, a couple of inches over six feet, with a square jaw and thick, dark eyebrows that matched his mahogany hair.

Zannah gave him an uncertain smile but couldn't think of anything to say. She felt completely out of step, as if she'd put her boots on the wrong feet and was walking backward through thick mud. She hated this feeling.

After a few seconds, he moved away from her. "Why don't we start with saddling and bridling?"

Zannah frowned. "But Belinda's already saddled."

"Maybe I did it wrong."

While she tried to control the "you've got to be kidding me" look that was fighting to take over her face, Zannah checked the cinch and the position of the saddle. "No, you did it exactly right."

"How do you know?" he persisted. "You weren't here when I saddled her."

She held out both hands, palm up. "But I can see the result, so I know you did it correctly. Why do it again?"

"Because the customer is always right?"

Either that or slightly deranged, she thought, but she manufactured a smile even as her bewilderment gave way to growing annoyance. "Of course. If you feel at all uncertain, we'll start again." She stepped back. "Since you put Belinda's saddle on, it should be easy for you to take it off. I'll watch and give you pointers if they're needed."

"Fair enough." He paused. "So, what do I do first?"

"Make sure she doesn't wander off while you unsaddle her." Zannah gestured toward Belinda's head. "That's why there's a halter under the bridle. You tie her to the fence using the halter. If you take the bridle off, she'll think it's time to run and she'll be gone in a flash. Belinda is laid-back, but she loves to run after a trail ride, and you'll have a hard time catching her. You don't want to tie her up with only the bridle, because she could pull on it and hurt her mouth. Don't tie her too tightly. As soon as she's secure, you can take off the saddle."

Brady nodded as if satisfied with her answer, tied up the mare and fumbled a little as he unbuckled the cinch strap. Zannah didn't step in to help. When it came to most aspects of horsemanship, it was necessary to learn by doing.

Grasping the saddle with both hands, Brady lifted it off, placed it on the fence, then removed the saddle blanket. When he tossed it over the top rail, it slid to the ground. Brady crouched down and reached between the fence rails to retrieve it.

Belinda looked around, snorted, shook her head and kicked out with her rear right hoof. She grazed Brady's backside, throwing him off balance.

"Hey!" Brady yelped, scrambling to stand up while Zannah grabbed Belinda's halter to bring her head down and around.

"Belinda," Zannah said firmly, her voice pitched low. "We don't kick the guests."

The unrepentant mare shook her head.

"Don't pretend like you don't know what I'm talking about," Zannah insisted, but Belinda only twitched her ears.

"What was that all about?" Brady asked, dusting off his jeans as he came back to them.

"I don't know," Zannah answered, mortified. "I'm so sorry. She's never done anything like that before."

"That you know of," Brady pointed out. "Haven't you been gone for a while? Only came back a few months ago?"

"Well, yes, but how did you know that?"

"You must have said something last night at the barbecue." Brady met her gaze squarely.

"No, I didn't." She never told the guests that she was new at running Eaglecrest, because she didn't want them to think she didn't know what she was doing. Her uneasy feeling about Brady Gallagher hardened into solid suspicion.

"Let's get back to saddling this horse." He tossed the saddle blanket over Belinda's back. She stood waiting, the picture of tranquility.

Zannah didn't mention that he hadn't removed and replaced the bridle. She wanted to get this lesson over and done.

Brady smoothed the blanket. Belinda flicked her tail up and caught him across the back.

"Has this horse got it in for me?" he asked.

"Of course not. She probably thought she felt a fly, or…something."

Brady's mouth firmed. "See if you can calm her down while I get the saddle."

"Calm down, Belinda," Zannah said dutifully to the serene animal.

After a moment, Brady came back and put the saddle in place. He scooted it too far forward, and Zannah was happy to correct him, taking the emphasis off the mare, who shook herself and flicked her tail again.

This time, Brady was ready for her, holding up his arm to block the sweeping tail.

"It takes a while to learn to adjust a saddle," Zannah said. "But you'll get the hang of it."

Following Zannah's instructions, he settled the saddle into place, buckled and tightened the cinch straps and untied the halter.

"That's perfect," Zannah said, checking the tack. "You did a good job, as I knew you would."

He lifted an eyebrow at her. "Except for crouching down behind her."

"That's true, and I don't know why she kicked out…"

"Yeah, yeah, she's never done that before."

Eager for a change of topic, Zannah said, "Let me see you mount. Remember to relax. She's really a very easygoing horse. Once you get used to her, you'll love her, I promise."

"I'll hold you to that."

As he lightly grasped the reins, he placed his left foot into the stirrup and threw his right leg over Belinda's back.

He gave a self-assured nod, squared his shoulders and shifted in the saddle. That was when Belinda exploded.

Feet dancing, she twisted and turned as Brady held on to the reins and tried to get her under control.

As everyone else turned to see what was happening, Zannah leaped for the horse's head but couldn't grab her before she lifted her front hooves off the ground and dumped Brady into the dirt. Free of her burden, she streaked across the ground and headed for the foothills.

Horrified, Zannah ran to Brady, who lay stunned, blinking up at the sky and trying to catch his breath.

"Are you okay?" she asked, crouching beside him and reaching to help him sit up.

"Ye…heh…hes." He finally managed to get a deep breath. "I…have…haven't been thrown…like that…in twenty years." He shuddered slightly as he filled his lungs with air again and breathed out as he turned to her with a firm gaze. "We're going to have to do something about that horse."

"What do you mean?" Zannah was only half listening as she gently placed her hand on his jaw and turned his head so she could check for bumps and gashes. She was relieved to find none. Across the corral, she saw Phoebe start their way but waved her back to indicate that everything was fine.

"We can't have a skittish animal like that in our string, especially not if we've got small kids and inexperienced riders around."

Zannah straightened and looked into his eyes to check that both pupils were the same size. That done, she finally focused on his words. "She's not skittish. At least, she never has been before, not until she met you—and what do you mean *we*?"

"I mean *we* because I'm about to become part owner of that animal."

Zannah frowned and shook her head in puzzlement. "You mean you want to buy Belinda?"

While Zannah stared at him, he stood up easily and offered his hand to pull her to her feet. "I didn't want you to find out this way, but hello, Miss Worth," he said. "I'm pretty sure I'm going to be your new partner."

CHAPTER TWO

"PARTNER?" ZANNAH ASKED. "What are you talking about?" Her expression concerned, she studied him for a second, then asked, "I didn't find a bump, but did you hit your head?"

Brady dusted off his jeans and shirt as he tried to gauge her reaction. She was staring at him in complete puzzlement, her golden-brown eyes examining him as she tried to understand. He certainly hadn't meant for her to find out this way. It was time to explain.

"My head is fine. Your father and I have almost reached an agreement for me to buy into Eaglecrest. We still have a few details to work out, but we shook on it."

Her face cleared as she gave a burst of laughter. "That's hilarious. My father would never accept an investor in the ranch—except for me, of course." She turned to see where

Belinda had gone. "I didn't take you for a joker, Mr. Gallagher."

"Call me Brady," he reminded her.

She waved a hand. "Sure, sure, Brady. Listen, part of learning about horses is learning to catch one. There's a patch of grass by the river that's Belinda's particular favorite, so if you're not injured…"

"Zannah, what did you do?" Gus Worth demanded as he hurried up to them. He gave his daughter a fierce glare, then turned to look Brady over, checking for injuries.

"Me?" Zannah's voice came out in a squeak as she stared at her father, clearly dumbfounded at what she seemed to see as an unfair accusation. "I didn't do anything to him. Belinda threw Mr. Ga…um, Brady, but…"

"Belinda's never thrown anyone in her life," Gus insisted. "You did something to scare her."

Zannah clapped a hand to her chest. *"Me?"* she asked again. "What on earth are you talking about?"

"I told you not to get prickly with him."

Brady watched Zannah go from puzzled to flabbergasted. He wasn't liking the way this was playing out. It was his own fault, though.

He'd let Gus decide too many of the terms of this agreement, including keeping it a secret from his daughter. But it had been his own idea to come to Eaglecrest as a guest to see how the operation ran—both the ranching and cowboy college sides of things. And he really shouldn't have blurted out the news of the impending partnership. His only excuse was that he'd been rattled by his unexpected flight through the air and meet-up with the ground.

"No, Gus," Brady said, holding up his hand. "I'm sure I did something to scare the mare. I haven't ridden in a while, and..."

Zannah turned on him suddenly, her gaze narrowing. "You haven't ridden in a *while*? You said you don't know much about this, and I assumed you meant riding, horses, ranching, but you also said you hadn't been thrown like that in twenty years."

"I may have understated the facts," Brady answered. He resisted the urge to look away from her stare, which reminded him so much of his fifth-grade teacher. Mrs. Price could get the truth out of even the shiftiest kid simply by locking eyes with them. Zannah didn't look a thing like his old teacher, but she seemed to have that same ability, which was probably why Gus was withering before that look.

Zannah's hands rose to rest at her waist, her shoulders squared, and she rocked back slightly on her heels. Her color began to rise as she asked, "And exactly why would you have done that, Mr. Gallagher?"

Brady cast a quick glance at Gus, who was regarding his daughter as if he was ready to duck and cover.

"I wanted to see exactly how you run this place, including how you deal with in-experienced riders."

"And as a paying guest, you would have seen all of that, experienced all of that, but you're not a paying guest, are you?" She gave her father a furious look. "Is that why I couldn't find any paperwork on him?"

Gus's gaze shifted away from her. "Now, honey, I didn't want you to get upset."

"What is it, in the simplest possible terms, that you didn't want me to get upset *about*?"

Gus looked away, and then back. "If Brady likes what he sees here, he's going to buy in to Eaglecrest."

Zannah stared at her father, her expression

fixed, then shifted her attention to Brady. The two men watched her expectantly, waiting to see what she would do. Brady thought this must be similar to waiting for a volcano to erupt—first a puff of steamy smoke, then a full explosion.

"No, he's not," she snapped.

"Now, honey, I knew you'd react like this. That's why I didn't tell you. We're having a bit of a cash-flow problem…"

"Which I only discovered in the past couple of weeks, and haven't even begun to solve— Oh!" she said, straightening. "This deal is why you didn't want me to take over the bookkeeping, isn't it?"

"Well, see there. Now you won't have to," Gus said in a falsely hearty tone that made Brady cringe. This was rapidly going from bad to worse. "Gallagher here has had all kinds of business experience. Haven't you, Brady? He'll have everything straightened out in no time."

Brady flinched at Gus's tone. He sincerely wished this conversation was taking place somewhere, anywhere other than this public area of the corral.

Her expression incredulous, Zannah turned

to Brady. "If you're such a hotshot business-man, why would you want to invest in an operation that's losing money?"

"It's a challenge." Brady pressed his lips together. It was a lifelong habit he'd never been able to break, even though he knew it looked like a smirk. He was growing more and more uncomfortable and truly angry with Gus. Brady had made it clear that there would be no deal until he saw Eaglecrest's books, but Gus hadn't been forthcoming with the financial records—and now it appeared that Zannah was the one with that information, but she was struggling to make sense of it. He had absolutely no intention of buying in to a sloppy operation or of getting in the middle of a family squabble.

Still, there was something that drew him to this place. He had to be careful and make sure his attraction to the ranch didn't overrule his good judgment.

He'd made his reservation at the cowboy college a couple of weeks ago with Gus and had carried through with it in spite of growing uneasiness with his potential partner's business dealings and insistence on secrecy.

In spite of all that, Brady still wanted to see how they ran the place.

As far as Gus himself was concerned, Brady didn't know if the man had been trying to fool him or his daughter. Maybe he was only fooling himself.

Zannah obviously thought so, too. Her eyes lit with fury. "It's a…a boondoggle, and it's not going to happen."

"Zannah, you need to think about this rationally," Gus said.

"*Why? You* obviously haven't. You…you did this behind my back…didn't even tell me." Her hands fisted at her sides, and tears filled her eyes. "How could you *do* that? And how could you spring it on me like this?"

Brady's gut twisted in dismay. She deserved an explanation, but Gus ducked his head and half turned from her as if he wanted to make a break for it. "Well, honey, I…"

He was interrupted by Phoebe riding up. She said, "Zannah, we're ready to start the short trail ride. Do you want me to go catch… Hey, what's wrong?" She dismounted, rushed to Zannah's side and placed an arm around her shoulders. "What happened? Are you hurt?"

Zannah shook her head, but no one answered. The riding teacher regarded both men with an aggressive glint in her eye.

Gus had told him about all the staff, so Brady knew Phoebe and Zannah were cousins. The two women looked very much alike, with their curly dark blond hair caught up in ponytails. They were of similar build, of medium height, lithe and strong. From a distance, it would be difficult to tell them apart.

And they could muster up identical unyielding stares from their tawny brown eyes.

"Uncle Gus? Mr. Gallagher?" Phoebe asked.

Zannah straightened and drew in a shuddering breath. She responded to Phoebe with a shaky smile. "It's okay. We can talk about it later. Go ahead on the trail ride. The guests are ready." She nodded to where the others were waiting, standing by their horses or already mounted, watching the drama playing out across the way. She gave Brady a look that was much steadier than her voice. "As far as Belinda is concerned, I'm sure she's gone to her favorite place. Mr. Gallagher will go get her. After all, it's not a good idea to lose newly acquired property."

"What?" Phoebe asked.

"Never mind." Zannah summoned a smile. "Have a good ride."

"What's going on?" Phoebe asked, surveying the small group.

"I'll explain later," Zannah answered. "As soon as I understand it myself. If I ever do."

Phoebe regarded them with a confused look, then glanced over to where the other guests were waiting for her. With a nod at Zannah, she returned to her horse. "Oh, okay." She pointed at Zannah. "But don't think I won't keep asking until I get all the details. See you later."

Gus turned and walked away rapidly. Brady almost envied the man his escape. Zannah sent an annoyed look after her father and turned one on Brady that could have singed his eyebrows off if he'd been standing any closer.

"So?" he asked. "How do we track down Belinda?"

"We walk." She gave him a disparaging glance. "And let's hope those new boots don't give you blisters."

"I'll be fine," he answered, hurrying to catch up as she took off at a double-quick pace. He was taller, but she was faster, and she had the advantage of intense fury to speed her along.

"So," she said over her shoulder as he reached her. "How long have you and my father been planning this…"

"Boondoggle?"

"Deal," she responded, then added, "Underhanded deal."

"A few weeks. Listen, Zannah, this is only an investment and, like I said, a challenge."

She stopped so fast and rounded on him so that he had to do some fancy sidestepping to keep from running her down. Color was once again rising into her face. He was beginning to be fascinated by how fast that could happen.

"To you, it's an investment. You don't know anything about this place, which has been in my family for ninety-five years. You want to know about a challenge? Try running a cattle ranch during the worst of the Depression, or during a drought so bad that even the San Ramon River becomes nothing but a trickle, or when the price of beef falls so low that there's no such thing as a profit margin and the only thing you see for miles is red ink."

She stabbed a finger in his direction. "Now *there's* a challenge for you."

She whirled around and stomped away from him, but he doggedly stuck with her.

"Zannah, you have every right to be mad," he began, but she waved her hand as if she wanted to swat him away.

"I don't want to talk about this anymore right now," she said. "And *you* can call me Miss Worth."

That almost got a laugh out of him. Instead of answering, he followed along as they moved onto a rough slope where he had to concentrate on where he was stepping, fighting back a loud groan as he slid on loose gravel. She'd been right about the boots. Blisters were forming.

FURY, PANIC AND feelings of betrayal warred within Zannah as the truth of what her father had done soaked into her mind. Her thoughts chased each other as she tried to pinpoint an emotion on which to focus.

Hurt was number one, she decided. How could Gus have decided to sell half of Eaglecrest to someone, especially someone they didn't know? She cast a glance over her shoulder and saw that Brady was concentrating on his feet, trying to keep up with her. She had walked this path so many times, she barely had to think about it, but the tenderfoot behind her would take a tumble if he wasn't careful.

Who was this guy, anyway, and where had he and Gus met? How much business experience did he have and was any of it in ranching? Or hospitality? How much money was he willing to risk in case she wasn't able to get Eaglecrest's finances stabilized, let alone show a profit? And would he expect to be involved in the day-to-day operations?

Right now, she could see Belinda in her favorite grazing spot by the river. The first order of business was to find out why she'd thrown Brady, then get her back home.

"There she is," she said, pointing.

"I see her," Brady answered grimly.

Zannah stopped and looked at him. "There's no point in being mad at her. She only did what horses do when they want to get someone off their back. It's instinct."

"I know that, and I'm not mad at her." He made a funny little gesture with his lips that

Zannah couldn't interpret, then said, "Are you going to show me how to catch her?"

"Sure, it's easy now that she's had a little bit of a run and a snack. Although, just so you know, it's not a good idea to let a horse eat with a bit in its mouth. It makes for a dirty bit, and they can't chew very well." She smiled sweetly. "But you probably already knew that, because you've had experience with horses before. Since you're here to see how we run the place, you might like to know that's the kind of thing we always tell our guests."

Brady raised an eyebrow. "I'll write that down."

"See that you do."

Zannah walked over to Belinda, who didn't even lift her head from the patch of sweet grass to acknowledge the newcomers. Taking hold of the halter, Zannah spoke to Brady over the mare's neck.

"Come hold her while I check the saddle to find out why she threw you."

Brady took the halter but said, "You watched me saddle her."

"Obviously not closely enough."

She undid the cinch straps and removed the saddle. After setting it on the ground, she lifted it to examine the underside, running her hand over the surface and tilting it up to the light.

"Nothing here."

Next she removed the saddle blanket and flipped it over. "Ah." She held it up for Brady to see. "Sand burrs," she said. "They must have stuck in the blanket when it landed on the ground under the corral fence."

"Mea culpa," he said. "My fault."

"Why yes, it is." She handed the blanket to him. She knew it was partly her fault, too. She'd been so anxious to solve the problem she thought Brady was having that she hadn't focused enough on the mare. "Here. Pick them out while I check her over. Then I'll resaddle her, and we can head back."

Zannah took the halter rope from him and held it while she ran her hand over the mare's sides to make sure there were no burrs stuck in her hair. She found one, and Brady found several in the blanket. Zannah double-checked it, too, before replacing it, along with the saddle.

"There," she said. "We can start back now." She began walking, but Brady hung back. "What's wrong?"

"Okay if I ride?" He gave that odd twist of his lips again. "Your prediction came true. I've got blisters."

Zannah didn't even bother to hide her grin. "Sure." She handed over the halter rope and reins. "Feel free. Are you going to join the trail ride?"

"No, I'll take her to the barn and check to make sure there are no more burrs. Besides, there'll be plenty of time for trail rides later. I'm going to be around for a while."

"So it seems," she murmured.

"We could ride double," he offered, but she shook her head. The thought of sitting behind him, arms around his waist, was one she didn't want to contemplate, and she *really* didn't want to be the one in front, with his arms around her.

"I could do with the walk." She lifted a foot to indicate her well-worn boot. "And these stopped giving me blisters years ago."

She watched as Brady mounted in one smooth motion. "So you *can* ride?" she asked, noting that he was doing everything right that she'd noticed him doing wrong earlier— sitting straight but relaxed in the saddle, hands easily holding the reins and halter rope, calves snug against Belinda's ribs.

"Yeah. Learned years ago on my aunt and uncle's farm. It's like riding a bicycle. You never forget." He touched his heels to Belinda's sides and gave the reins an encouraging shake. The mare took off at a lope with her new, almost part owner giving every appearance of an expert rider.

She watched him go. She could admire a good horseman, but she didn't appreciate having been played.

GUS HURRIED INTO the ranch office, closed the door behind him and considered locking it. He'd known Zannah would be furious with him. He couldn't blame her for that, but there had been no other way out for them. He was convinced of that. Besides, there was something else he had to do, something important, and this was the time to do it.

He didn't have to hide his project anymore. Zannah knew he was getting an investor now. If it didn't turn out to be Brady Gallagher, it would be someone else with equally deep pockets. She would learn about everything else in due course.

Opening an old steamer trunk that he kept beside his desk, he removed the books and maps he'd been keeping secret, enjoying the scent of leather that clung to the items and scratching his nose at the stir of dust that rose to tease him. He opened the desk drawer that Zannah had cleared earlier and used his forearm to sweep everything from the desktop into it so he'd have more room.

He slammed the drawer shut and eagerly settled into his chair. It thrilled him to know that he didn't have to hide these things away anymore but could study them at his leisure.

He quickly became lost in them, making notes as he worked, and barely heard when the door opened and someone came in. He didn't even look up until his daughter said, "Dad. It's time to talk."

When she repeated her statement, Gus had to blink and pull his mind back from the past in order to focus on her.

"Not now, honey. I'm…"

"Ducking me." Hands on hips, she stalked up to the desk. "How could you accuse me of doing something to make Belinda throw Gallagher?"

He looked away from the hurt in her eyes.

"I'm sorry about that, Zan. I guess I was worried. I overreacted."

"But why?"

He gave a small shrug and gestured to the items spread out on his desk.

Zannah looked at the maps and books. "And what on earth are you doing with old geological survey maps?"

His answer came quickly. "I'm planning what I'm going to do next."

"Next? After what?"

"After I turn Eaglecrest over to you…and Gallagher."

"Over to me," she corrected. "Not Gallagher." Her hands rose to her waist and she gave him the kind of no-nonsense stare he used to get from her mother. Esther had never let him get away with being evasive, and their daughter had that same talent.

"I know you're the sole owner, but I've always considered Eaglecrest to be mine, and Casey's, too. He doesn't want to run it. He and I have talked about this." Her voice broke as tears swam in her eyes.

Gus felt a sharp pang of regret as she went on.

"When I made the decision to come home,

learn to run the ranch, I thought you and I would be equal partners."

"Well, now you'll be fifty-fifty partners with Gallagher. He'll be buying in for half, but you'll get your half free and clear. It's your inheritance, your legacy."

Before she could object, he rushed ahead. "I know the ranch is in trouble, Zan. Has been for a couple of years. I kept things afloat by the skin of my teeth. It's slowly gotten worse and worse since your mother died. She was the money manager. And, yeah, I know I've had ten years to get it right, but I was never any good at it." He shrugged, embarrassed. "I always knew that, and now I've dumped the whole mess on you."

"But I can get things back on track. I know I can. We've got long-established guests who love coming back year after year to learn more about ranching, and—"

"But that's only part of the business. You don't ever know what's going to happen with the price of beef."

"We've weathered fluctuations in the market before. We can do it again."

He shook his head. This was something he absolutely knew. "Honey, ranching can beat

the stuffing out of you. It's rewarding. Sometimes it's even fun, but it never gets easier.
Never."

"I'm not afraid of hard work." She swung
out a hand to encompass everything outside the
office. "I started helping out when I was five.
I learned to curry horses while standing on a
stepladder, and I was practically born knowing
how to ride. This place is our heritage—Mom's
and yours and mine, Casey's and Vanessa's and
their kids'."

"I know, and that's why I'm only taking on
a partner, not selling outright. Besides, Gallagher or some other investor will make things
easier on you."

"On me?"

"I don't want to see you working yourself
to death on this place the way…" His voice
trailed off as memories welled up.

"The way Mom did," Zannah finished for
him, her face stricken.

"Ye…yes." He cleared his throat. "And her
father before her, and *his* father."

"But this is different. I came back specifically because I *want* this responsibility. I want
to do this."

"Your mom did, too. Even after we knew

she was sick, she wanted to stay here." His gut clenched at the memory.

"It was her home."

"Yeah, hours away from the best doctors, the best medical care."

Zannah nodded, and Gus watched her face carefully. He knew he was screwing this up, but he had a goal in mind, an important one.

"There was no cure for her. We knew that from the beginning. And it's been ten years, so why are you doing this now—taking on a partner, putting us through this upheaval?"

"When you got your degree in social work and went to work for the state of Nevada, helping people, families in need, I was relieved. You wouldn't make much money, but it was away from here, from being tied to the ranch."

She flinched. "But it beat the stuffing out of me in a different way." Looking puzzled, she shook her head. "What do you mean, tied here? Is that how you feel? You've worked on this ranch since you were sixteen. I thought you loved it as much as Mom did. As much as I do."

"I did when I was younger." He glanced around. "Before it got so…hard. Now, I guess, *obligated* might be a better word. Ninety-five years of obligation. It weighs on you after a while, and I don't want it to be such a heavy burden on you. That's why we need an investor. I asked around about Gallagher and his family. They have a solid background in business. I've told him he's free to explore other moneymaking options."

"Forget Gallagher," she said, waving that aside. "I understand what you're saying, but I'm…mystified about why you didn't tell me this before, as soon as I came back home, or at least when I took over the books."

Gus avoided her gaze, wishing he could have kept all of this to himself. "In for a penny, in for a pound," he murmured.

"What?"

"I talked to Lucas Fordham about buying Eaglecrest."

"Fordham? Seriously?" Zannah's voice fell to a whisper, and the color drained from her face.

Miserably, Gus nodded. "I was only considering my options, but he didn't offer fair market value for the place—not even close."

"Because he's not interested in the ranch itself, only the river access where he can stage

watersports and tear up the environment."
She shook her head, her gaze never leaving
his face. "I can't believe you'd even consider
Fordham. He's ruined his own family's property with his motocross racing course and all-
terrain vehicles chewing up the ground. The
fact that it's all on private land is the only
thing that's kept him from endless violations
of environmental laws—but to turn him loose
on the river. That would affect the whole valley and everyone in it."

Gus held up his hands, palms out. "I know.
I know, and that's one reason I started talking to Gallagher, and…"

"Why did you talk to Fordham about it,
and Gallagher, before telling me? And you
didn't even tell me. I found out completely
by accident."

"I wanted things to be settled, before I told
you."

"But why? Why now? Taking on a partner?
I thought you and I were partners."

He took a deep breath. "I had an—episode
last winter."

As he'd feared, concern, bordering on terror, filled her face as she asked, "What kind
of episode?"

Gus jerked a thumb toward his chest. "I thought it was my ticker—heart attack."

"Oh, no. Why didn't you tell me? Why didn't Sharlene tell me?"

His gaze darted away from her pale face. "She didn't know. No one does. I was out in the truck, pulling the stock trailer, coming back from delivering a couple of heifers to a man over in Kenner. I felt like I had a bull sitting on my chest. Drove straight to the hospital. It wasn't my heart, though, only stress. I decided right then I needed to make some changes." He gave her a cautious look. "Didn't tell you or your brother because I didn't want you to worry—after everything that happened with your mom and all. It's the same reason I didn't tell you about the ranch finances and Gallagher and everything. Didn't want you to worry 'cause it seems like you're just now getting your feet under you…"

She waved her hand to stop him. "Never mind that. Are you okay now?"

"Yeah. Doc said I'll be fine. Need to take it easier."

"Which is why you decided to take on a partner."

"To make things easier on you, too. I told Gallagher that I'll only agree to the deal with him if he'll be here throughout the summer, at least, to help you run the place…"

"Run the place? He knows nothing about the ranch."

"It's a business. He's run businesses before. He'll learn."

Zannah stared at him. He knew she was having a hard time taking this in, but he was wound up now, eager to tell her all about his plan—the one that was going to make them rich, richer than either of them could imagine.

"And what are you going to be doing while I run Eaglecrest, with the help of a man who knows absolutely nothing about the place?"

This was the moment he'd been waiting for. His eyes were shining as he said, "I'm going to find the Lost Teamsters Mine."

CHAPTER THREE

ZANNAH COULDN'T HAVE been more surprised if Gus had whipped out a top hat and pulled a rabbit from it. She expected him to laugh at the shock he'd caused, but he only stared at her, wide-eyed and smiling as if he'd said something brilliant.

"The...the Lost Teamsters Mine? That's a myth!"

"I used to think that, too, but now I'm sure I know how to find it. Come on, look at this." He gestured for her to come to his side of the desk. "See? I've got proof."

As if she was in a dream, she walked around and looked at the yellowing map.

"This is a geological survey map from the 1930s. See?" He ran his finger up between two ridges. "This is Two Horse Canyon."

"Yes, so?"

"Look at the elevation of the ridge on the west side." He flipped to the next map, a much newer one. "Now, look at the elevation of the same ridge on this map."

Zannah studied them for a few seconds, placing a finger at the designated spot on each map. "What am I looking at?"

"The ridge is ten feet shorter since the first map was drawn. How do you account for that?"

"Erosion? The ground settling? Rock slides?"

"Or maybe a cave-in of a mine entrance." He looked at her in triumph, all but dancing in place.

"And you think it could be the Lost Teamsters Mine?" She shook her head. "Isn't that a little far-fetched?"

His jaw set defensively, Gus said, "Legend says it's in Two Horse Canyon."

"Legend," she said faintly. "No one has ever found a speck of proof that it even exists."

"And they wouldn't, either, not if the cave entrance had collapsed soon after the teamsters left there. So many rock falls have changed the landscape that people didn't know what to look for."

"People have wandered around in those

canyons for more than a hundred years, followed every possible lead, no matter how crazy it sounded. No one found any credible proof of the mine's existence."

Obviously disappointed that she wasn't as excited as he was, Gus began folding up the maps. "They quit too soon."

"Or they came to their senses."

Zannah didn't know what else to say. Her head buzzed with all of today's surprises. It took her a few seconds to focus on what her father was doing. When she did, she saw a familiar name in faded ink on the back of one of the papers.

"Henry Stackhouse," she said, pointing. "He didn't quit too soon. He spent his whole life—*wasted* his whole life—looking for that mine. Even when he was sick, knew he was dying, he kept at it."

With sadness, she thought about the man who had once been a fixture around the ranch. Gus had let him stay in a cabin on the place and do odd jobs. He was an excellent carpenter and a licensed electrician who had brought all of the electrics on the ranch up to code, but whenever he'd saved up a little money, he'd disappear for weeks at a time, all his supplies packed onto his faithful old donkey, Kayetta. He'd been like a figure straight out of the 1800s, always glad to pose for tourists, or to spin yarns about the lost treasure, though his tales were carefully crafted to throw off anyone who was actually interested in looking for the teamsters' mine. Whenever he was at Eaglecrest, he and Gus spent a great deal of time together. Now Zannah knew what they'd been talking about.

"He was on the right track, though."

"He died last winter, and—"

"Left me all his papers."

She threw her hands in the air. "But if Henry's maps and notes and papers had been worth anything, wouldn't he have found the treasure years ago? And seriously," she went on before he could answer, "it's a far-fetched story every treasure hunter tells. Five teamsters with their string of mules laden with supplies getting caught in a storm and taking refuge in a cave where they happened upon a gold strike. A cave and a gold strike no one else has ever been able to locate. Even the two teamsters who survived the fight over the gold couldn't find it again. Doesn't that all sound oh-so-convenient, and just plain crazy?"

"Maybe, but that doesn't mean it isn't true." Gus held up one of the folded maps. "It only takes someone with time and patience to figure this out."

"Henry certainly had time, he had patience…" Horror washed over her. "Oh, my gosh. You've got gold fever."

"Don't be ridiculous. Only naive fantasists get gold fever."

She gave him a pointed look, and he answered with a frown. "I'm interested, and I want a change from what I've been doing. I probably don't have enough time left to spend years on this, but I can…"

"Don't have enough time left. What… what do you mean?" Zannah's voice began to shake. "Is that why you've been thinking about Mom, and…and medical care? Are you *sick*?"

"Nah, I'm fine. I told you, that episode was nothing but stress." He finally seemed to focus on her dismay, and his tone softened. "But I'm almost seventy, and I see time passing by without me doing all the things I planned to do. The things your mom and I talked about that we never did."

"So looking for the Lost Teamsters Mine is on your bucket list?"

"Right at the top."

"I didn't even know you *had* a bucket list."

"Well, I haven't written things down, but this is what I want to do, and I've earned the right to do it. I've worked hard all my life. Don't you think I should be able to do what I want?"

"Well, yes, of course I do, but..."

"I know it's a lot to take in, and I was going to tell you all about it sooner, but the time was never right, and then Gallagher wanted to come this week, and I didn't get the chance to talk to you."

"Gallagher," Zannah said, her thoughts circling back to their potential new partner. "Exactly what is he offering?"

"Capital. You've been doing the books, so you know how badly we need the money."

"Oh, how can I know that? I haven't seen all the receipts or paperwork." She gestured to the pile of receipts she'd unearthed in his desk earlier. "Are there any more I need to know about?"

He squinted at the stack and tilted his head to one side. "I don't think so, but you don't need to worry about that right now. You've got guests to see to, and I want to get back to work." He glanced at Henry's maps.

"So, when are you planning to go looking for the gold?"

"Soon as I can get this deal done with Gallagher. Then I'm outta here. Don't know how long I'll be gone."

Zannah stared at him for a long moment. "Who *are* you?" she finally asked.

That brought his head up. He met her gaze straight on. "A man who wants to do something different, something that…matters."

She threw her arms wide. "Eaglecrest matters. The family business matters. *I* matter."

"And I've spent nearly fifty years taking care of all those things. Taking care of everything. Now I want to do something else."

Zannah's mind spun as she tried to follow his thinking. "I know you've always been the rock everyone on the ranch depended on, the one with all the responsibility. When was the last time you took a vacation? Maybe you need a rest."

"Nah, that's not it. I'm going to do this, so drop it, will you?"

Zannah started to argue but realized she wouldn't get anywhere by pushing him further. She needed a break from him and the many surprises he had revealed today. Frustrated and feeling dismissed, she took a deep breath. "Don't forget that Casey is bringing your granddaughters soon."

"I know," he responded.

"And I still need your help with the guests. Tomorrow is the long trail ride. Phoebe and I will need your help, since Juan will still be gone."

"I know that, too." He met her eyes. "Zannah, one more thing."

"What?" she asked, reluctance dragging the word from her.

"If Brady Gallagher is going to invest, he'll have to know everything that's going on here, all about our money situation, how it comes in and where it goes."

"Too bad you didn't let me in on all that," she snapped.

Her father's face hardened into stubborn lines. "And he needs to have free rein so he can make any changes and improvements he thinks are necessary. After all, it's his money."

So hurt and angry she could barely speak, Zannah whispered, "We don't need a stranger to—"

"My mind's made up."

Mystified and hurt, Zannah watched him for a few seconds longer. "All right, then, I'll see you later."

A grunt of assent was her only answer as she left the office and closed the door behind her. It was doubtful that she would see her father for the rest of the day. While she and Phoebe and the rest of the staff worked with the guests, she guessed he would spend his time studying his treasure trove of documents.

Her head spinning with all of the shocks she had received so far today, she stood for a moment, lifted her face to the sun and let the warmth soak into her skin. She listened to the sounds of the ranch—horses whinnying; the two border collies, Rounder and Coco, barking to make sure everyone knew they were on guard duty before they collapsed on the front porch of the main lodge and fell fast asleep; the soft breeze that picked up the whump,

whump, whump of the windmill that pumped water into the stock tanks.

She had missed all of this so much when she had gone to college, starting later than her peers because she'd wanted to be home for her mother. Watching vibrant, beautiful Esther waste away had been unbelievably hard, especially since she'd felt so alone for so much of it. Sharlene had helped, but she'd been busy with the housekeeping duties and taking up the kinds of responsibilities with the guests that Esther had once handled. Gus had simply been absent. Her mother seemed to understand, saying Gus didn't handle illness and death very well, and he was better with animals than he was with people.

Still, Zannah knew it must have hurt her mother to know that Gus wasn't there for her when she needed him most. To his credit, he had been in the sickroom every spare minute during Esther's last week of life, but he and Zannah had never really talked about his thoughts and feelings during that time. They were a family that didn't really get into the deeper emotions.

It had taken Zannah years of reflection to admit that when she had finally left Eaglecrest to go to the university in Las Vegas, she had been escaping from the memories, from her anger at her father, her grief for her mother. She'd pursued a degree in social work because she'd wanted to help people. After five years, she'd known that even though she loved her job, she wasn't cut out for it. She had worked with so many families in distress but felt she was never quite up to the task. A series of tough situations and a near tragedy had made her long for the peace and stability of Eaglecrest. She finally admitted to herself that she had to go home. The ranch was the family business, and her heritage.

Eaglecrest had been founded by her mother's family in the early days of the twentieth century. The Graingers' last surviving member had been Esther. When she had married Gus, who had come to Eaglecrest as a ranch hand, Esther had gladly shared ownership of the ranch with him. Since Casey's interest was in science, Zannah had expected to inherit it fully someday. Now everything had changed.

Confusion and anger were only two of the emotions buffeting her. She had to calm down and think about this.

Brady had obviously done some research

on the place, and on the two businesses they ran. He had also done research on her. It was only fair that she return the favor. She knew she wouldn't get those answers from her father.

Zannah glanced up when she heard riders approaching. The group was back, and she knew Phoebe would need her help. It was the perfect distraction for now. After the guests had eaten lunch, rested for a while and were settled into new activities, she would talk to Brady Gallagher. He'd better have some answers for her.

BRADY EASED OFF his boots and socks, then ruefully examined the blisters and sore spots on his feet.

"Tenderfoot," he muttered, the old-fashioned description fitting him perfectly. From past experience, he knew the best treatment was to let air get to his feet. In a little while, he'd go looking for a first aid kit, but for now, he propped his feet up on an a well-worn ottoman and looked around at the decor. He had stayed in many hotel rooms over the years on family vacations, college trips with the baseball team, then for work when he'd started his first job in one of the family businesses.

All those rooms had been specifically designed and decorated so that the occupants couldn't possibly make a lasting impact on them. This place was different. Besides the usual queen-size bed, there was an old desk and dresser that looked as though they had been restored with great attention to detail and a desk chair with a cushion that matched both the leaf-patterned drapes and the chair where he was sitting. It felt as if it had lovingly cradled many weary bodies.

Instead of stark white walls dotted with dings and scratches, this room was painted a soft green that invited the occupant to relax. Instead of generic prints of forgettable landscapes, there was original artwork on the walls. They were colorful paintings and drawings with a Western theme. Some of them were amateurish, but two of the paintings were views of the multihued mountains and were of excellent quality. He had been unable to locate a signature on them, but the unknown artist had real talent. He knew his own refined mother would have been honored to hang them in her home.

In addition, there were some beautifully nuanced black-and-white photographs of the ranch in all four seasons. They were grouped together on the wall above the bed and appeared to have all been taken from the same spot, looking down on the main lodge, at roughly the same time of day with long shadows forming on the east side of the building as the sun dropped behind the mountains to the west.

Last night after the barbecue, he had knelt on the bed and examined them carefully. He didn't know who the photographer was, but love for Eaglecrest was evident in every detail of the pictures. The welcoming hominess of the ranch shone through.

Brady smiled. There was something about this ranch, this entire area, that drew him, even before he'd seen it. Too bad he couldn't put a name to the sense of longing he felt. Maybe it was nostalgia for something he wished had once existed for him, a different upbringing than growing up in the hustle and bustle of the various cities where they'd moved as his parents pursued business opportunities.

He shook his head. It was crazy. He had a

wonderful family. He'd had a great life, every advantage, but something about Eaglecrest pulled at him. He couldn't quite put a name to it. How could he feel nostalgic about a place he'd never been before?

On the wall by the door, there was a bulletin board with a list of the ranch activities, emergency numbers, instructions on what to do in case of a visitation by unwanted creatures such as rattlesnakes and scorpions, and a dozen thank-you cards and notes from former occupants of the room to the owners and staff at Eaglecrest. Some must have been written on a computer and then printed. A few were written by an adult hand, others in a childish scrawl. His favorite was from a boy named Arlo, who insisted no one should ride his favorite horse, Voyager, until he and his family returned to Eaglecrest. Brady doubted that the kid got his wish.

His phone rang, and he answered it to hear the voice of his brother Finn.

"How's it going, little bro?" Finn asked.

Brady chuckled. "I'm sitting here looking at a board full of thank-you notes from guests to the staff."

"That sounds promising."

"Yeah, people actually seem to like camping out, gathering cows during a rainstorm and developing saddle sores."

"You sound like you're either puzzled by that or envious."

"Yeah," Brady said. "I know."

Finn didn't respond, obviously waiting for Brady to go on. When that didn't happen, he said, "It's an adventure—which is what you're supposed to be having, right?"

Brady looked down at his blisters. "More right than you know. How is it going with you?"

"Haven't found a suitable business yet. Everything I've come up with so far is too run-of-the-mill to meet Dad's requirements."

"It can't be that hard to find a financially strapped company related to the entertainment industry that you can invest in and turn around in one year."

"You only say that because Eaglecrest Ranch practically fell into your lap," Finn grumbled.

"It pays to keep in contact with old college buddies."

"Uh-huh," Finn responded on a sigh. "You've always been a lucky so-and-so. Running into Garrett Flanders at that alumni meeting last month was pure luck."

"Yup."

"And he conveniently came out with the information about Eaglecrest?"

"He's in the cattle business, too, in New Mexico, not far from here across the state line. Anyway, Gus and Garrett's father, Jeff, are friends. Gus told Jeff he was looking for a partner—something Gus hadn't shared with his daughter, by the way."

"What?"

Brady explained about the day's events.

Finn whistled through his teeth. "Sounds like a bad start with her."

"Gus warned me she's really attached to the place, although I didn't think that was the case when I first heard about the ranch a few months ago. She wasn't even here. Sounds like her decision to come home was very recent."

"Well, watch your step. People are attached to their home places."

Brady chuckled. "We wouldn't know anything about that."

"Mom and Dad are slowing down now,

though. They've been in their current house for almost two years."

"Yeah, but Mom was talking about sprucing up the exterior."

Finn groaned. "A sure sign she's getting ready to sell. Do you think Mom and Dad will hire housepainters this time?"

"Why would they when they've got three able-bodied sons?"

Finn groaned again. "I can already feel the muscle spasms."

"Me, too. Say, have you heard from Miles?"

"He checked in with Mom and Dad a few days ago. He's in Colorado somewhere but won't say what he's pursuing. You know he always plays it close to the chest."

"'Cause he's afraid we'll steal his thunder."

"I told you we should have been nicer to him when we were kids. It's our fault that he never learned to share."

Laughing, Brady agreed, said goodbye and hung up the phone. He was just getting ready to find some kind of treatment for his blisters when someone knocked at the door. Crossing the room, he swung the door open to see Zannah standing on the mat with a white metal case under her arm and a determined look on her face.

Brady gave her an uncertain glance. "Um, hello, Zannah. What can I do for you?"

She swung the case around so that he could see the red medical symbol printed on the front. "First aid."

He reached for it. "Thank you. I was just about to go find—"

She pulled it away. "I'm the official administrator of first aid around here. I'll do it."

"There's an official administrator of first aid?" He had to fight to control his grin.

She lifted her chin. "That's right, and I'm here to take care of your injuries."

He gave her a skeptical look. "You want to bandage my feet?"

"Not really, but I do want answers. Treating your blisters is my way of getting those answers."

Brady stepped back to let her in. "I'm hoping that's not a promise of torture to come."

Zannah rolled her eyes. "Oh, please. It's only in bad action movies that the torturer announces his intentions."

Brady grinned and shut the door behind her.

"Sit," she ordered as she flipped open the

kit. She motioned for him to put his bare feet on the ottoman while she pulled on a pair of thin latex gloves. Glancing around the room, she said, "I would ask if the cabin is comfortable, but, in your case, I really don't care."

"Um, harsh," he said. "But I do find it very comfortable." He pointed to the two paintings he had been admiring. "Who's the artist?"

She couldn't conceal a flash of pride as she answered. "My dad's sister, Stella. Phoebe's mom."

"She's very talented."

"We know," Zannah stated in a no-nonsense tone. "She owns a bakery in town. We get all of our baked goods from her."

He probably shouldn't be enjoying this so much, he thought, especially considering she was armed with alcohol wipes and iodine. Something about the defiant way she held her head, though, and the direct stare she was giving him, made him want to prolong this encounter. "And the photographs over the bed. They're very good, as well."

She glanced at the pictures, then shot him a swift glance before answering, as if she was trying to test his sincerity. "Thank you," she finally said.

"You're the photographer?"

"Yes. It was a youthful hobby I don't have time for anymore."

"You're good. You should take it up again."

She gestured to his feet. "Shall we get on with this?"

"You seem to have recovered from the surprise you received today."

"Not even close. I didn't get any satisfactory answers from my father, so it's your turn." She leaned over his left foot and tilted the worst blister toward the light. After examining it, she used a cotton swab to clean the surface, and another to spread on a thin coat of antibiotic cream. She looked over the other spots and said, "These only need air and time to heal. Do you have a pair of sandals or flip-flops you can wear for a couple of days?"

"Yeah, but I can't wear those and participate in all the cowboy college training and activities."

"Why, yes, that's exactly right."

"So I'll have to spend my time going over the books, seeing what it will take to make this place profitable."

"Why Eaglecrest?" Zannah asked, replacing the items in the first aid kit and snapping the lid shut. "Sure, your background is in business, but your family owns auto parts stores, travel stops on the interstates, a car dealership. Why on earth do you want a ranch?"

"Oh, so, you've been busy doing research this afternoon." He leaned back, tented his hands over his chest and smiled at her.

Zannah stood up from the ottoman and moved across the room. "We may be behind the times on some things, but most of the time, we do have good internet access."

"I told you, investing in Eaglecrest is a challenge."

"You're not afraid it's going to be a money pit?"

"The challenge is to make sure it isn't."

She glanced away. "You have no idea what you're getting yourself into."

"No, and that's the point. My dad is a big believer in diversifying both our skills and our income. He issued a challenge to my brothers and me, to find a business that is involved in the entertainment industry in some fashion and turn it into a moneymaker."

She stared at him. "You think ranching is entertainment? I'll tell you what, you go out looking for a stray calf during a storm in freezing weather, then come back and tell me how *entertaining* it was."

"Ranching is only part of the challenge—"

"What's the rest of it?" she broke in. "What, exactly, do you get from this challenge?"

"Are you kidding? I've got two brothers. I get bragging rights."

She rolled her eyes. "A sorry excuse."

Brady gazed at her for a few seconds, then said, "It all has to do with funding. Whichever one of us is the most successful this time, using our own money, will be fully funded by our dad for the next one."

"So what happens to the losers?"

"Finish the project and move on."

"So the stakes are very big for all concerned." She paused, obviously thinking that over before she asked, "Is there a timeline? A deadline? A specific amount of profit?"

"Yes, we have to show major progress within six months, and a complete turnaround within a year."

"Is that even possible?" she asked, alarm in her voice.

"If we work nonstop."

Before she could ask more questions, he said, "And we're a very competitive family."

"You must be."

He sat forward and looked at her intently. "Well, then how about this? With foreign markets opening up for American beef, there are going to be opportunities like this industry hasn't seen in years."

"That doesn't make it any easier."

"I'm not looking for something easy."

She gave a dismissive wave of her hand. "Yeah, yeah, I know. You're looking for a challenge."

"Not only the cattle business, but also the cowboy college. How many of the guests who have participated have actually become ranch hands? If they can afford what you charge to teach them about riding, vaccinating and rounding up cattle, they're probably not looking for those skills as a career choice. No, they're pursuing a fantasy, the cowboy mystique that's such a huge part of our identity as Americans." He shrugged. "Entertainment."

Zannah studied his face for several seconds before she said, "To you it's a moneymaker." She tilted her head toward the other cabins. "To them, it's entertainment, a chance to participate in a fantasy, the Old West. To me, it's my heritage, my family's way of life for nearly one hundred years. Good times and bad times, experiences you can't charge on a credit card or buy with a check."

Brady considered her. "And yet your brother wasn't interested in staying here, running the place."

"Not that it's any of your business, but no. He's a botanist who works for a firm in Phoenix that's developing a method to increase crop yield in desert areas."

"So you're the one who will keep the place going."

"That's right."

"For whom?"

"My family, my nieces, whoever comes after me, whatever children I have."

"So, how do you plan to do that with a negative cash flow? Without a partner, an investor to help you?"

"I can deal with the cash-flow problems," Zannah insisted. "If I'm given a little time."

"Do you even *know* all the cash-flow problems yet? Gus indicated he's been a little lax in the bookkeeping."

Zannah blinked. "He *told* you that?" A pang of distress pierced her as she wondered why her dad would have told that to a complete stranger when he'd barely been willing to admit it to her.

Brady's face softened as he answered. "I guess he felt like he'd have to be completely honest with a potential investor."

But not with his own daughter, she thought again, hurt and consternation growing. While she searched for a response, he went on.

"Would you have fought him on it if you'd known his plans?" His tone wasn't unkind.

"Tooth and nail," she admitted. "And even more so knowing his reason for doing this is so he can go look for a mythical gold mine."

"Um, he told me he wanted to pursue his own interests."

Zannah shook her head, struck again by the sense of being betrayed by her father.

"He's looking for a partner so he can go prospecting, and you're looking to win a bet. He's being selfish and you're being—"

"Businesslike?"

"Frivolous."

Brady raised an eyebrow at her. "Look, an infusion of capital will make everything easier." He spread his hands wide. "I'm here, checkbook in hand."

"Yes, you are." And there wasn't a thing

she could do about it. She watched him ease back into the chair, his body relaxed, his eyes steady, as if he expected her to fall right in with his and Gus's schemes.

In her previous career, she had dealt with many tough situations, often faced down hard men. She'd always had backup, though, a colleague or even a police officer. This was completely different. Brady wasn't hostile or apologetic or intimidating. He was calm, professional and solid, with those brown eyes of his watching her with complete reasonableness. His whole demeanor seemed to invite her to be equally reasonable—which made her completely unwilling to do so.

Suddenly swamped by exhaustion, Zannah turned away. "Once you see the books, you might decide it's not worth the trouble. Good night." She gathered her first aid kit and hurried to the door.

She swung the door open, but before she stepped out, she looked back at him. "On second thought, to help you make the final decision to invest in Eaglecrest, you need to learn how hard the work of running a ranch really is."

Brady's dark eyes watched her warily. "Uh-huh, and—"

"If your blisters are better in the morning, you can take over the horse-grooming tasks that Juan Flores usually does. He'll be gone for a while." She paused. "You do know how to groom a horse, right?"

"I'm learning that you appreciate honesty, so I'll tell you I don't have a clue. Never done it." His lips flickered in a grin. "When my brothers and I rode at our uncle's farm, he did all the horse grooming. I'm a quick study, though."

"You'll have to be," she answered. "Mr. Gallagher, have you ever been up close and personal with a cow?"

"You mean like I got up close and personal with a horse today? No, not really."

"I see. We'll soon take care of that, and you might easily change your mind."

Before he could respond, she stepped outside and closed the door behind her.

Brady watched her go as he wondered if there were any online videos about horse grooming.

CHAPTER FOUR

ZANNAH SAT ON the side of her bed and stared dejectedly at the wall of photographs and paintings opposite her. Old black-and-white photos that she'd had printed on canvas showed the early days of Eaglecrest—the first house, which was not much more than a cabin, cowboys lounging on the front porch of the bunkhouse as the long shadows of the trees stretched out nearby. Photographs of family weddings, including her parents' and grandparents', were carefully placed along with images of her and Casey as children, riding and roping, trying to learn and keep up with their father and the patient ranch hands who actually knew what they were doing and were willing to teach their skills to two eager kids.

Her favorite photo was one she had taken herself. It showed her nieces at about three and four years of age, each of them holding one of their grandfather's hands. He was bending down to accommodate their much shorter stature as they took him down to the corral so he could tell them about the horses.

A knock on the door had her sweeping away tears and calling out, "Come in," with a quavery voice.

She turned as Phoebe stepped inside. Her cousin had showered and changed clothes. She was now wearing her evening outfit— yoga pants and an Eaglecrest T-shirt.

"I finished teaching the yoga class and was about to head home," her cousin said as her concerned gaze took in Zannah's face. "Are you okay? Uncle Gus told me what's going on."

Zannah threw her hands in the air. "So *now* he becomes Mr. Chatty."

Phoebe came and sat beside her. "He seems to think this is a great idea, that it'll solve all the financial problems. I knew money was tight since he canceled repaving the main road last fall, but I didn't know how bad."

"I'm only now finding out." Zannah looked back at her wall of memories. "It's all changing now."

"And you hate change."

"Yes. All those years I was in college in Las Vegas, then working—"

"At a job that didn't suit you."

Zannah gave a small shrug. "True, but all those years, I knew Eaglecrest was here. That Dad and Sharlene and you and Aunt Stella were all here, would always be here. That gave me stability—knowing I had someplace to go."

"You romanticized this place, fantasized it into being more wonderful than it is," her levelheaded cousin pointed out. "Because your job showed you so much of the worst in people."

"I know," Zannah admitted. There was no point in lying, especially not to Phoebe, who could cut through any nonsense in a hurry. "In spite of all my college courses—"

"In which you excelled."

"Book learning sure doesn't prepare a person the way being on the front lines does. I began to catch on when I had my internship, but throughout all the training, I still had a pie-in-the-sky idea that I was some kind of guardian angel or…or a knight on a white horse who would charge in and instantly make people's lives better, rescue every child in need, turn some abusive spouse into a saint."

"That was a heavy load to be expecting of yourself." Phoebe gave Zannah a searching look. "You realize that whole fantasy was because you felt like you should have saved your mom, right?"

Zannah gave a self-deprecating little shrug. "We've had this discussion before. Numerous times."

"And I only mention it now because you're still dealing with it."

"I always will be. I know that now. No one could have told me that at the age of twenty. I thought I could deal with it by having a complete change, running away. I thought it would be okay if I was near family. Since Casey and Vanessa were in Vegas, it was good, but when they got jobs in Phoenix, that all changed."

"So you went through all that upheaval and you're back home facing another one."

"Yes."

Phoebe reached over and gave her a hug, then stood up. "The question now is how are you going to handle all this?"

Zannah looked up. "What do you mean?"

"Uncle Gus heading off to look for the Lost Teamsters Mine. I can't wait to hear what Mom has to say about that, by the way. He's determined to do it, so you can't stop him."

"I realize that." Zannah crossed her arms tightly.

"Oh, don't get defensive. I'm only saying that you can't change his decision, and as for the situation with Brady Gallagher, you can't fantasize it away. Even though you hate change, you have to accept it. You have to make it into a situation you *can* accept."

"We're the same age," Zannah said in a marveling tone as she stood up. "How is it you're so much wiser than me?"

Phoebe winked. "More time on the back of a horse. Who was it that said, 'The outside of a horse is good for the inside of a man'? Or in this case, a woman."

"I don't know. I'll look it up."

Phoebe laughed, and Zannah focused on her cousin. "I'm sorry. I've only been thinking about myself. This will affect you and everyone else, too. How are you feeling about it?"

Phoebe shrugged. "I'm taking a wait-and-see approach. If Gallagher's expertise improves things and makes it easier for you, I'm okay with it. If not, we'll have a problem. By the way, if this is actually going to happen, you and Gallagher need to call a staff meeting and let everyone know their jobs are secure. The news has already spread through the staff like a brush fire."

"Oh, of course, I should have thought about that."

"It's been a busy day."

"Don't I know it."

With a grin and a wave, Phoebe left the room. Zannah looked back at the wall, seeing not the past but the future. Things were about to shift, but maybe it wouldn't be all bad. There were still plenty of memories to be made.

BRADY STOOD BESIDE the table in the barn where he had spread out various horse-grooming items. He glanced first at his phone, then at the tabletop. He hoped that he had everything he needed. He had watched six different videos last night, and the information was crowding out anything else in his head. He knew his first priority should be looking at the books, but he was intrigued by the reality of getting up close and personal with the animals, which were such a huge part of operations here at Eaglecrest.

He knew he could ask Phoebe for help, but she was tied up with the guests on the long trail ride. And he'd assured Zannah he could do this. He picked up what the online videos had described as a curry comb but what he thought looked like a medieval torture device and turned to see which horse looked like it would be most likely to appreciate being groomed by a complete novice.

Yesterday's foe lifted her regal head over the top of the stall door and fixed him with an unblinking stare.

"Not you, Belinda. We have history. And you know what they say—'Never go back to a woman who dumped you.'"

"Who says that?" Zannah asked from behind him.

Brady glanced over his shoulder. He was becoming accustomed to looking foolish around her. "My brother Miles. And he would know. It's happened to him a few times."

Zannah smiled as she walked up to him. She was dressed in work clothes—short-sleeved T-shirt, jeans and boots, and he wondered briefly if she ever got out and had fun. His gaze swept up to her face as he gauged her mood. She looked rested, he decided, and more cheerful than she'd been last night.

"I wondered if you would be out here since I didn't see you in the office."

He told her his reason for starting with grooming.

"Sounds like a good idea." She looked at the items on the table, then pointed to his phone. "Have you been watching videos?"

"Yeah, and I think I know where to start." He held up the curry comb. "I start with this, right, to, uh, get out the, um…" He glanced at his phone. "Dirt and dead hair."

"Well, you could, but you'll be chasing your horse all around the corral." She nodded toward the big doors that opened to the outside.

"What?"

"We talked about this yesterday, remember? Your first step is to secure your horse. It's best to use a quick-release knot."

"Right. Of course. I don't know how to make one. I should have paid more attention in Boy Scouts."

Zannah grinned. "Would you like me to show you?"

Brady recognized the question as the peace offering it was. "Sure."

"Good. This should be easy, since you're a quick study."

He chuckled as she went into a nearby stall and came out leading a palomino mare. The plaque on the stall door said her name was Buttercream. He gathered the grooming tools, returned them to the wide-mouthed bucket where he'd found them, then picked it up and followed Zannah to the corral.

"By the way, how are your blis— Oh," she said as she looked down and spied his comfortable old sneakers. "Number one rule, even more important than tying up your horse, is never wear sneakers when you're working around large animals. They're not sturdy enough to withstand the weight of a horse stepping on your foot."

"And boots are?"

"More than something designed for walking or looking cool on a basketball court."

"Got it." She was right, and he should have thought of that.

He shrugged. "So what do I do? You told

me not to wear my boots, then assigned me to groom horses."

"Well, obviously, I should have thought that through a little better. Now, watch and learn."

Zannah guided Buttercream to the corral fence and took the lead rope. Brady watched carefully as she demonstrated how to tie a quick-release knot. After she showed him a couple of times, he felt that he had mastered it, smugly tying one that passed her critical inspection.

"By the way," she said. "Phoebe reminded me we need to call a staff meeting to tell everyone what's going on, that my dad is looking for an investor, and it might be you, but their jobs are secure." She gave him a pointed look. "Their jobs are secure, right? We don't want anyone quitting."

Brady nodded. "I was going to suggest that. It's usually the first step when we buy into a new business."

"You mean take over."

He let that slide as he went on. "But things haven't happened that way here."

"No kidding," she murmured.

"Set up a time to meet with the staff. It will

be better coming from you, but we'll have to present a united front."

Zannah's lips tightened, but she nodded and turned back to the task at hand.

"Grooming isn't difficult, but if you do it right, it's a good workout for you," she said, picking up the curry comb. "You only have to remember to cover the entire animal, and to follow the steps."

Brady took out his phone.

"What are you doing?"

"Recording the steps," he answered, tapping the device to turn on the video recorder and aiming it at her.

"Excellent plan. That way, I won't have to give you another lesson." She turned back to her task, instructing him as she did so, showing him where to stand, cautioning him about letting the horse know exactly where he was with each step, then having him practice.

Brady didn't know what to expect at the upcoming staff meeting, but he knew it wouldn't be easy. He decided to cross that bridge when he came to it. He leaned against the fence and steadied the hand holding the phone along the top rail. He found that he didn't have to focus on recording but could allow himself to be entranced by Zannah's no-nonsense approach to the task, her firm but gentle touch, the way she praised Buttercream for her beauty and docile nature.

Zannah's own hair was in a braid, no doubt to keep it out of her way. It slid back and forth across her shoulders as she moved. He admired the way her biceps flexed and stretched as she worked.

This kind of task was second nature to her, something she had no doubt done her whole life. He'd only known her a couple of days, but she didn't seem like most women he knew. They all had busy lives and careers, families that needed them, their own interests, causes they fought for. Gus had told him that she had graduated from college and worked as a social worker, but he hadn't elaborated on why she'd left that career and returned home. Now it seemed that her whole focus was Eaglecrest.

None of their so-far testy conversations had been personal, but he wanted to know more about her. Ranching and cowboying were a whole new world to him, and he was eager to learn whatever she could teach him. He knew they would have to become friendlier in order for that to happen, but he wasn't sure how to do that. He'd never tried to partner with a woman before, and with Zannah, he felt like he'd jumped straight into the deep end. He probably needed to think of her as a business partner first and a woman second.

When he found his attention wandering to her hips as she bent to brush Buttercream's legs, he brought himself up short.

"I, uh, think I get the idea," he said as he stopped recording. "I will, um, go and take a look at those books."

"What?" she asked, looking around.

"See you later," he called over his shoulder as he hurried toward the corral gate.

"Don't forget that we're getting up close and personal with some cattle later on."

"Can't wait," he called over his shoulder.

"BUTTERCREAM, WHAT DO you think bit him?" Zannah asked out loud as she watched him swing through the gate and disappear around the corner of the barn. "He moves pretty well for a man with blistered feet."

The mare answered with a gentle swish of her tail, as if to say, "Don't know, don't care."

Zannah shrugged and finished her task,

then went to notify the staff about the meeting. There would have to be two—morning and evening—so that everyone could choose the one that fit their schedule best. This was a big deal, though, so she knew the first meeting this evening would be packed.

When that was done, she went to assist Chet Barnes as he instructed some of their younger guests in the basics of roping while most of the adults were gone on the long trail ride. They started out by learning to make a Honda knot in a rope that would allow them to have a loop loose enough to throw but flexible enough to tighten when necessary.

Cow horns attached to hay bales simulated an animal to be roped. Several guests stuck with it all afternoon, while a few decided to take a break and sit in the shade drinking prickly pear lemonade.

Zannah had always loved watching Chet teach. He had been working at Eaglecrest and teaching cowboying classes for twenty years. He was slow talking and gentle, especially with the little kids. Six-year-old Liam Bardle followed Chet around, a faithful shadow, trying to emulate his new hero, even going so far as to try and stand and walk exactly as Chet did, the toes of his boots pointed in a little.

When Liam managed to get a loop around one of the cow horns, he was overjoyed and glowed under Chet's quiet approval.

As she gave help where it was needed, Zannah thought about everything that had happened. She was still deeply hurt by her father's secrecy, but she was putting that aside for now. Her more immediate problem was learning how to deal with Brady, make him see matters from her perspective.

The biggest disconnect between them was that to him, Eaglecrest was a business, a means to an end, probably a short-term commitment. To her, it was family, her heritage and history.

She didn't know if she could make Brady understand that. She had lived her entire life thinking her father understood it—after all, he and her mother had taught her how important the ranch was to them all. Their family, all four of them, had worked together toward the goal of keeping the ranch successful. To have Gus throw it over like this was beyond her understanding.

Zannah straightened suddenly, startling a

few guests. She gave them a reassuring smile and moved away from the fence as she tried to deal with the anger she was feeling. She wasn't simply angry with Gus, but with herself. Ever since this bombshell had been dropped on her yesterday, she'd been reacting, not acting.

She had to make sure she was fully involved in everything that happened in order to avoid any further shocks, or at least anticipate them. She had to focus on Eaglecrest, not on her own resentment. This wasn't happening just to her. Besides, nothing would be solved by avoidance.

After signaling to Chet that she was leaving, she turned and strode purposefully toward the office. She may have been dropped into the middle of an unwanted and unplanned partnership, but that didn't mean she was going to be willfully ignorant of what was going on.

When Zannah reached the office, she swung into the room so fast that Brady jumped and looked up from the pile of papers on the desk.

"Oh, uh, hello, Zannah. Somebody chasing you?"

"Came to see how you're doing with the books." She strode across the office so forcefully, he scooted the chair over a few inches. Grabbing another chair, she pulled it over and sat beside him. "So, how *are* you doing with the books?"

Brady gave a soft laugh as he answered, "I feel like I'm hacking my way through a paper jungle."

"I know the feeling." She moved her chair closer and took control of the computer. "Let me show you what I was able to find in all of this."

For the next two hours, they sorted through papers and found several unpaid bills and a few checks that needed to be deposited.

At the end of that time, Zannah sat staring in consternation at the debt Eaglecrest had accumulated.

Brady rubbed his hands over his face and shook his head. "Well, at least now we know. Finding this out is part of due diligence. It's a mess, but Gus hasn't tried to hide anything."

"*How* have we stayed out of bankruptcy?" she asked shakily.

Brady pointed to the pile of unpaid bills. "I'm guessing that some of these people are your dad's friends, ones who knew he'd pay them when he could. Most of them are fairly small. I think he moved money around to pay what absolutely couldn't wait, like utilities."

Zannah put an unsteady hand to her forehead. "Yes, and they must have known or suspected we were in trouble." In frustration, she formed her hands into fists and pounded them against her knees. "*Why* didn't anyone tell me?"

"I don't know anyone around here yet, but I'm guessing they didn't want to cause him embarrassment. They were being good neighbors."

"Maybe, but you can't run a business like that. We can't, and our neighbors can't."

Brady stood and closed the laptop into which they had been entering data on a spreadsheet, then stacked up the folders where they had filed the papers they'd uncovered.

"That's true. Come on," he said, reaching down to tug her gently to her feet. "I think we've looked at enough red ink for today. Why don't you show me some more of the ranch?"

She stared at him, trying to sort out her thoughts about what they'd found. Seeing what they faced, she didn't know why he wasn't already packing his bags and hitting the road. That was what she wanted, wasn't it? But she knew Gus would simply find another investor—maybe even Fordham. That was unthinkable.

"Zannah?" Brady prompted her.

She blinked. "Oh, all right. Time for you to make the acquaintance of a few bovines."

Zannah quickly texted Phoebe and Chet to tell them where she'd be.

"Um, which horse will I be riding?" His face was a model of reluctance. His hands twitched then settled at his waist. She wondered if he was resisting the urge to rub his backside where he'd landed in the dust yesterday.

"None. We're only going over to the nearest pasture." She gave him an innocent smile. "Surely even a blistered tenderfoot like you can go that far."

"I'm sure I can," he answered firmly.

Zannah had to admit she liked the way he always had an answer to give her.

As they crossed the yard, she looked around automatically, checking to see what everyone was doing. It was always important to make sure everyone was busily engaged in something productive, not given idle time to get into trouble, especially kids.

She said as much to Brady, who replied,

"Probably need more activities for them. Does anybody do hot air balloon rides around here?"

"No, and we aren't going to be the ones to start."

"Be profitable."

The fact that he was sounding so reasonable—yet again—annoyed her even more. "Balloons would frighten the livestock, send them running."

"Stampede, huh?"

She didn't like the way he said that, as if it was something to be shrugged off lightly. "You haven't lived until you've tried to turn a herd of panicked cattle."

"Okay, okay," he said, lifting his hands in surrender. "We'll put that idea on the back burner."

"Where it can set itself on fire," she retorted, ignoring the grin he was giving her.

Once they reached the pasture, Zannah opened the gate, then closed it behind them. There were about three dozen head nearby, eating and relaxing. She loved the peacefulness of the scene.

"All right," Brady said, looking around in exactly the way she thought a businessman would when assessing what he needed to learn in order to make a profit, then felt a little ashamed of that thought when he went on. "Start with the basics. What kind of cows are these?"

"Cattle," she corrected. "Cows are females. Before their first calf is born, a cow is called a heifer. Males are called bulls or steers."

One part of Zannah's mind wondered why someone would be willing to invest a significant amount of money in an industry he barely knew. Another part was glad he was willing to learn.

"What breed are they?"

"Mixed breed, but mostly Angus-based beef."

She walked up to a cow who was lying in the grass with several others.

"You don't have to worry about approaching a cow the way you do with a horse. They can see almost three hundred sixty degrees and smell you coming as much as six miles away."

She knelt down and laid a hand on the animal's rump. Brady crouched beside her.

"Do they have names?"

"They're not milk cows, Brady. They're beef cattle. You don't give a name to something you plan to eat, or sell to eat."

One of the nearby cows made a rumbling noise.

"Did she just fart at us?" he asked, laughing. "There goes the ozone layer."

"Are you a third grader?" Zannah asked. "That was a burp, which is what the real concern is to the environment."

"Burps," he said, around a laugh. "Wait till I tell my brothers."

"Great. A whole family of third-grade boys."

Brady stood up. "I think I've seen enough for now." He bent and offered his hand to help her up.

Zannah was capable of standing up on her own, but she knew he was being polite. She placed her hand in his, aware of how smooth it was against her growing calluses. Self-consciously, she pulled away, and, as she did, she saw a faint smile flicker on his lips, making her wonder if he knew what she was thinking.

"What's next, Zannah?" he asked.

Her gaze shot up to meet his. For a second, she didn't know what he meant. Was he asking what was next for them? No, of course not, her common sense corrected her.

She made a production of dusting off her jeans. "What do you mean?"

"What else do you need to show me here at Eaglecrest now that I've gotten up close and personal with cows?"

"We need to go for a ride, see the full scope of the ranch and all its operations."

"Horseback?"

She had to smile at the dread in his tone. "No, although you and Belinda need to kiss and make up at some point. But today, we have a four-wheeler with nice padded seats. Come on. I'll show you."

As they left the cattle behind, she went on, "I'll take you for a ride around Eaglecrest and you can see the entire property."

"You'll drive?"

Zannah shot him a sideways glance as she tried to decipher his bland expression and even tone.

"It's *my* four-wheeler."

He gave her a steady look.

"At least until you write a check and are a real partner," she added, annoyed. "I've been driving quads on this ranch since I was twelve."

He held up both hands. "I believe you."

But still, he questioned her ability. Somehow that was more irritating than anything else he'd said or done in the two days she'd known him.

She threw her hands in the air. "Then why are you determined to doubt that I can drive one?"

His lips gave that odd little twist she'd noticed a couple of times before. "I'm not. I'm doubting my ability to let someone else take the wheel."

With a startled laugh, she said, "Get used to it, Gallagher. I'm not sure what kind of jobs and situations you've been in before, but this is a whole new world." She raised her eyebrows in a challenging look and thrust out her jaw. "This is Zannah's house."

She didn't wait for a response but walked faster toward the garage. Brady had to quicken his pace to keep up.

In the garage, she walked to the newer four-wheeler. After checking the gas gauge and the tires, she snagged a couple of bottles of water from a cooler by the door, handed one to him and slid behind the wheel.

"We've visited the herd, but there's plenty

more to see. Buckle up," she ordered, her irritation still simmering.

He meekly obeyed, then grabbed onto the roll bar to steady himself as they began to move.

"Does anyone drive that one?" he asked, pointing to the older quad she'd passed over. It was bigger and would have accommodated his long legs better.

"Needs work. It's not in the budget right now."

"Hello," he said, pointing a thumb toward his own chest. "Car dealership, auto parts stores. I've got some mechanic's skills. I'll take a look at it."

"Good. I won't have to pay you, then. And, since you're determined to be essential to this operation, you won't mind paying for any parts you need out of your own pocket."

"I'll be sure to keep the receipts."

"You do that, and then give them to my dad. That way I'll never see them and won't have to reimburse you."

Brady answered with a crack of laughter as she wheeled the vehicle out of the yard and onto a narrow track leading away from the ranch buildings.

CHAPTER FIVE

BRADY TURNED HIS body in the seat so he could watch her and the scenery at the same time. Cedar and pine trees, cottonwoods and willows slipped past as she told him about the terrain, what to expect when it rained too much for the creeks that fed into the San Ramon River to handle the overflow, the floods they'd had and the droughts. Her love for the ranch, and her pride in it, echoed in every word she said. It was obvious that even during the years she'd been gone, she had kept up with the goings on at the ranch.

The country they were rolling through was breathtaking, but Zannah was much more intriguing as she talked about the struggles her family had overcome to stay on Eaglecrest and make it successful.

"I'll take you over to the original homestead sometime. It's amazing to look at the small scale of that house and realize that all of this started there." She lifted a hand from the wheel, and with a sweeping gesture, indicated the area around them.

Brady admired the pride in her face, the quiet joy she took in Eaglecrest. An odd feeling sifted through him, and it took him a minute to realize it was simple envy, something that he, with his admittedly privileged life, had never felt before. It was so foreign to him that it took him a while to pinpoint the reason.

A sense of place, he decided. His family had moved often because of his father's business interests. There was no one place he could point to and say, "That's mine. It's been in my family for decades." Somehow that hadn't mattered until he'd arrived here.

Knowing he needed to give this a great deal more thought, he smiled at Zannah and said, "Sure. I'd like to see the original homestead."

He was going to ask more about her ancestors who had first settled this land, but right now they seemed less important than Zannah herself. While she was relaxed and driving over the land she loved, she might be willing to answer some personal questions. If he could ask in something other than a ham-fisted way.

"I understand how much you love it here, so what made you leave? Did you ever intend to come back?"

She shot him a glance. "How much has my dad told you?"

He lifted his hands in an innocent gesture. "That's it. That's all Gus told me, which is why I want to know more."

Zannah looked at him again, as if she was measuring the sincerity of his question. She was a smart woman. No doubt she would tell him barely enough to be polite and to satisfy his curiosity, but not enough to show she really trusted him.

But she surprised him by saying, "I don't know that I even had a long-term plan. Social work was something my mom and I had talked about often. It's a way to help people without being in medicine or teaching. I knew I wasn't suited to either of those professions."

"But it's as emotionally draining and demanding."

"Yes, but—" She paused, gathering her thoughts. "That was one of the reasons it appealed to me. It took up all my mental and physical energy, and even more so when I realized the job and I didn't fit each other."

"So," Brady said slowly, "instead of trying to make things easier for yourself, or phoning it in like some people do when they are overwhelmed, you tried harder to succeed?"

She shot him a swift sideways glance and hesitated before she responded, as if she was examining his question for hidden traps. He could tell her there were none. He was simply curious.

"It affected people's lives," she said with a little smile. "And their taxes paid my salary."

Brady was going to ask another question when she turned suddenly onto a steep, deeply rutted track that appeared too narrow for even a four-wheeler.

Realizing their personal conversation had come to an abrupt end, he glanced down at the sheer drop-off on his side of the vehicle, and said, "Um, Zannah, are you sure you should...?"

She ignored him and gently pressed on the gas.

The upward track was even more spine jarring than it had first appeared. Brady held on tight.

They topped a ridge and rolled onto a wide mesa that gave stunning views of the valleys below. The White Mountains, row upon row, disappeared into the distance. Zannah stopped the quad, and Brady, enthralled, stepped out to experience the full impact of the scenery.

"This is amazing," he said, turning in a slow circle to take it all in.

Zannah came to stand beside him. "My family used to bring picnics up here in the summers when I was a kid. It was the perfect place to play, although we lost many a Frisbee and softball over the side." Her fond smile took in the whole area, which he guessed was about ten acres. "It was never too windy up here because of that cliff." She nodded toward a high ridge that rose up behind them, the only feature keeping the view from being a full 360 degrees of breathtaking majesty.

"Does this place have a name?"

"Sure." She gestured for him to follow her, and they walked several hundred feet to the north. She pointed to a through-and-through opening near the top of the cliff.

"My great-grandfather thought Eagle's Eye

or Needle's Eye was a little too obvious, so he called it Hawk's Eye."

"Perfect," Brady said. "Hawk's Eye on Eaglecrest."

"It's a very special place to our family. We still have picnics up here when my nieces come. Joelle and Emma will be here in a few days, and I know they'll want to come up here. Maybe we'll invite you, too."

"I'd like that," he said absently, his mind racing ahead with plans and possibilities.

They spent the next half hour on Hawk's Eye Mesa, walking around, examining the topography, looking over the sides and into the valleys.

"Is there a source of water up here?"

Zannah frowned. "Well, no. We're at the top of the mesa. I've heard that there's an underground aquifer at the bottom of the cliff. But even if we located it, the cost to pump water up here would be astronomical, so we've never tapped into it. I suspect it's as elusive as the Lost Teamsters Mine."

He wandered away, his feet moving slowly as his mind raced. He was aware of her gaze following him, but he was lost in his own thoughts. He began to feel excited, the way he always did when a plan started to form in his mind.

When he pointed out a trail much less steep than the one they'd ascended, Zannah said, "We used to come up that way, but it washed out at the bottom a few years ago, so we can't use it anymore."

"That's too bad. It must have been much easier." Brady walked over to study the rutted track that had brought them to the top.

Watching him, Zannah said, "Worried I can't get us back down?"

He loved the challenge in her voice and couldn't resist a comeback. "I can drive if you want me to."

"I've got it, thanks. You ready to go?"

"Yup."

They bumped over the track that took them to the better road they'd been following earlier.

"We've had success raising hay in this little valley," Zannah said, stopping at a pullout that overlooked a lush, green meadow.

"Is this ready for harvesting?" he asked.

"You mean baling? Almost." She shifted into lowest gear. "We have several fields planted like this, because we'll need at least

a thousand bales of hay in the winter. Let's
take a closer look."

"Down there?" he asked. The front of the
vehicle pointed straight up into the air as she
drove over the road's edge, then straight down
onto what looked like another steep decline
with no track or trail to follow.

"Yes, it's much better to be able to see everything up close." She gave him a bright
smile as she drove over some rocks that tilted
the vehicle far to the right.

Brady tried to estimate how close they
were to tipping over, but Zannah didn't even
break a sweat as she turned the wheel to the
left and eased them down the slope.

"I was fine from the top. I can see…" His
voice trailed off as he considered that silent
prayer might be a better use of his time than
talking. Or screaming.

Brady tightened his grip on the roll bar and
braced his left hand against the dashboard as
he shot a look at Zannah's face. Her bottom
lip was caught between her teeth. Her face
was alight with excitement. Her hands were
steady on the wheel, and her foot only rode
the brake enough to keep them from descend-
ing too fast.

Everything about her, from the look on her face to the way she was sitting, told him she was enjoying this immensely.

When they arrived at the bottom, she gave him a triumphant look, and he realized how much he had underestimated this woman. However, he didn't plan to make the mistake of telling her that.

DURING THE NEXT few days, life at Eaglecrest settled into a routine. After a pair of uncomfortable meetings with the staff, who asked many questions and got only a few concrete answers, they carried on with business as usual, while Brady, with Zannah's help, tried to figure out what Eaglecrest's business as usual actually was. The two of them finished sorting through all the papers and put the collected information into the bookkeeping program.

Every day since those meetings, she had seen Brady talking to staff members, asking Chet about the horses, his days on the rodeo circuit and his success in teaching roping. He'd also spent time with Phoebe and even sought out members of the kitchen staff. He was getting to know people who seemed to appreciate his efforts, although they were still hesitant to trust him—exactly as she was, Zannah thought as she went about her daily tasks. She knew he wasn't simply being friendly but was performing his due diligence of finding out exactly how everything and everyone at Eaglecrest worked.

She asked him about it when they were both in the office one afternoon.

"Is this how you always work? Talking to all the employees, getting to know them?"

He gave her a surprised look. "Of course. I long ago learned it's all about the employees. If they're not happy, they won't stay."

"And that will kill your profits."

Brady answered with a steady look that made her feel ashamed. "It's more than that. It affects their lives. Although," he added thoughtfully, "it's different here since, for some of them, this is their home. In a way, they're tied to the land." He shrugged. "Never experienced that before."

"Because your family moved so often?"

"Yeah. It's made me rootless, I guess. Finn and Miles, too."

He changed the subject, but Zannah was troubled by his admission. How soon would it be before his itchy feet caused him to move on? She knew there were conditions of winning his dad's challenge that had to be fulfilled, but what if he lost? How soon would it be before he sold out and left? And if that happened, where on earth would she get the money to buy him out?

The thought made her feel panicky, so she forced herself to focus on each day and not borrow trouble from the future.

Gus was busy getting ready for his expedition and had little time for the ranch or the cowboy college. He was present, but it was as if he was already gone. Zannah missed him and, on the rare occasions she saw him, wondered who he had become.

She was still angry with him for keeping their financial problems a secret and still profoundly hurt by the way he had brought Brady in.

Part of her wanted to sabotage Brady, turn the staff against him, but that would only harm everyone involved.

Even if she hadn't already known it was wrong, all she had to do was recall the kinds of conflicts she'd witnessed in her previous career to stop all such thoughts of sabotage.

Someone always lost in that kind of confrontation.

Her thoughts returned to Gus, who truly would have been gone already if he wasn't waiting to see Casey, Emma and Joelle.

She said as much to Sharlene one morning when Brady had been at the ranch for six days. They were taking inventory of the housekeeping supplies.

"You're right. He'll be gone as soon as he's seen Casey and the girls. He's become a man on a mission," the older woman said.

"Yes, I know."

Sharlene placed a box of guest soaps on the shelf and turned to give Zannah her full attention. "You understand with your head, but not with your heart."

"What do you mean?"

"He's always worked hard. That's why he wanted you and Casey to get college degrees, so you two could have an easier life. When you decided to come back here—"

"He was disappointed?"

"No." Sharlene shook her head vigorously. "He saw it as his chance to turn things over to you and do something else for a while. I'm sure that, since he had provided all he could for you, including your college education, and you had decided to come home, he feels he can do what he wants." She laughed ruefully. "Silly me. I thought he'd take up a hobby like whittling. I never thought he'd be stricken with gold fever."

Zannah considered that as she opened a box of tiny shampoo bottles and placed it behind a nearly empty one. "What if he never wants to be involved with the ranch again?"

"Then he'll have the retirement he deserves, and he'll know you have a reliable partner to help you."

Partner maybe, Zannah thought. Reliable, she wasn't too sure. With Brady's big variety of interests and ideas, she didn't know if he'd want to stick around here and shoulder the workload Eaglecrest required.

"Zannah," Sharlene said gently, "you've reached the point where you simply have to accept what's happening."

With a rueful smile, Zannah admitted, "I know that with my head, but not with my heart."

"There you go again," Sharlene said with a smile. "Throwing my own words back at me."

Zannah shrugged. "I understand that he feels like life is passing him by."

Sharlene paused in what she was doing and looked at Zannah. "Yes, he's said as much."

"Yeah, to me, too. I don't think I'd want to be his age, or even close to his age, and feel like I'd never followed a dream or pursued something that was important to me."

Sharlene didn't respond but stood with her hands resting on a shelf for a while. Zannah was going to ask if she was okay when she gave a shake of her head and finished her task.

Afterward, Zannah walked outside and looked around to see what was going on. Everyone seemed to be busy.

She saw Brady enter the garage with a couple of men she didn't recognize. Curious, she followed them and found them loading equipment into the larger of the two four-wheelers, which Brady had put back into working order.

When she walked in, all three men turned to look at her, but only Brady's expression grew wary.

"Oh, hey, Zannah," he said, attempting to stand nonchalantly before a large case he'd loaded into the back of the quad. "I thought you were helping Sharlene."

"I was," she answered as she walked up to him. She made a big show of standing on tiptoe to peek over his shoulder. "Whatcha doin'?"

He reached out an arm to block her view. "I'm taking my friends here on a tour of Eaglecrest."

One of the men gave Brady a curious look while the other engaged in a coughing fit.

"Oh really?" Zannah ducked under his arm to see what he was trying to hide. The case he'd put in the quad was printed with words, which she read out loud. "'Warner and Baker, Surveyors.'" Beside it was what looked suspiciously like a tripod.

She gave him a level stare and then turned to smile at the two men. "I'm guessing you're Mr. Warner and Mr. Baker."

"Yes, miss."

"Well, it's nice to meet you," she said far too sweetly as she shook their hands. "I'm Zannah Worth, owner of Eaglecrest."

Both men looked at Brady, who responded, "Part owner." He gave them a hearty smile. "Why don't you two climb on in? I'll be right back." He took Zannah's arm and hustled her toward the open doorway, where she jerked her elbow out of his grasp and rounded on him.

"You've got some explaining to do, Brady. Why are there two surveyors here?"

"They always work in pairs," he hedged.

"You *know* what I mean," she responded in a low, angry tone.

"They're going to survey Hawk's Eye Mesa."

"Whatever for?" She drew in a quick breath. "You're not thinking of *building* something up there? You can't!"

"It might be the perfect place."

"For—?"

"Homes, vacation homes, condos. We're not sure yet."

She slapped her hands onto her hips and leaned closer to him. "*I'm* sure that it's not going to happen. Where did you get such a crazy idea?"

"We'll talk about this later."

"We should have talked about this already."

"There's a good reason we haven't, Zannah, and you're demonstrating that reason right now."

"Which is?" she asked, her voice tight with anger.

"Your unreasonableness."

Furious color washed into her face at the unfairness of that statement, and she sputtered. "Un...un...unreasonableness? I..."

"According to my agreement with Gus, I can explore any further moneymaking possibilities before we actually sign the papers. I have to know this place will turn a profit."

"Not by building on Hawk's Eye!"

He jerked a thumb toward the quad. "It has to wait, Zannah. I'm paying these guys by the hour."

Sucking in a quick, furious breath, she said, "Fine. I'm coming with you, but don't think this discussion is over." Turning, she stomped away.

"I wouldn't dare," he responded in a dry tone.

The trip to Hawk's Eye Mesa was made in an awkward silence with all three men sending wary glances at the angry woman accompanying them.

When they reached the top of the mesa, the surveyors got busy with their task while

Zannah grabbed Brady's sleeve and dragged him far away from them.

"Start talking," she snapped.

"I didn't tell you about this idea, because it might come to nothing."

"Well, I could have saved you the time and trouble by saying it's guaranteed to come to nothing."

"Why?"

Zannah threw her hands wide to encompass the mesa. "This is an unspoiled area that needs to be left alone."

"I repeat. Why?"

"Because that's—"

"The way it's always been done?"

"Stop interrupting me," she insisted. "Why didn't you tell me about this?"

"I already said, it's because I knew you wouldn't listen—at least not until I had a lot more to share. Right now, I'm only gathering information."

"I can give you information. What do you want to know? How important this place is to my family? The priceless memories we have of times here with my mom?" Along with her anger, she felt betrayed because she had shown him this wonderful place, so precious to her, but he saw it only as another money-making opportunity.

"We can't pay the bills with happy memories. Zannah, you've seen every unpaid invoice that I've seen."

"Well, yes, but we haven't even begun the conversation about how to pay everything off."

"We're starting it now." He took a deep breath. "We're going to need much more than I had anticipated."

Zannah stared at him. "Am…am I going to lose Eaglecrest?"

"No," he said quickly. "No, but *we* have to be practical about how we can raise capital."

"And you think developing Hawk's Eye Mesa is the way to do it?"

"Right now, I think it's the only way."

"There are other areas on the ranch." She turned in a circle. "Look at it. It's untouched, pristine."

"Which is why it's perfect."

She shook her head, trying to form words for an argument at the same time she forced back the tears she could feel starting.

"Look, Zannah. People would certainly buy property anywhere on the ranch to build a summer home or weekend place, but we could ask premium prices on lots up here because it *is* pristine and untouched."

"It will be ruined."

"Not if we—"

"No. We're not doing this." She turned away, scooping her cell phone out of her pocket as she did so. "I'm calling my dad. He'll back me up."

"I don't think so."

She glanced down at the screen. "Ha," she exclaimed, waving the phone at him. "This will kill your plans right now. That cliff over there doesn't just block the wind, it blocks cell phone service, but don't worry about that. Maybe you can put up a lovely cell phone tower, too."

SHARLENE FINISHED CHECKING the guest rooms and turned to her newest employee, Lauren Blake. She had been recommended by a friend in town, who had told Sharlene the young woman was new in the area and in need of steady employment and a place to stay for herself and her young daughter, Rebecca.

"You did an excellent job today, Lauren. I

loved the way you fashioned the hand towels and washcloths into little cowboy hats. Did you think of that yourself?"

Lauren nodded shyly. "It came to me, so I tried it. It looked like a blob until I used the washcloth to make the crown of the hat, then put a crease in it."

"Very clever. It adds a nice touch."

"Thank you."

As Lauren took her cart of cleaning supplies and moved on to the next room, Sharlene gave the younger woman a critical look. She was tall and far too thin. Her little girl was seven but small for her age. Although Sharlene knew only a few sketchy details, she knew two of them had come from Los Angeles in a car far older than Lauren herself, and they had experienced rough times. She was glad to give them a safe haven.

She started toward her tiny office on the ground floor, thinking about the number of people who had found Eaglecrest to be a safe haven. A big believer that hard work was more valuable than coddling a new employee, Gus had always been willing to give people a trial period, working with them until they learned the ropes and often watching in annoyance as they took their fresh skills and went to work for someone else. She had received many an earful about the ingratitude of some people.

On the other hand, he didn't want people around who didn't want to work here. Pride of place had always been uppermost in his mind.

Until recently.

Sharlene entered her office and located the list she'd compiled of the housekeeping supplies they needed, then called her supplier and placed an order. She had a dozen things that needed to be completed, but she did none of them, instead sitting at her desk and looking out the window at the beauty of the mountains in the distance. That was one of the best things about living here—there was a gorgeous view from every window.

She had loved living and working here, but things were changing. Her conversation with Zannah weighed on her mind.

Before she could become too lost in thought, the door opened and Gus strolled in, his arms laden with those blasted charts he'd been studying for weeks.

"Hey, Sharlene, look at this," he insisted, dropping the maps and charts onto her clean desktop. One of them rolled toward her, and she put out a hand to stop it.

Somehow, seeing his single-minded focus, as well as the heedless way he'd dropped the dusty papers onto her desk, hardened something in her.

"I'm really not interested." She pushed the documents away. "This is your project, your obsession, and you're welcome to it."

He looked up and blinked. "What?"

"You've become obsessed with finding that blasted mine, and you have a perfect right to do that, and I have a perfect right to not hear a word about it."

His face crinkled in puzzlement. "Huh?"

"You heard me."

He took off his hat and resettled it on his head in the characteristic gesture he used when gathering his thoughts. "But you've listened to me every time I've talked about it."

"Not anymore."

"So you're against me now, too, are you?"

She rolled her eyes. "Oh, of course not. But I am against the way you've handled all of this."

He took off his hat again, but this time he

tossed it onto her desk. "Has Zannah been talking to you?"

"Not much. She's too busy trying to stay afloat in the lake of selfishness you've dropped her into." Sharlene picked up his hat and smashed it against his chest.

His mouth dropped open as he stared at her. "Well—I—I—what—what's the matter with you?"

"Not a blessed thing that a break from you won't cure." Angrily, she snatched the maps and charts from her desk and shoved them back into his arms, causing him to take a step back and view her with growing alarm.

"Are you leaving? You—you can't."

"If you can, I can."

"But—but I was counting on you to be here to take care of things."

"Like I've been doing for ten years?"

"What's gotten into you?"

"I'm suddenly seeing things clearly." She clapped her hands onto her hips and tilted her head to the side as she studied him. "I spent ten minutes this morning convincing your daughter that she simply needs to accept what you're doing and that if it doesn't work out, you can retire and enjoy the rest of your life."

"Um, thank you?" he said uncertainly.

"But now I realize I've given you far too much credit in this. It's a terrible habit I've developed over the years, because I felt like I had no choice. I was bound by a promise."

"And that's bad?"

"Not entirely. Esther was the best friend I've ever had in my life—from grade school to her deathbed."

"Yeah, I know that."

"Before she died, she made me promise her that I'd look after you and Zannah—Casey, too, if need be—and I was happy to make that promise."

"And I was glad you made that promise, 'cause it made her last days easier."

"I guess I'm a little slow, because when I first realized that your plan was to go off into the mountains and chase after a fairy tale, I thought it would be all right, that you'd come to your senses, but that isn't going to happen, is it?" She tapped a finger on the rolls of paper she'd shoved back into his arms. "You're actually going to do this."

"Well, yeah. I haven't made any secret of it." His face flushed. "Okay, I'm not making a secret of it any longer."

"So, maybe I want to do something like that, too." Sharlene turned to pace the small room, coming back to stand before him once again.

"You want to look for gold?"

"No. I want to do something different, like you want to. My promise to Esther has kept me here, but I'm reaching retirement age, and I need to think about my future. There were things I wanted to do, places I wanted to go, but I'd promised Esther I'd look after you."

"But you're not leaving, are you?" he asked again.

"I don't know yet. I don't know that I would want to do that to Zannah, but be warned. Once she and Brady get their partnership worked out and things are going smoothly, you might come back from your hunt for gold and find me gone."

Gus gulped in a lungful of air as if someone had jerked a rug from beneath his feet and he'd landed on his backside. "Now, don't be hasty, Sharlene."

"Like you? I already said I won't leave Zannah in the lurch, so don't worry." She waved a dismissive hand at him. "And, by the way, if you keep treating your hat like that, you'll have to take it into town to get it steamed and reshaped so you'll look spiffy for your trip to nowhere. Now, run along. I've got work to do."

She strode to the door and held it open while he scooted past her. Once he was outside, she closed the door and walked away with the sharp, firm steps of an angry woman.

Behind her, she could hear him mutter, "What did I say?"

CHAPTER SIX

"THE NEXT STEP is to get the Environmental Protection Agency out here," the surveyor named Tony Baker was saying. He looked from Brady's intent face to Zannah's rebellious one. "Actually, that should have been your first step. I'm guessing you two have never been involved in a project of this magnitude before."

"No, not like this."

Brady shot a glance at Zannah and sighed. "Or any building project," he admitted.

Baker looked around. "So, what is the scope of this project?"

Zannah faced Brady. "I'd like to know the answer to that question, as well. If it's not too much trouble," she added with a falsely sweet smile.

Her annoyance with him had only grown while they were on the mesa, staying out of the surveyors' way and doing their best to avoid each other. She had finally sat down on a flat rock, chin in hand, and brooded.

He should have known better than to think about this project without giving her a heads-up. His dad had always used the old-fashioned phrase *In for a penny, in for a pound.* Once a project was started, go at it all out to see if it would work. If not, move on, but don't waffle.

"High-end homes or condos in a resort setting. There's no room for a golf course—"

"Golf course?" Zannah asked around a strangled noise.

"No, there's not," Baker said. He pointed over the side of the bluff. "Maybe down there." He walked over to take a look. "At least a nine-hole course. Be a big draw in this area."

"Over my dead body," Zannah muttered.

"I hope we don't have to go that far," Brady answered, then flashed her an apologetic look. "Sorry. We're in the exploratory phase right now."

He braced himself for more arguments from her, but she simply gazed at him with a profoundly disappointed and puzzled look on her face, then turned away. She went and sat in the quad, her head down, staring at her hands.

Seeing her distress caused regret to stab at him. He thought he'd done his best to explain, but she simply didn't understand.

HE DIDN'T UNDERSTAND, Zannah thought. This morning's actions proved that. And somehow she'd failed to make him understand. After they had gone through the books, discussed every purchase and every bill, she'd thought he grasped how important it was that Eagle-crest continue on the way it was, but with better financial management.

She'd been wrong.

The trip back from Hawk's Eye Mesa had been virtually silent, and as soon as Brady stopped the four-wheeler beside the survey-ors' truck, she jumped out and went looking for her father.

She found him in the office, writing a list of the supplies he needed to take with him into the mountains. When she whirled inside and shut the door, he jumped.

"What bit you?" he asked, starting to his feet.

"Brady Gallagher, of course."

"What?"

Her words tumbled over themselves as she told him about Brady's plan.

When she came to a halt, he looked at her for a second, then said, "Is that all?"

"Is that *all*? It's Hawk's Eye."

Gus frowned and sat back in his chair. "I don't like the idea of building on Hawk's Eye."

For the first time, Zannah felt a spark of hope. Finally, someone was listening to her.

Eagerly, she moved around to sit on the corner of the desk nearest him. "Me, neither. It's not right to develop it into a rich man's hideaway."

"Rich man's?" Gus paused to consider. "So these will be exclusive, high-end places. Be interesting to see how he does it."

"Dad!" she said in alarm. This conversation was going sideways fast.

Gus brought his attention back to her. "Has he taken any money, signed on the dotted line with any buyers? Or contractors?"

"No."

"Do you think he'd do that without telling you?"

"Yes. He certainly got the surveyors out here on the double."

"But has he done anything else, used ranch money for anything?"

Some of the steam began to dissipate from her anger. "Well, no. We all three know the ranch has hardly any money, but isn't it enough that he started this without telling me?"

"Sounds like all he's doing is exploring an idea. Something he has a right to do as part owner, or even as a prospective partner. He can make plans, hire surveyors, get the EPA out here. I'm guessing he's paying for it."

"I suppose."

"It's his money," Gus pointed out. He sat down and picked up his list. "He has the right to use it how he wants."

"But we're supposed to be partners, right?"

"Zannah, a partnership has to be built. It doesn't appear out of nowhere."

Astounded by the unfairness of that statement, Zannah was speechless for a moment. Finally, she said, "Funny you should say that, because that's exactly how this partnership got started."

Gus hunched his shoulders, and she bolted off the desk, turned on her heel and stalked out.

Once in her bedroom, she sat on the side of her bed once again and stared at her wall full of family memories.

Her gaze landed on the drawing her aunt Stella had done of the original homestead. It was something she'd created from old photographs and family oral history descriptions. She'd given it to Esther as a gift many years ago and it had come to Zannah after her mother's death.

Zannah had always loved it because to her, it represented continuity and history, but also the future. Her family had been here for more than ninety years, and they were a solid part of the land.

Brady simply didn't understand because his family had always been on the move, always pursuing greater opportunities.

Well, no, she thought, her ideas coming together. He didn't understand because he'd never been a part of something like Eaglecrest. His experiences with family business were strictly financial. From what little she knew about it, the Gallagher business model had been one of finding a struggling company connected to the auto industry, buying it, building it up, selling it and turning a profit.

He didn't know what it was like to love a place wholeheartedly because it was part of him.

Zannah shot to her feet. She'd been going about this all wrong. Time to change that.

"So, WHERE ARE you taking me?" Brady asked, not for the first time.

"I already told you, someplace I should have taken you days ago. Be patient."

"Hey, between the two of us, I don't think I'm the one who has trouble with patience," he said, pointing to himself, then to her.

She didn't respond. She was driving the quad, and she had to concentrate as she slowed down to make the turn onto an over-grown track. They bumped over rough ground for half a mile, then came to a stop beside a small wash that could only be called a creek in the rainy season.

"Here we are," she announced, swinging out of the vehicle.

Brady followed and came to stand beside her. He rested his hands on his hips as his gaze swept the area. "Where we are is—?"

"The original homestead." She smiled as she looked around. "Where my great-grandparents built their first cabin, started their family." Flashing him a proud smile, she said, "Come on. I'll show you."

Brady followed her as she walked over to a cleared area of ground. A forlorn-looking pile of stones showed where the fireplace had once been. It was the only part of the cabin that was still recognizable.

"Up close, you can see that this was where the house stood. Part of it burned, and they tore it down when the new ranch house was built in the 1960s, but the ground still shows where the foundations were built." She pointed to a depression in the earth several feet from the ruined fireplace. "There was a root cellar, where they stored preserved food, but it was filled in so no one would accidentally fall. I think there must have been a trap-door over it at some point."

Brady walked around, studying the ground. She was thrilled that he was taking this little excursion seriously until he looked up and said, "So the scars will always be here."

"Scars? What do you mean?"

He pointed to a long, dark stain that ran

around the perimeter of the house. "This must be where they dug the foundation, because the ground has been disturbed, the natural vegetation eradicated. It will never go back to being the unspoiled meadow it was when your family first arrived here."

"Does it need to?" she asked, reminding herself that the reason they were there was because he didn't understand.

Brady stood with his thumbs hooked into the back pockets of his jeans. "No, but it illustrates the point I've been trying to make— that things change, progress is made and matters can never go back to the way they were before the change."

"Don't you think that depends on *how* the change was made?" Zannah asked, frowning. This was not the kind of reaction she had expected or wanted from him.

"Look," he said, swinging his arms wide to take in the lush meadow. "This place is different than it was before your family came, probably different than it was a few years before that. Lightning strikes probably caused wildfires. Elk, deer and maybe even bison grazed here, changing the landscape, probably trampling the grass, changing the path of the creek."

"So?"

"None of those things permanently wrecked the landscape, ruined the beauty of this meadow." He turned back to look into her eyes. "And building homes on Hawk's Eye Mesa won't ruin it, either, Zannah. I'll make sure of that. But we have to look forward to projects that are going to help us establish a firm financial foundation. And the sooner, the better."

"I know we need more money, but—"

"And now you also know how much we need, and I do mean both of us have to work to find a solution." Brady breathed a heavy sigh, then straightened and squared his shoulders like a man facing an impossible task. "Look, I get that you don't want me for a partner, but fighting me on every suggestion? Every opportunity? How is that going to help save Eaglecrest?"

Zannah waved a hand in the general direction of the mesa. "How is that project going to give us the immediate help we need? It will be years before it pays off."

"Not necessarily. Once we have the plans

in place, we can advertise to the kinds of people who can afford to invest in a substantial down payment."

She shook her head. "Still, *years*."

"Do you think that's what your great-grandparents thought when they came here, built a house, planted a garden, started running cattle, had kids of their own, out here in what must have been the back side of beyond? They took a risk, and it paid off. Are you saying you're not as courageous as they were?" He paused, waiting for that to sink in. "I refuse to believe it."

Her stunned brain couldn't seem to form a coherent sentence. He had her cornered, and they both knew it. He knew she wouldn't say that she wasn't as brave as her ancestors. It infuriated her that he had so neatly turned the tables on her.

When she didn't answer, he went on. "It's only exploratory, Zannah. If it looks like it will be too costly, too difficult, we won't do it."

"Speaking of exploratory, I need some clarification."

"On?" he asked, eyeing her warily.

"On boundaries. On how much you're

going to explore and decide on without discussing it with me."

When he started to speak, she held up a hand. "I know it's an equal partnership—at least, it will be at some point—and I know my dad has given you free rein to explore more moneymaking opportunities, but I need to know what you're thinking." Frustrated, she clenched her hands at her sides. "I need to know—I mean, hiring surveyors to go up on Hawk's Eye—that's something I should have known about."

His expression softened. "Zannah, I—"

"You must have worked with partners before. There has to be communication—"

"You're right," he broke in. "I should have told you what I wanted to do, but, honestly, I knew you'd fight me on it."

She looked away. He was right, and they both knew it. She took a deep breath and said, "About the idea of developing the mesa, it might take years to find that out, and even more years to see a profit."

"We won't know until we make a start."

"And how do we do that? From what I can tell, you don't know any more than I do about construction."

"I do know a few things. My family has built several businesses from the ground up, so I know how to get started. First, we clear the site, level it out, find any problems with rocks or caliche."

"What about utilities? The kind of people you're hoping to sell to won't want to live in a cabin without electricity or running water. Getting back to nature has its limits for most people."

"We'll find solutions," he said. In a gentler tone, he continued, "I know what you want, Zannah."

Uncertainly, she met his eyes. "What?"

"You want to know how it's going to end before we even start. I'm afraid that's not possible."

She didn't like that he understood this about her, but he was already aware of how she felt about change in her life. There were people who ran toward new experiences with open arms. She simply wasn't one of them.

She was aware of Brady watching her as she brooded for a few seconds.

Then he said, "Maybe Gus shouldn't have told me you don't like change, but if we're going to be partners, it's something I need to know."

"You're right. He shouldn't have told you that, and I *don't* like change." Her gaze met his, then skittered away. She hated that he knew such a thing about her.

"But I also know you've been through big changes and survived."

Defensively, she glared at him.

Brady took a deep breath and lowered his head a little as if he was determined to get through this no matter what. "Like when your mother passed away. You could have stayed here at Eaglecrest, maintained your old life, worked at what you'd always known, avoided any more changes, but you didn't. You went to college and worked in Vegas before coming home."

Zannah wrapped her arms around her waist as she said, "What's your point?"

"My point is that change is inevitable, and it isn't always bad. It's something you learn to live with. You're a different person now, and Eaglecrest is different, too. Changes have to be made, or Eaglecrest won't exist at all." He gave her a firm look. "And I already know *that's* a change you couldn't live with."

Zannah pressed her lips together as she thought it over. At last, she said, "All right, then. We can explore the development of the mesa, but promise me that even in the planning stages, it will be environmentally friendly, ecologically responsible, will fit the landscape and…and be beautiful. If the plans fail to meet any of those standards, we won't do it."

Solemnly, he raised a hand. "I promise."

She looked at him for a few seconds, sure she saw a suspicious twinkle in his eyes, but his expression was a model of seriousness.

"Okay, then," she finally said.

"Good." As they walked back to the quad, he asked, "So why Las Vegas?"

"What?"

"Why go to college in Las Vegas, live and work there? I mean, that must have been a huge change."

"It was, but that's where my brother and his wife were, and I wanted to be near family. Then they had Emma and Joelle, which made it even better. Once they moved to Phoenix a couple of years ago, it was too hard. Why?"

"Just that you don't seem like a Vegas girl."

"I'm not. I'm home now." She paused. "And what exactly is a Vegas girl like?"

The look on her face must have told him he'd better tread carefully. He considered her for a second, then said, "Big city, neon lights." He released a gusting sigh. "Never mind. I'm going to shut up now. Let's get back. Isn't your brother arriving this afternoon?"

"Yes."

"From what I've seen of your family so far, you probably have certain traditions to follow when he arrives, right?" He smiled. "My mom always makes my favorite cake when I come home—or wherever their home is currently."

"Well, yes, we do," Zannah said. She used to take first-day-home photographs, but that had fallen away years ago. She wondered where her best camera was.

Brady glanced at the sky. "And it looks like it's going to storm."

She hadn't paid any attention to the weather report that day, an oversight she shouldn't repeat. A sudden storm could be dangerous when they had guests out on a trail ride.

THERE WAS VERY little talk between them on the return trip. Zannah concentrated on the rough track she had to follow, her mind heavy, full of everything she had experienced since the day Brady Gallagher had landed in her life.

She had little time to dwell on it all, though, because as soon as they got to the main house, twin human tornadoes erupted through the front door and into her arms.

"Aunt Zee! Where have you been?" Joelle demanded.

"We've been waiting for hours and hours!" Emma added.

The girls wrapped themselves around her, one on each side, and looked up at her expectantly. She hadn't seen them in weeks and was surprised that the tops of their heads were suddenly level with her chin. At nine and ten years old, they were growing into beautiful young women.

Both of them had their hair, dark like their mother's, pulled back into ponytails, and they were dressed in shirts, jeans and boots. They were ready for the ranch.

She gathered them close in a tight hug and planted kisses on their heads. "It hasn't been that long. We were only gone for a little while."

Brady walked up and she introduced him

to the girls. They each shook his hand politely and said, "Nice to meet you." Their parents had drilled good manners into them.

Brady smiled down at them. "Glad you're here. Your grandpa tells me you're a big help in the summer."

"Yes, we are," Emma answered in a matter-of-fact tone that made Brady chuckle.

He glanced at Zannah, and they shared a moment of amusement before she realized he had known her nieces all of one minute and he was already charming them the way he had charmed her father and probably everyone else he'd met at Eaglecrest.

She frowned, and he gave her a curious look before he turned toward his room to get ready for the evening's activities.

The girls immediately asked, "Is that your new boss?"

"Of course not." Zannah shot a glance after him, sure she could see his shoulders shaking with laughter. "He's my unplanned partner," she added, raising her voice.

"Come on," she said, looking back at her nieces. "Let's go get you two settled into your room. You've got the one right next to mine again."

"We know. Sharlene told us," Emma said, looking up at her aunt with a sweet smile. "Can't we have our own rooms now, Aunt Zee? Mom and Dad finally let us have our own rooms. We don't have to share at home anymore."

"Yeah," Joelle added. "I like having my own room."

"Sorry, my loves, but we don't have any extra rooms for you. You'll have to share."

"Oh, okay," they said together, but reluctance dragged at their voices.

"If we have to," Joelle added.

Zannah chuckled at their aggrieved looks, and glanced around. "Where's your dad?"

"He's in the office with Grandpa. They're looking at some dirty old papers and maps."

"Of course they are."

AFTER SHE HELPED her nieces settle in, Zannah headed toward the ranch office, only to be caught up short by the suddenly darkening sky and the sight of Robert and Greta Bardle running toward her.

"Have you seen Liam?" Greta called out frantically as she approached.

"No. What's wrong?"

"He's upset because this is our last day here," Robert answered. "We think he's run off to hide."

Greta cast a frantic look at the sky. "We've got to find him. It's going to rain. He'll be lost, cold and scared."

Zannah knew that the billowing clouds and gusting wind promised much more than rain. A full-on storm was coming.

"Do you have any idea which way he went? Did he say anything that might help us find him?"

They shook their heads. Robert answered, "He was upset when Chet said goodbye. Liam was crying and holding on to Chet's legs, but Chet had to go, said he had business to take care of in town. We peeled Liam off him, and Chet rode away. Maybe heading back to the barn? But Liam was with us then."

"We went inside to pack," Greta added. "It wasn't until fifteen minutes later that we missed Liam."

"Now, since you don't know the area very well, I'll contact Chet and see if he's seen Liam, then get the staff to begin searching," Zannah said. "We know the area very well. You stay in your cabin in case he comes back and we'll be in touch as soon as we find him. I promise."

The worried parents exchanged looks, but Zannah called on her years of social work training and experience to calm their fears. "We've mounted successful searches before, and since he's a small boy, he can't have gone far in fifteen minutes. Besides following Chet to the barn, are there any other places that he really liked? Places where he might go to hide?"

"Any place Chet was," Robert answered.

Zannah smiled. "A true case of hero worship. Chet is an experienced tracker, and so is Phoebe. We'll get them to help find Liam. And we'll call the sheriff's office. They will send a deputy and will call in a professional search team if necessary, but we'll do everything we can on our own while we wait for them."

Her reassuring tone, as well as a solid plan of action, seemed to calm them. It was a skill she had learned when dealing with emotional situations as a social worker. After she got a few more details from them, the Bardles went back to their cabin to wait for news.

Zannah headed for the office at a run, trying to outpace the storm that was swooping in, and startling her father and brother, who were examining Henry Stackhouse's old papers.

"Dad, Casey. I need your help." Quickly, she told them what was happening.

Casey headed for the door. "I'll get the staff together to help out. Let's meet in the dining room in ten minutes."

"Okay," Zannah agreed, grateful that her brother, the scientist, still knew exactly what to do in an emergency on the ranch.

She turned to her father. "After we get the staff together, it would be best if you stayed here to keep track of everyone's whereabouts and to coordinate the search."

To her grateful surprise, he didn't argue, but began gathering up the walkie-talkies that had been sitting on their chargers on a shelf by the window.

"Let's go," he said. "It'll be dark in two hours. We don't have time to waste."

Word had spread quickly about the little boy's disappearance, so almost every employee and guest was gathered in the dining room, awaiting news and instructions. Joelle and Emma were there with Sharlene, bright-eyed with excitement.

Brady, Phoebe and Casey were standing together, talking quietly as they waited. As soon as Zannah and her father walked in, Gus called for quiet.

"Thank you, everyone, for coming in, but at this point, we need only experienced staff to help find Liam. We'd like all the guests to return to their cabins to wait for news. We can't take a chance on having someone else get lost." He glanced at Zannah, who nodded her agreement.

"Zannah?" came a hesitant voice from the crowd. Lauren, the newest member of the housekeeping staff, was nearby, holding the hand of her small red-haired daughter, Rebecca.

"Yes?"

"Will you need me?" She glanced around uncertainly. "I wouldn't know where to look, and with this storm, Becky will be scared."

"Oh, no. We have plenty of help. Go on to your cabin. We'll know where to find you if we need you."

Lauren gave her a grateful smile, scooped up her daughter and hurried out.

Zannah looked after her for a second. There had been something in her demeanor that went deeper than concern for the missing boy or the coming storm. Something much more fearful.

She was brought back to the present crisis by a sharp crack of lightning, followed by a roll of thunder.

The remaining guests left quickly for their own cabins.

The staff gathered around, waiting for their assignments. Zannah directed them to different areas of the ranch while Gus handed out the walkie-talkies. When she asked about Chet, she was told that no one had seen him, and attempts to phone him had been unsuccessful.

"He'll be in touch, Zannah," Gus assured her. "He always checks in around seven, but with this storm coming, his phone may not be working. I'll coordinate from here," he said, indicating his walkie-talkie.

"Okay, Dad."

Casey warned his daughters to stay inside with Sharlene before heading off with his partner.

Zannah was right behind him when Brady caught up to her. "I'm coming with you," he said.

"I can travel faster and farther on my own."

"I'm sure you can, but two pairs of eyes are better than one."

"I don't—"

"Want to waste time arguing," he finished for her. "Me, either. Let's go."

She knew he was right, so she pelted out the door, Brady at her heels as they started for the barn. Fat drops of rain began hammering them as they went.

Inside the barn, they began a systematic search of each stall and every nook or cranny big enough to hide a little boy. They climbed into the loft, sifted through piles of loose hay and double-checked the sliding bolt on the double doors through which the hay was loaded in. The bolt was secure, too high and heavy for a small boy to open.

"Nothing," Zannah said when they met once again at the front door of the barn. The brief rain shower had stopped, but rolling black clouds overhead told them another was on its way.

Brady used the walkie-talkie to contact Gus, who said no one else had found Liam, but they were expanding the search area. A deputy had arrived and was talking to the Bardles, and the search team had been alerted. Gus reported that he had still been unable to reach Chet.

After signing off, Brady glanced across the yard to a small building half-hidden behind some trees.

"What's that?" he asked, pointing.

"It was a pump house for the water system at one time, but we don't use it anymore. All the equipment's been removed. After Chet's parents died, Dad let him store their things in there. Chet's been going through it slowly." She paused as a memory clicked in.

"What?"

"He's still settling their estate. That's probably why he went to town."

"Do you think he went in that building today?" Brady asked, starting across the muddy ground. "Maybe Liam followed."

"Maybe, but Chet keeps it locked, and he's got the only key."

"Still worth a look."

Zannah followed as he hurried to the door. As expected, it was locked. They walked the perimeter, looking for another way in, and ended up back at the door.

"There's a window up there," he pointed out, pulling a small but powerful flashlight from his pocket and shining the beam upward.

"It's so dirty, you wouldn't be able to see anything." Zannah glanced at the sky. "The rain is coming again, and it's getting dark fast."

"Then we'd better not waste any time."

She frowned as she looked up. "Okay. There's a ladder in the barn. Come on."

They returned to the barn at a run, but the ladder wasn't propped along the back wall as it should have been, or anywhere else they could see.

"Now what?" Zannah asked on their way back to the pump house.

"I have a plan." Brady studied the muddy ground, then looked up at the window again. "The door is seven feet tall," he murmured to himself. "The space between it and the window is about a foot. The window looks like it opens from the bottom and swings upward. Might be locked from the inside, but we'll chance it." He tilted his head from side to side and rolled his shoulders like a prizefighter preparing to enter the ring. "Yeah, this will work."

"How are you going to climb up there?" Zannah asked.

"I'm not." He turned to her. "You are."

CHAPTER SEVEN

"WHAT DO YOU MEAN?" She looked at him in alarm, then visually measured the distance to the window. "I'm too heavy."

"I'll bet you don't weigh more than a buck forty."

"I weigh one hundred and twenty-five pounds, thank you very much," she said testily.

He waved a hand. "I can bench-press that much any day of the week."

She had a mental image of herself held aloft like a set of barbells.

"Or I could throw you up there." He flexed his shoulders and tilted his head from side to side once again.

"No."

"Oh, come on," Brady said, his face tightening in exasperation. "Do you really want to stand here arguing? Liam might be inside, in distress, scared and hungry, crying for his mom and dad, afraid he'll never see them again."

She quickly shook her head. "No, no, of course not, and you don't have to lay it on so thick, Brady. How are we going to do this?"

He held his hands out, fingers interlaced. "I'll boost you up and you can look in the window. Use my flashlight."

"Okay."

She took the flashlight, tucked it into her pocket, then placed her hands on Brady's shoulders and her right foot into his hands, murmuring an apology for the muddy state of her boots.

"Don't worry about it. We're both going to be a lot wetter and muddier by the time this is over."

He lifted her easily, then stood with his back to the door so she could peer inside.

"See anything?"

Zannah tried to shine the flashlight through the window. "No. As I thought, this window's too dirty."

"Can you get it open?"

"Only if you can boost me up a little higher."

He managed to heave her up a little bit more.

She scrambled for a hold on the window ledge, but there wasn't enough area to grasp.

"Um," he said, sounding winded. "I may have overestimated my ability to hold you up like this."

"What do you suggest we do?"

"You'll have to stand on my shoulders."

"In my boots? How much punishment can you take?"

"On second thought, maybe you'd better get down and take them off."

Before she could answer, he lowered her to the ground and stood, rubbing his lower back, then his shoulders as she leaned against the side of the pump house and pulled off her boots and socks.

She dropped them and said, "Okay, but you're going to get covered with mud."

"I'm already covered with mud. Come on. Quit worrying about—"

"Unimportant things." She flapped a hand at him. "I know. I know." Looking up, she said, "I wish my family had been in the circus instead of the cattle business."

The walkie-talkie crackled with reports from the staff members—no sign of Liam. This gave added urgency to the situation, so

Zannah once again placed her foot in Brady's hands, then twisted to swing a leg around his neck and sit on his shoulders. He steadied himself against the door.

"Don't move," Zannah cautioned as she carefully tilted to one side and lifted her foot to place it on his shoulder.

"I don't plan to. I've got a buck forty–pound woman on my shoulders."

"One twenty-five!"

Annoyed, she placed a hand on his head, digging her fingers into his thick hair.

"Ow! What are you doing?"

"Getting a grip," she answered sweetly. "Now, stand still."

She got her other foot in position, then steadied herself against the wall. To her surprise, she was able to stand up easily and reach the window.

"I still can't see anything, and you're right, the window is latched from the inside." Frustrated, she rattled the window in its frame.

"I'll have to break it, but that might send glass flying over a frightened little boy."

"Do you have an alternative plan?" he asked in a dry tone.

"No. Okay, here goes," she said. "I'll use

your flashlight. Keep your head down in case glass falls on you."

"Not only is my head down, but the rest of me will be pounded in like a railroad spike if you don't hurry up."

"All right, all right."

She held the flashlight with the metal handle pointing toward the glass and lifted her arm over her head. "Here goes," she said.

"What are you guys *doing?*" asked a small voice from roughly the level of Brady's thigh.

Brady jerked in surprise. Zannah, who was already off balance, pitched to the side. The flashlight flew from her hand and she scrambled for a hold on the wall, but her hand slid down the rough surface and she snatched it away, full of splinters. Her feet slipped and she had a moment of panic as her arms flailed. By sheer luck, she slid down onto Brady's shoulders.

"Watch out," he yelled, though she wasn't sure who he was talking to. He took a few awkward steps as he tried to keep from going down, and finally thumped up against the side of the pump house. Zannah's elbow hit the wall, picking up even more splinters.

"Ow," she said, grasping Brady's head with

her uninjured hand, then muttered, "Sorry," when he yelped in pain.

Both of them were breathing heavily as they looked down to see Liam Bardle staring up at them.

"That was funny," he said, grinning a gap-toothed little-boy grin. "You guys are funny."

"Liam, where have you been?" Brady asked as he helped Zannah to the ground.

"Everyone's been looking for you," Zannah added. Grateful to be on solid ground again, she wiped her feet the best she could, then quickly donned her socks and boots. She knelt before the boy. "Are you okay? Where were you?"

He looked away. "Hidin'. I'm good at it. I was hidin' 'cause I don't wanna go."

"So you followed Chet?"

"Yeah." Liam pointed to the pump house. "In there, but I hid, then he left, but I wanted to stay." He pulled a granola bar from his pocket. "I'm gonna camp out."

Brady looked at the padlocked door. "How did you get out just now?"

"I heard bumping and people talking, so I came out."

"I mean, how did you get out of there?"

"In the wall." He pointed toward the back of the building.

"Show us, Liam," Brady instructed him.

They followed him around to the back while Brady radioed Gus to report the boy had been found safe and well. When they reached the back of the building, Liam pointed to a loose board they hadn't noticed in their search of the perimeter.

Bending down, Zannah swung it aside and saw that the wide plank's opening would have given her plenty of room to wiggle through. Shaking her head, she stood up.

Giving him a stern look, she said, "Liam, I'm glad you were safe, but you gave everyone a bad scare."

He hung his head. "Yeah, I'm gonna be in time-out till I'm old." He glanced up at her and Brady. "Like you."

Zannah laughed, and Brady rolled his eyes at her.

"Let's get you back to your family," he said.

"Can I ride on your head like she did?"

"Sure. I'm already several inches shorter than I was an hour ago, so it'll be easier to lift you up. I might take up a new career as a pack mule."

"Well, you've certainly got the mule part down," Zannah responded brightly. "At least the stubborn part. And do I need to remind you whose idea it was for me to climb on your shoulders?"

"Nah. I'll remember for the rest of my life."

He grinned at her as he lifted Liam and swung him onto his shoulders.

"Yay," the boy shouted. "Giddy up!"

It was almost full dark by the time they reached the Bardles' cabin. Robert and Greta rushed out with their two daughters to sweep their son up and check him for injuries. They thanked Zannah and Brady, then took their adventurous boy inside with the sheriff's deputy accompanying them.

At that moment, the skies opened up again. A heavy rain began pounding down on them. They both started to run toward the main house, but Zannah hit a patch of mud that sent her skidding.

Brady grabbed her hand. She sloughed around in a circle, then came to a stop as she bounced up against his chest.

He didn't waste any time but picked her up and ran with her, carrying her the last few yards to the front porch of the main house.

Gulping for air, she looked up in surprise as he set her on her feet. "I thought you'd had enough of carrying me today."

He swiped rain from his face as he said, "That's what partners are for. Aren't you glad you've got a partner?"

"Oh, um, maybe," she answered, out of breath and trying to figure out what had happened. In confusion, she pushed wet hair out of her eyes, then flinched at the pain in her hand. She looked down at it.

"What's wrong?" he asked, tilting her palm toward the glow from one of the bright porch lights.

"Splinters." She pulled her hand away. "I think I've got some in my elbow, too."

"Want me to pull them out? Looks like the official first aid person is out of commission."

Zannah looked up at him. His wet hair was plastered to his head, and rivulets of rainwater ran down his face. He swiped them away good-naturedly with the sleeve of his also-sopping shirt. Through it all, his eyes were bright with laughter. Her gaze fell to his lips, which were curved in a smile directed at her.

All of the emotional ups and downs of the past week settled into a feeling of solid rightness, as if where they were at this moment was exactly where they were supposed to be.

Zannah felt that momentarily, a different kind of storm would break, one that wasn't related to the weather. She had the crazy thought that it wouldn't be a bad thing, because they were cocooned in some kind of safe haven they had created.

Confused and alarmed, Zannah pulled her hand away and stepped back.

"Nuh…no. I can handle it."

"Oh, come on, the ones in your elbow, too?"

"I'll get Sharlene to help me."

Whirling around, she dashed the few steps across the porch and into the house, shutting the door behind her.

THE NEXT MORNING, Gus stood beneath the shelter of the awning above the back door and looked out across the ranch as he sipped a cup of coffee.

He had already been out to check for storm damage. He was chagrined to see that the main road onto the ranch from the highway had been washed out in several areas because of the force of the storm, and because he hadn't been able to afford repairs last winter.

He had strung yellow caution tape and closed the main gate, even posted detour signs.

Anyone coming or going would have to take an older, much longer route to the highway, but that road was in marginally better shape than the washed-out one.

Zannah and Brady would have to undertake the repairs, and soon. He felt guilty about the neglected repairs, but at the time he'd had no choice, no financial option. Now, with Brady's money, Zannah had that option.

He was making a conscious choice to leave it all to them, and he had to stick with that decision.

In the meantime, he would enjoy his coffee and the spicy cinnamon scent of rolls just delivered by his sister to the ranch kitchen. He knew he would get to eat one later. In the meantime, he was enjoying the fresh-washed scent of the air, drinking coffee and wishing he knew why the hell Sharlene was so mad at him.

Sharlene had come into view around the corner of the farthest cabin, empty now of guests, ready to be cleaned and prepared for the next family. She was pushing a heavy laundry cart down the sidewalk toward the commercial washers and dryers housed in the utility room. Ordinarily, he would have hurried over to help, but he knew it would make her even madder than she already was.

Sulkily, he watched as she turned the cart over to the new girl. What was her name? Laurie? They talked for a few minutes, then Sharlene started toward her office, pulling one of her never-ending lists from her apron pocket and making some notes.

A few weeks ago, he would have known everything that Sharlene knew about this girl, but as he'd become more and more involved in his plans, he'd lost touch with the day-to-day details of both the ranch and the cowboy college. He knew that should bother him, but he had a right to do what *he* wanted to do for once. Didn't he? Wasn't that why he'd encouraged Zannah to come home when he realized her job was killing her? She had the right to live a life that she loved. Wasn't that why he wanted to take on a partner? He also had the right to live a life, to do a job that he loved.

He wished everyone else could see that. He also wished he didn't feel so guilty about it. More than anyone else, he felt that he was letting Sharlene down.

He would give her a little time, then try to talk to her. It was true that she and Esther had been best friends. Before Esther got sick, they would take overnight trips to Las Vegas during the slow winter season and come back richer or poorer than they'd been when they left—and always with hilarious stories of their adventures. He'd never been jealous of the fun they'd had. Because he and Stella had been raised by alcoholic parents who loved to gamble, nightlife had no appeal for him. Being a rancher was enough of a gamble. Also, he'd understood early on that marriage to Esther meant that Sharlene would be in their lives forever.

Heartbroken after Esther's death, they had leaned on each other and held up Zannah. They had been a unit of three, supporting and assisting one another. When his daughter had gone off to college, he and Sharlene had become a unit of two, getting each other through the days, then the weeks, the months and the years.

One day, he'd realized that Sharlene hadn't been only Esther's best friend, but his, as well. He still remembered the shock of that realization, which he'd never shared with anyone.

But now, even Sharlene was leaving him. Them, he mentally corrected himself. Or at least, she was talking about it. But she couldn't do that, he thought, fuming internally. He was counting on her.

As much as he didn't want to risk her wrath, he knew he had to talk to her. He decided to wait a little while, finish his coffee and enjoy the crisp freshness of the rain-washed morning.

Later, he returned his cup to the kitchen, ate the cinnamon roll that had been saved for him and talked to the kitchen staff for a few minutes about the incoming guests. Both Zannah and Sharlene were wrong about him and his interest in Eaglecrest. He still cared about it, about everything that went on, but he wanted to care about other things, too.

He stepped outside once again, took a deep breath and headed toward Sharlene's office, only to be brought up short by the sound of a man's voice coming from inside.

"It's a big decision," he was saying.

The door was open a few inches, so Gus leaned closer, completely unashamed to be eavesdropping. After all, whatever decision

Sharlene made would affect him and everyone else on the ranch.

"It's long past time for me to make it, though, don't you think? Everyone else has already moved on this, taken the chance."

"That's true."

"But it's a big step." Worry echoed in Sharlene's voice.

"Let me know what you want to do."

"I will. Thanks, Jim. And thanks for stopping by. I could have come to you."

"It's my pleasure, Sharlene. I was already out this way."

There was a silence that Gus thought was far too long for someone who was getting ready to leave. Was this guy kissing her goodbye or something? His stomach made an odd little flip as he thought about that.

Footsteps approached the door, and Gus barely had time to step back a few feet before it swung open and a man of about his own age emerged. He saw Gus and nodded at him, then walked away, carrying a briefcase.

As he watched the man leave, Gus's mind flicked quickly through all the people he knew locally and decided he'd never seen this guy before. He wasn't from Raymond,

Arizona. Maybe not even from the surrounding area.

How could he find out who this guy was?

Sharlene was smiling what Gus thought looked like a secret little smile as she watched him leave, but it disappeared when she turned and saw him.

"Who was that?" he asked.

"My private business," she answered sassily, turning back into her office. "And none of yours."

"Does that guy have something to do with you wanting to leave?"

"Why do you care, Gus? You won't be here." She sat down in her chair and picked up the phone. "I realize you no longer work here, but I do, and I've got plenty to do."

The dismissal hung in the air between them, but Gus wasn't ready to go. Instead, he sat down in the chair facing her. She appeared to think better of making the call and put down the phone.

"What do you want, Gus?" Sharlene asked, smoothing her hair away from her face, then folding her hands patiently on top of her desk.

"I want to know what you plan to do."

"I'm not at liberty to divulge that at this time," she answered coolly.

Gus pressed his lips together as he stared at her, trying to figure out what he needed to say. He'd never been in this place before, not with Sharlene. She was reliable, steady, dependable.

"You're needed here, Sharlene."

"So are you, but that doesn't seem to be stopping you from doing what you want to do."

"I've worked this ranch most of my life."

"So have I."

Frustrated at her untroubled tone, he sat forward. "People are depending on you."

She smiled but didn't look happy. "Ditto," she responded. "But that's not stopping you from going off and doing what you want to do."

He pounced. "So you *are* going off somewhere? Can you wait until I get back? How about if I give you a raise?"

"How about if you quit trying to spend money you don't have?" She stood up suddenly and leaned over the desk. "You have something to do that's important to you, Gus, and so do I. We'll go our separate ways."

She looked so angry that he stood up automatically and backed away from her. "I thought you'd always be here."

"So did I." Sharlene sighed and shook her head. "We were both wrong."

"So, DAD'S GOT gold fever, hmm?" Casey said as they rode out together to check the stock and the road damage after the rainstorm. Joelle and Emma were busy helping the staff get ready for new guests. They had rushed to their favorite spot for gathering wildflowers and were busily creating bouquets for every room and cabin.

Zannah groaned. "Yes, a serious case. What do you think of him hunting down that old myth?"

"I think it's nuts, but he's determined."

"I know. It's mystifying to me."

They rode along in silence for a few minutes, heading toward the pasture where the cattle had bedded down for the night. Zannah switched her reins from hand to hand, easing the irritation to the one that had been full of splinters the night before. Sharlene had helped her remove them, but her flesh was still tender.

She had slept badly, tossing and turning,

telling herself it was because her hand and elbow hurt, but really because she had been thinking about the crazy moment in last night's rain when she had been so drawn to Brady, momentarily willing to let him tend to her wounds, to comfort her. It was the last thing in the world she wanted, but she couldn't shake her curiosity about what might have happened.

Early this morning, she had awakened thinking about Brady, prompting her to recall his comment about traditions. She had uncovered her favorite camera in her closet and prepped it for some candid shots of Casey and his daughters. The simple activity had given her a sense of peace and purpose he had known she needed.

She was grateful to have Casey beside her. Like most little girls, she had adored her big brother. When they were young, he had seemed to love Eaglecrest as much as she did, but in high school, a biology teacher had inspired him to look at the wider world, to see what someone with his interests and talents could do to create hardy strains of grasses and other plants to provide for animals and humans alike. She was proud of him and his accomplishments, but she missed him, missed having a big brother to rely on.

Casey gave her a sidelong glance as if he was weighing his next words very carefully. "Sounds like your new partner has big plans, Zannie."

"I know."

"And you don't like them at all, do you?" Casey looked at her with the kind of wisdom and indulgence he'd shown her all her life.

"I guess I've made that obvious, haven't I?"

"To absolutely everyone."

Zannah grimaced and shrugged, hearing the truth but wanting to ward it off.

Casey pulled up on the reins, then twisted in the saddle to face her. "Listen, I'm not going to tell you how to feel about this. You're smart and mature and you'll figure out how to handle whatever happens."

"But?" she prompted.

"But I'll listen if you want to vent, want to complain, want to indulge in self-pity."

"Thanks, I guess," she said uncertainly because she could hear another but coming.

"But only if it ends up being constructive. Only you can decide that. If you want to keep Eaglecrest—"

"Unchanged," she added for him, then held up her hand. "I know. I know. I have to accept change." She gave him a desperate look. "But *Hawk's Eye*, Casey. It's beautiful, clean, untouched."

"And not helping to pay the bills," he added drily.

"You sound exactly like Brady," she grumbled. "And Dad."

"That's fine with me if it helps you quit stewing over this."

"Stewing is a little harsh," she protested.

Casey let that go, obviously ready to make another point. "And you can't hang onto the past or try to preserve this place for my girls. If they want to live and work here, fine. If not, fine. They may want something completely different. Emma, for example." He grinned and shook his head in bafflement. "She's decided she wants to be a rock star. Thinks all she has to do is find that magical place where they create rock stars and she'll be made into one. She says she'll allow Joelle to be a backup singer."

Zannah laughed. "Big of her. Um, am I right in supposing they've got the Worth family musical talent?"

"Sadly, yes. Which means none that we can find. Vanessa's holding out hope, though, that one of them will play her old violin."

"Whatever they do, they'll be good at it."

"I know they will." Casey nudged his horse and they began moving again, soon arriving at the pasture, seeing the cattle up and milling about, finding abundant water this morning, as well as fresh grass.

He looked around with interest. Zannah could see the scientist in him assessing the grass and the ground where it was growing.

After a few minutes, he went on, "You will, too, Zannie. Stay here, go, run off and join the rodeo. Whatever you do, you'll be fine. Make sure it's what you want, and that you're not staying here, preserving this place for our long-dead ancestors. I love this ranch, but I always knew it wouldn't be my life like it was for Mom's family, and for her and Dad. You've got to think of Eaglecrest's future, sure, but not at the expense of your own."

"You're a botanist, for crying out loud. How do you know so much about psychology?"

"I don't," he answered with a self-assured grin. "I just know you. It's my big-brother superpower."

CASEY RETURNED TO Phoenix, and the subsequent days fell into a routine with the girls helping wherever they could. To his delight, Gus discovered that his granddaughters were a ready audience for his tales about the Lost Teamsters Mine.

"So, they could never find it again?" Joelle was asking as the three of them examined the geographical maps.

Gus knew they couldn't really understand the topography. The dizzying lines indicated elevations, but it meant nothing to a couple of little girls. They knew what gold was, though.

"No."

"They didn't take a picture of it?" Emma wanted to know.

"They didn't have a camera, and it was more than a hundred years before cell phones were invented," he answered, getting a kick out of their goggle-eyed amazement.

This was what he'd wanted all along, somebody to listen, ask questions, be as enthusiastic about this as he was. He would have been happiest if it had been his daughter or Sharlene. Casey had been polite and indulgent, but clearly not interested.

Even getting Brady to be as enthused as he

was would have been nice, but there didn't seem to be time for it. Once Brady had become fully involved in the running of the ranch, he had limited time for Gus.

He'd also begun to ask uncomfortable questions about the search for the mine, like how long Gus would keep up the search and how many months or years he planned to devote to it.

Couldn't a man have a dream without a timeline attached to it? Gus groused to himself. Thank goodness for these girls. They were enthralled without being judgmental.

He pulled out a large sheet of paper and spread it on the desk. "One of the remaining miners did draw this picture of the cave entrance," he said, showing it to them.

Joelle frowned. "It could be any old cave entrance. There's a bunch of them up there." She nodded toward the mountains.

"How are you going to find the right one without getting lost, Grandpa?" Emma wanted to know.

Realizing he might be scaring them, he answered with a confident smile. "I've got maps, see?" He gestured toward the yellowed documents.

"Yeah, maps are good," Emma said. "Mrs. Gomez made us learn about them in school. It was hard."

Their matching looks of skepticism didn't change, so he added, "Also, my phone has GPS, so I'll be able to find my way with no problem."

"Sometimes cell phones don't work up there," Emma pointed out. "Maybe you can't find your way home, or other people can't find you if you're lost."

Joelle gazed at him solemnly, a line of worry forming an exclamation point between her brows. "You'd be gone forever."

Touched by their concern, Gus gave them each a hug. "Hey, I won't let that happen."

Suddenly Emma brightened and Gus felt encouraged until she asked, "If you don't come back, can I have your room?"

CHAPTER EIGHT

"It's GREAT TO have you back, Juan," Zannah said, smiling at the young man who had been gone for several days. "How's your mom?"

"Much better." Juan set aside the bridle he had mended with a strip of leather and said, "She's still weak from that lung infection, but she's getting stronger every day."

Carolina Flores had worked for them years ago but had moved on to a better-paying job in town. Still, she was considered to be part of the Eaglecrest extended family.

"Good," Zannah said quietly. "That's a big relief."

Juan's deep brown eyes searched her face for a few seconds. He gave her a gentle smile, and added, "Don't worry about her, Zannah. She's going to get well."

She nodded and smiled, knowing he was trying to assure her that his mother was in no danger of dying. He was a gentle young man, barely twenty-one, who planned to become a veterinarian specializing in large animals. He was saving money toward that goal and Zannah wished there was some way they could help him. She knew that two weeks off from work had set him back. His mother had been off from her job in the county recorder's office for over a month, so money was tight for the whole family.

"I understand there's a new boss here?" he asked. "Some guy who took over some of my chores."

"In a manner of speaking. He's an investor."

Juan picked up the bucket of currying tools. "Well, I guessed he's not a horse groomer."

"He learned his skills from online videos," she answered, and the two of them shared a chuckle.

"At least he was willing to try," Juan pointed out.

"Yes, I suppose that says something in his favor."

Juan shot her a curious glance as if questioning her choice of words. She was questioning them herself. Thinking that over as she headed out of the barn, she suddenly turned back. "Actually, he's more than an investor. It looks like he's going to be a full partner, or so my dad says."

"Good," Juan said, nodding slowly. "You'll need the help with Gus being gone."

"So they keep telling me."

"You sound like you don't believe that," Juan said. "Nobody else does, either."

"What do you mean?"

"He's made some suggestions no one seems to want to try."

"Like what?"

"Like trying to find ways to reduce waste in the kitchen."

"How did that go over?"

"Not well. Cook's not willing to try it."

"No one said anything about it to me."

"Why bother? They know you're on their side." Juan turned away. "I'd better get to work before someone tries to tell me how to do my job."

Zannah went outside, mulling over what he'd said. Brady hadn't talked to her about it. Probably because he knew she wouldn't support him.

She regretted that her attitude was affecting the staff. Her only excuse was that she was still scrambling to find her way in this new situation.

She checked in with Chet and Phoebe, who were introducing their newest guests to the routines of the ranch and to the horses they would be riding and caring for during the next few days, then went into the office.

Brady sat at the desk, engrossed in a computer program.

The room was stifling, so she left the door open and rounded the desk to open the windows. As a warm breeze stirred the papers on the desk, he looked up from the screen. He rubbed his eyes for a few seconds before giving her an ironic smile.

"You've been here for a while now. What do you think of all the hard work that goes into this place?"

"It's hard," he admitted.

"But you're not ready to quit?"

"Nah, I like a challenge, remember?"

He tilted his head and grinned in a way that made her heart do an odd little dance. She straightened and said, "As hard as this has been, it can get worse."

"You're right about that," he agreed, indicating the stacks of paper and the computer screen. "It helps to have a clear picture of the receipts and all the bills that need to be paid."

"Which side is winning?" she asked, sitting down opposite him, leaning back in the chair and stretching her legs out in front of her.

"I think you know, Zannah."

When he didn't go on, she glanced up to meet his gaze. "What?"

He stood up and stretched, then came to sit on the corner of the desk. He propped one knee up, then idly swung his foot back and forth.

Momentarily, Zannah was mesmerized by the motion. It was such an unconsciously male thing to do that she couldn't look away. She had grown up around men who had been strong, self-confident and capable in their chosen fields. She had worked with men who were good at paperwork and the onerous details of government work. She had dealt with some of the worst kinds of men, ones who only understood brute strength and handed out abuse.

Looking at Brady, though, she felt unexpected warmth for him, for his strength, his willingness to learn, his business knowledge, even his wealth of ideas—though she rarely agreed with them.

Helplessly, she had to admit he was also really sexy. Startled at where her thoughts were going, Zannah finally pulled her attention away from his body and back to his solemn expression.

"It's time for us to discuss more ways to come up with additional income."

"I thought your Hawk's Eye Mesa project was supposed to solve our cash-flow problems." The thought still stung.

"We're still waiting on the environmental impact report, and Hawk's Eye is not a sure thing, remember? It might not pay off until next year, or the year after that."

"Brady, I—" She stopped herself, recalling that she had to quit her habit of becoming defensive at every one of his suggestions. "What did you have in mind?"

He blinked as if he was surprised at her sudden about-face. "There are only certain things we can control. There's nothing we can do about the price of beef."

"It's been pretty good lately."

"But we have to sell at market price, which only goes so high, and then, from what I can see, it can fall as easily."

"This looks like it will be a good year, though."

"So I hear, but even if we sell a major part of the herd, it won't get us what we need." He paused for a second, obviously judging her reaction. Zannah kept her expression neutral.

"We need to raise fees for the cowboy college side of things."

"Raise fees? It's already pretty expensive. There are other outfits that don't charge as much as we do. Won't our guests go to them instead?"

"The notes on the bulletin board in my cabin tell me you have—*we* have—loyal customers who come back year after year and recommend us to their friends."

"But will that keep up if we charge more? Will we be pricing ourselves right out of the market?"

"I don't think so. People want a quality experience and they get it here." He lifted his hand and made a sweeping gesture toward the mountains. "And I'm betting there are few places that have this kind of spectacular view."

Zannah shook her head. "I don't know. All

these changes. You've only been here a few weeks. The deal isn't formalized yet—"

"And I'm still learning the ropes. Literally," he said, nodding toward a coil of rope he'd been using to practice his skills. "We haven't made my buy-in official yet because I had to learn as much as I could about the business. But the truth is, we're drowning in a river of red ink and we've got to turn this boat around."

Puzzled, Zannah stared at him. "Boat?"

"Never mind. I know I'm mixing my metaphors. My point is, we've got to come up with additional income."

"Raise fees, hmm? How much were you thinking?"

OUTSIDE THE WINDOW, Joelle and Emma leaned in to listen. Ordinarily, the conversations of adults didn't interest them very much, but this was different.

"What do you think Brady means?" Joelle whispered. "What river of red ink?"

Emma shrugged and turned in the direction of the San Ramon. "That one, maybe?"

"You think it turned red? Ick."

"Don't know. Let's go look." Emma started

off because as the oldest, and bossiest, she felt she had the right to lead the way.

It was more than half a mile to the river, but they hurried, then stood gazing down at the water that looked the same as ever to them.

The two girls looked at each other and shrugged.

"Grown-ups," Emma said, shaking her head.

BRADY WALKED OUT onto the wide terrace at the back of the main lodge and said good night to the guests who were leaving the getting-to-know-you party.

Across the room, he saw several employees, including Chet and Juan, sitting around a table. They were laughing and sharing stories. It was obvious that they all knew each other well, had all been part of the same staff for a long time. They were friends, with Juan Flores as their leader, even though he was younger than most of them. Brady had already noticed that Juan had a warm, friendly personality and an ability to make people feel comfortable and welcome. It made for a tight-knit group among the staff. Brady understood that, as well as their reluctance to let a new boss in.

"Good thing I like a challenge," he murmured, walking up to them. "How about if I buy a round of drinks?" he asked.

Juan looked up and grinned. "How about if you give us all a raise?"

Everyone laughed, including Brady, who pulled out a chair and joined them. "Let's negotiate."

DARKNESS HAD LONG since fallen by the time Zannah convinced her nieces that it was time to leave the getting-to-know-you party with all of their new guests and go to bed.

They knew better than to argue with her, because their father had warned them that if they caused any trouble, he would be right back to get them. They had to content themselves with mutinous looks at their aunt.

She mollified them by reading an extra chapter of their current favorite book. They objected to their bedtime story, but she knew it was resistance only for show. They loved the bedtime ritual she had established with them when they were small.

Once the chapter was finished and they

were settled into their twin beds, Emma looked at her sister, who nodded.

"Aunt Zee? Where's the river of red ink?"

"What do you mean?" Zannah paused as she was reaching for the light switch and looked from one girl to the other.

"We heard you and Brady talking in the office."

"I didn't see you."

"We were outside the window."

"That's called eavesdropping."

"Yeah," Joelle agreed. "We were eavesdropping."

Zannah laughed and came over to sit at the foot of Emma's bed.

"We know it's not the San Ramon," Joelle continued, turning on her side and propping one arm under her head. "We went down there to look for it."

"Red ink is only a saying people use meaning they're spending more money than they're making."

"Huh?"

"Like last year when you two had a lemonade stand in front of your house. You earned money, right?" In answer to their nods, she continued. "But if you'd made less than you spent on your supplies, that would have meant you were in the red."

"So, Eaglecrest doesn't have money?" Emma asked.

"We have some, but we need more."

"Oh, don't worry about that. Grandpa will find the lost mine, and we'll have all that gold," Joelle said with assurance.

"Let's wait and see if that happens," Zannah hedged. She wasn't going to discourage their belief in his ability to find the mine, even if no one else really thought he would.

Zannah looked from one to the other of them. "Did Grandpa tell you that?"

"No," Emma answered breezily. "We know he'll find the gold and we'll all be rich."

"Let's hope so." Zannah's mind clicked back to the beginning of this conversation. "Wait. Did you say you'd gone down to the river?"

The girls exchanged looks in response to her sharp tone, then Emma answered for both of them. "Sure. How else were we going to see the red ink?"

"You know you can't go wandering off by yourselves without telling anyone where you're going, don't you? Don't ever do that again."

"It was only to the river."

"Which can be very dangerous after a rain like the one we had a few nights ago."

When they didn't respond, she prompted them, "Promise me you won't go down to the river by yourselves again."

"We promise," they answered in unison, but they exchanged the kind of look she had seen from them many times, as if they were silently communicating something other than agreement with her.

For her own peace of mind, she ignored that as well as their reluctant tone, gave them each a kiss and flipped off the light as she left, hoping she had extracted a promise they would keep.

SHARLENE CHECKED HERSELF over in the mirror, then turned to the side to evaluate how she looked. Facing front, she gazed into the reflection of her own eyes and said, "You know you're being ridiculous, right? You probably won't be able to say anything to change his mind." Looking down, she fluffed the skirt of the red summer dress that had been in her closet since last year—waiting for a special occasion.

She loved the dress because it was exactly the kind of thing she would have bought in the old days when she had gone shopping with Esther.

"I don't know how special this is going to be, but it's certainly going to be some kind of occasion."

With a shake of her head, she turned away. The price of being single her whole life was that she spent way too much time talking to herself, way too much time alone once the day's work was finished. It might have been different if she had been in the main house with Gus and Zannah, because there would have been people around all the time. She had her own place, though, not quite a cabin, but a very small house that she had enjoyed fixing up.

It had been different when Esther was alive. They usually met in the evening after work to drink tea and discuss what had happened that day and what needed to be done tomorrow. These past ten years had been hard without her best friend, but Sharlene knew she had to stop pining and move on.

If Gus could do it, so could she.

She slipped on some sandals and smiled at

her own vanity. She hadn't worn these since the last time she had a date, and that had been last summer.

"It's all changing now," she murmured and went out looking for Gus. Of course, he was in the first place she looked—the office. As usual, he had those blasted maps and papers spread out over every surface. She still didn't understand what he hoped to learn from them, but she also didn't want to ask because she had something to say.

Sharlene closed the door behind her and quietly turned the lock so they wouldn't be disturbed. Her stomach fluttered with apprehension as she stepped into the room.

Gus glanced up to see who had entered the room, and his eyes widened with a mixture of surprise and alarm.

"Uh, hey, Sharlene. You going somewhere?"

"Yes, to see you." She strode across the room and stood before him.

His look grew wary, unsure of what was coming. "I thought you were mad at me."

"I am."

His brow wrinkled.

"I want to talk to you, then I'm going into town to meet with my new partners."

"Partners?"

"Several of us are getting together to invest in a business."

"What kind of business?"

"A bed-and-breakfast. We're going to fix up the old Mosely house and open it for guests."

"What?" He stared at her.

"Lucas Fordham bought the place years ago and is willing to part with it for a song."

"Yeah, a song entitled 'I'm a Broken-Down Old Fire Trap—Enter at Your Own Risk.'"

"Nevertheless, we're going to make a go of it."

Sharlene could almost hear the gears turning in his head as he tried to determine how this would impact him and Eaglecrest—but mostly him.

"You're not leaving here, are you? I mean, somebody else will run the place, right?"

"No. I'll be the one running it. I've been working here for thirty years, Gus. I think I know a few things about looking after guests."

"Sharlene, you can't."

She heard an edge of panic in his voice. Good. He needed to learn that he wasn't the only one who could keep secrets and spring surprises on his unsuspecting loved ones.

"Sure, I can. It will take a few months to get the place ready, and others in our investment group will look after those details, but once it's done, I'll be handling the day-to-day operations. Zannah and Brady will have plenty of time to find my replacement." She paused, watching his face, gauging how he was absorbing this news. "I'll suggest Amanda Clayborn to them. She's been here for a couple of years. She's smart and conscientious and knows almost everything about my job."

Gus made an odd gurgling noise, then his knees seemed to give way and he collapsed into the desk chair. The papers he'd been holding when she walked in fluttered to the floor.

It was a few seconds before he could say, "But why, Sharlene?"

"You mean why now, when you're about to go off and chase a fantasy?"

He didn't even bother to argue that the lost mine wasn't a fantasy. He simply nodded.

She took a deep breath and plunged in. "When Zannah came home, I was thrilled, because I was so worried about her and that job that was killing her. She's blossomed since she's been back. She's happy, content, settling back into a routine."

"Yeah, I know."

"But there was no way she was ready to take on the running of the ranch, much less a partner."

"Well, maybe my timing was a little off," he responded in a gruff voice she knew all too well. It was the voice that said he was sorry, not sorry.

"I had no idea you were planning to go off treasure hunting."

His face took on its usual stubborn, closed look as he looked away, but he said, "I didn't want anyone to know until I was ready." He glanced up. "And yeah, I know I messed up telling everyone."

"No, you messed up by not realizing that you've already got a treasure."

"What do you mean?"

"I mean this place, this legacy, your family, your granddaughters."

He jutted out his chin. "I know that, but I'll be back, and—"

"And me." Her heart was pounding so hard in her throat she thought she might pass out, but she took another deep breath and said, "Me, Gus."

His face went completely blank. "Well, yeah, we're friends and I hope we always will be."

"Gus, I'm in love with you. Have been for years."

"With *me*?" His expression went from surprised to stunned in the blink of an eye.

"That's right." She was relieved to feel her heart settling into a normal rhythm. "And it's about time you knew it. You can't be the only one around here with surprises to spring."

"Um, I—" He opened and closed his mouth a couple of times, then sank back in his chair, his gaze fixed on her face. His eyes were so glassy, she was afraid he would be the one to pass out.

"After Esther died, we were both devastated, depended on each other because we had both loved her so much. Seems like you and I did everything together—looked after Zannah, encouraged her to go off and make a new life for herself."

"Yes, but—"

"You needed me and I needed you. I had always liked you because you were good to Esther and she was important to me, and you

were a good father, a hard worker. You were
building something to be proud of here at
Eaglecrest. Gradually, I began to realize that
I felt more than friendship and affection for
you. It was true love."

The color washed into his face. He covered
his mouth with his hand, then dropped it to
the desktop as he stared at her.

Sharlene felt sorry for him. She knew from
recent experience what a jolt it was to receive
unexpected news.

"I… I don't know what to say. I never—"

"I know, Gus." She smiled at him, trying to
soften all the hard truths she was lobbing at
him. "I know this is a shock to you, and I honestly don't expect you to do or say anything,
but this is why I'm making plans to leave."

"But… I thought we were your family."

"And that I'd always be here. I know, but
things have changed. You've made them
change, and maybe that's a good thing. We
don't know yet, but I do know it's made me
think about my future. I have to take care of
myself, provide for myself, like I always have,
but now I'm getting older and it's more urgent."

Gus propped his elbows on the table and
ran his hands through his hair, then looked

up again. "We would always take care of you, Sharlene. We're family." His voice trailed off.

She gazed at him for a few seconds, choosing her next words. She intended to say everything she needed to and never have this conversation again. This was hard on him, but it was hard on her, too. She had never expected to have this discussion, in spite of the endless sleepless nights and hours she had passed thinking of exactly the right things to say.

She took a breath and plunged in again. "You know that I never wanted kids of my own because I had to help my mom raise my five little brothers and sisters after my father left. If it hadn't been for Esther, for our friendship, my growing-up years would have been even more miserable than they were. I was so grateful that you gave some of my siblings jobs, and my nieces and nephews, too. You helped all of them learn the value of hard work."

"Nah, I think they learned that from you."

She smiled. "Either way, I've loved being part of your family, of Esther's family, felt privileged to be a part of Eaglecrest, proud of it. But I've wanted my own place, my own business, for a long time. Now I'll have it. I certainly don't expect my family or yours to take care of me."

"And that guy who was in your office earlier? Who was he? I never saw him before."

"Jim Denton. He's a real estate broker. He's new in town, working with San Ramon Realty. He's handling the details of the transaction. Several of us have invested in this, people I've known forever. They unanimously agreed that I would run the place." She gave a small laugh. "I'm terrified but determined and excited."

"Why?" Gus lost his voice for a second, cleared his throat and started again. "Why are you telling me this now?"

"Because I don't want any regrets. You going off to hunt for the Lost Teamsters Mine has crystallized some things in my head, made me realize that life is too short to waste time not telling the people you love how you really feel." She attempted a smile, but she knew it must look shaky. "I don't plan to take this to the grave with me."

He nodded, but he looked confused. "I see. I… I guess I see."

Sharlene tilted her head to the side as she gazed at him. "I hope you do, Gus. We all have to make our own decisions, lead our lives the best we can. We're at an age where it's time for both of us to do that." She glanced at her watch. "I've got to get to my meeting."

Having the weight of what she'd told him lifted from her had her laughing and twirling toward the door. She knew she looked ridiculous, but she didn't care.

"So, you think this is funny?" Gus asked, surging to his feet, his face flushed with sudden anger. "Are you laughing at me?"

"No, of course not. I'm happy that I've told you, and I'm happy to be starting something new in my life. It's time to move on."

He came around the desk, obviously not ready to let this go. "Have you told Zannah and Brady you're leaving?"

"I'll tell them tomorrow, so please keep it to yourself until then. Tonight's meeting will provide a timeline, and I'll be able to give them an exact date."

"Well, be careful dealing with Lucas Fordham. He can be a real shark when he wants to."

Sharlene smiled again. "So can I."

With a wave, she went out. As she closed the door behind her, she felt a pang of regret at the lingering shock on Gus's face, but she knew she'd done the right thing.

CHAPTER NINE

BRADY LEANED AGAINST the corral fence, his forearms resting along the top rail as he watched Zannah, Chet and Gus prepare for the day's activities. The guests, some eager and some less so, were assembled with their horses, ready for what was to come next.

Chet and Phoebe had tied their horses to the corral fence while they waited for the word from Zannah to begin. They moved among the guests, checking cinches and saddles, speaking reassuringly to anyone who seemed nervous. Brady appreciated the matter-of-fact way they approached their work, secure in their knowledge and skills. They knew their jobs and were happy to share their expertise.

Ordinarily, Gus would have been the one to get the day's activities started. Brady watched the older man. He seemed deep in thought, though not with the excited, going-to-hunt-for-gold excitement he'd shown since the day they had met. He appeared to have a heavy weight on his mind. Maybe he was worried about all the details he still had to handle before he left.

Whatever it was, Brady wouldn't pry. He'd seen Zannah casting concerned glances at her father but knew there wouldn't be an opportunity for her to talk to him until much later.

Right now, the show had to go on. And that was what this was, he reflected. He'd taken a wild chance and really stretched the parameters of his own dad's challenge to his three sons. He had no idea what Finn and Miles had become involved in. They were playing things close to the chest. They knew where he was and what he was doing because he'd always been the most talkative of them.

As for him, ranching and a cowboy college were far different than what he'd imagined when he had accepted the challenge. Zannah had been right on the day they'd met. There was far more hard work than entertainment involved in the operations at Eaglecrest.

He'd had visions of turning this outfit around, exactly as his dad had mandated, making it a success, accepting the accolades from his folks and the envious comments from his brothers before moving on to another business, maybe something he actually knew.

When he came in, he had planned only on being the money man, the one who balanced the books and paid the bills, riding horses whenever he chose, having a good time on a regular basis, then moving on. It wasn't that he had itchy feet, he told himself. He simply hadn't been raised to stay in one place for a lifetime.

He admitted he *had* been having a good time, but he had also lugged hay bales and sacks of feed to stack in the storage shed, repaired the four-wheeler and unclogged the toilet in one of the cabins.

The joys of being the boss, he thought as he watched Zannah climb atop the wooden mounting block the less skilled riders used to get onto their horses. She raised her hand to get the group's attention.

"Good morning, everyone," she said cheerfully. "We're going to have a great day, and I promise you'll be completely exhausted by the end of it. Those of you who have been here before know what's about to happen."

"We're all gonna fall on our cans," one man responded.

"If you do, we'll pick you up, George—"

"Yeah, and put me right back on."

"Yup."

The guests laughed, and Brady straightened to look across at George Schallert, a man he'd met a couple of days ago. He was a divorced father from Phoenix who had brought his three kids to Eaglecrest every year for the past couple of years. He said it was something that he and his kids could do together that would ensure they had happy memories of time spent with Dad.

His kids, two boys and a girl, had partnered up with Emma and Joelle. He hoped they knew enough about riding to remain safe today, but if the real professionals—Zannah, Chet and Phoebe—weren't concerned, he shouldn't be, either.

Brady admired the way George focused on his kids but didn't appreciate the way the man's attention seemed to linger on Zannah. He'd noticed it last night and wondered if she had seen how his gaze had followed her around the room. He'd managed to be where she was several times throughout the evening.

Annoyed with himself, Brady brought his attention back to what was going on. Zannah was a strong, capable woman who could doubtless handle anyone or anything that got in her way.

And she was beautiful, too, he thought with a sense of longing, noting the way the sun glinted on the braid that swished across her back as she turned her head. He smiled as he realized the glint was because of a sparkly gold ribbon that had been plaited into it. He suspected that was something her nieces had thought up. He loved watching her with them. She was kind but firm, never talking down to them. He also liked the way she stood easily before a crowd, giving directions and good-naturedly fielding questions.

"Today is when we have to move some cattle from the north pasture to the south so the north pasture can begin growing again," Zannah continued. "Also, one of our staff discovered the fence is almost down in one corner of the north pasture near the road, so we've got to keep the cattle away from it until it's repaired."

"What causes something like that to happen?" George asked.

Brady knew he was only trying to keep Zannah's attention on him, but she smiled as she said, "Ground softened by all the rain we've had. Cattle leaning up against it, trying to get any sweet grass they can reach."

George nodded, smiling back, and Brady forced himself not give the man a disgruntled look.

"Then we'll move some cattle into the holding pen in preparation for loading them onto the gooseneck trailer to go to a buyer a couple of counties over." She looked around the group, then said, "Please remember that we have to move them slowly. A running cow is a cow that's hard for new riders to handle, and a running cow is one that's losing weight, reducing any profit we might make when he goes to auction. That's especially true of the ones that are going to a buyer this afternoon. Remember, cattle ranchers get paid by the pound."

Brady watched as she carefully surveyed the group, asking for more questions, making sure they understood what she was saying. Seemingly satisfied, she said, "Good. So mount up and let's get this workday started."

Some people needed help, but soon everyone was ready and the group started off. Chet, Gus and Phoebe spread themselves among the riders to monitor what was happening.

Brady mounted Buttercream and urged her forward so he could catch up with Zannah, who looked around curiously when he trotted up beside her and her favorite mare, Trina.

"Anything in particular we need to be looking out for on this ride?" he asked. "Any trouble that might happen?"

Her expression told him she wondered if he could be any actual help if something did happen. "Just what I said before. The fence is loose, and it's a hazard since it's near the road. The rest of the fence is good along there, but there's always the possibility of a break, or of cattle getting out. They're wonderful opportunists when it comes to finding a fresh patch of grass, and they've been known to knock down a sturdy section of fence to reach some."

"So, it would be a good idea if we rode along the inside to keep the cattle away until we get them all moved and settled in, right?"

"Yes, and by *we*, I mean *you*," she answered with a mischievous smile. "Then you can double-check the fence for any breaks or hazards."

"Got it, boss," Brady said, grinning.

The group stayed together well until they got to the pasture where the cattle were eating, lying in the grass or simply standing with their heads together. Brady wondered if they were planning to make a break for it.

He thought about saying that to Zannah, but as soon as they got close to the cattle, she stopped being the charming hostess and became a rancher ready to take care of business and get these animals moving.

Gus, Chet and Phoebe were still spread out among the guests, showing them how to work the cattle, using their horses to urge the animals toward the pasture gate. Within moments, the peaceful area was full of movement, loud whistles, running cows and riders chasing them, attempting to slow them down with their newly acquired skills.

Brady tried to keep up but found himself watching them, especially Gus, who seemed to have forgotten his troubles and was showing what a lifelong cattleman could do. He rode fast, whistling and shouting, waving his left arm in the air as he went. He signaled to

Rounder and Coco, the two cow dogs who had accompanied them, and they took off after a heifer who had decided to forge her own path. Then Gus pulled his horse around to bring another cow into line or let her have her head as she went after a runaway.

Zannah did exactly what her father did, showing the same expertise. Brady could only dream of having those kinds of skills someday, but the thought crossed his mind that if he won the challenge and then moved on, he'd never learn them.

"Hey, Brady," Zannah yelled at him and pointed to a heifer who was loping straight for him, hooves hitting the ground, ears flopping up and down. "Head that one off and get her back to the herd."

Brady snapped out of his daydream. "Oh, yeah, right."

He nudged Buttercream, who seemed to know a great deal more about moving cattle than he did. She took off at a run, throwing him back in the saddle. He fought to stay upright and finally managed to tug the reins to the right so that she turned to cut the heifer off.

The animal wasn't having it, though, and

made a quick dash in the other direction toward the fence. She ran along it, trying to get away from the pursuing horse and rider.

"Brady, keep her away from that corner. Don't let her get out on the road," Zannah yelled, coming up behind him.

"That's what I'm trying to do," he called over his shoulder, racing to get ahead of the panicked animal, who spun quickly and evaded him.

His worst fears came true when the heifer hit the corner fence post and it went down before her weight. She stumbled and went down with it but was up again in a flash, scrambling through the ditch and onto the wide-open space of the road, heading toward freedom, maybe even to town.

"Darn it, Brady," Zannah yelled as she flew past him on Trina and chased after the heifer. "Come on."

He didn't answer, too annoyed with himself, but he spurred Buttercream ahead to try and turn the cow so it would be easier for Zannah to stop her.

As he neared Zannah, though, he found himself riveted by the sight of her reaching for her rope with one hand while she held on to the reins with the other. In only seconds, she had played out a big loop and began twirling it over her head as she drew closer to her quarry. It was a motion so easy and natural to her that she might have been doing no more than tossing her hair over her shoulder.

Brady wasn't the least bit surprised when the loop landed around the cow's neck, flipping her onto her side. Zannah jerked on the rope while her well-trained horse slowed and pulled back. Once the heifer was on her feet again, Zannah headed toward the pasture, leading the animal back to captivity.

As she passed Brady, she couldn't seem to resist a triumphant smile. "And that's how it's done," she said.

He stared after her, smiling, mesmerized by the memory of what he'd seen, the easy way she had caught that heifer. He'd never seen anything like it, like her. Every day, it seemed that he learned something new about her. And every day, he wanted to learn more.

SHARLENE LOVED HIM, but she was leaving him, leaving Eaglecrest, her home, everything. If she loved him, all of them, how was it possible for her to leave him? Them?

Gus stood in an empty stall in the barn, staring down at the mass of items he still had to fit into his waterproof duffels. He had packed and repacked his gear. It had been ten years since he'd taken a lengthy ride into the mountains, when he'd made his cowardly escape from Esther's sickroom. Not his proudest moment.

This was different, though. He had a goal, something important to do.

He planned to take Daisy and Honus, the two most sure-footed horses in their string. They could carry him and at least two weeks' worth of food, as well as his tent and enough filled water bottles to tide him over until he located a source of fresh water near the search area. He knew of several streams that were no doubt swollen with their recent rains, so he wasn't worried.

If he ran out of supplies, he would call and ask Juan Flores to bring him more. He was taking several extra phone batteries and chargers with him and would save them carefully, even though he had promised his granddaughters that he would check in with them as often as possible and let them know when he struck gold.

"At least someone believes in me," he muttered.

Turning away from his task, he sat down on a stool and leaned against the side of the stall. "That makes a total of three people," he continued.

He heard the barn door open and close, and Zannah called out, "Dad? Are you in here?"

"Yeah, in Miler's old stall. You need something?"

She came and leaned on the door, her gaze taking in the clutter. "I need to see my father. Do you think you'll be ready to leave by tomorrow like you'd planned?"

"Not sure, but I've almost got this licked."

She laughed. "I can see that." Swinging open the stall door, she stepped inside. "Need some help?"

"Nah. Here, sit down." He stood to give her the stool, then sat on a hay bale pushed up against the wall. They'd sat like this many times since she was a little girl, discussing school, life, the ranch, almost anything—at least until she'd reached adolescence and it wasn't cool to spend so much time talking to her old dad.

There had been some rough patches during

her high school years, but they had weathered them and they'd all learned a few lessons.

Things had changed, though, when Esther died. He wasn't proud of the way he'd left most of the care to Zannah. He had no excuse except pure panic at the thought of losing his wife, then profound grief when it happened.

Sharlene was right. The two of them had held each other up and propped Zannah and Casey up in the bargain. It was an experience, a bond, that would never break.

Thoughts of Sharlene had kept him awake for most of the past two nights. He had to admire the amount of courage it took for her to tell him what was on her mind. She could have kept it to herself for the rest of her life, but she'd chosen to tell him she loved him. He still couldn't wrap his mind around it. It might be one of the biggest things that had ever happened to him.

He looked at his daughter, remembered the day she'd been born, so tiny and precious. He and Esther had thought they would never have kids before they were blessed with Casey, who had been born two weeks later than expected and arrived big and hearty, full of demands. Zannah, though, was tiny. She had released one cry after birth, but when the nurse had placed her on Esther's stomach, she had looked around and licked her lips as if to say, "I'm here, world. What do you think?"

All her life she had done almost everything he'd asked of her, and more, especially when caring for her mother. He was ashamed that he hadn't fully grasped how tough that was on her and how impossibly difficult her job in Las Vegas had been.

"Zannie, I'm proud of you," he blurted.

She looked up with a puzzled smile. "Thanks, but what brought that on?"

"Just thinking. I don't say things like that often enough."

She laughed. "You almost never say things like that."

"Shameful of me, since Stella and I never heard those words from our parents."

"I'm sorry. I know you two had a rough childhood." She reached over and squeezed his hand. "If it's any comfort, Casey, Phoebe and I had very happy ones."

He covered her hand with his, the rough calluses familiar to the touch, and gave her a grateful smile, then paused. She waited, watching him, obviously understanding that there was more to come.

"Life was better for Stella and me when our grandparents took us in, but when they couldn't keep us any longer, I was afraid we'd have to go back to our mom and dad. I couldn't go back to that, couldn't take Stella back." He paused, hating the memories. "This place was the saving of me—Stella and me both. When I got a job here, Esther's dad let me bring my little sister with me. She was only fifteen. We pretty much lived in two rooms, but we were our own bosses. There was no one to—" He stopped, seeing the pained look on his girl's face, the tears starting into her eyes. He didn't continue with his next words, which were "whip us."

"That's when you taught yourself to be a good man. Grandpa Grainger was an example, but you taught yourself."

Grateful that she understood that, he said, "Thanks, honey. I'm glad you came home to help out, to take over." When she started to speak, he said, "And I promise, it's not only because I want to go off and look for the mine."

"I'm glad to be here, to be doing this

again." She glanced around. "It's so good to be home."

He waited a few seconds, then said, "So Sharlene talked to you and Brady, huh?"

"Yes." Zannah gave a disbelieving laugh, then shook her head as if she still couldn't grasp it. "Yes, she sure did. I never saw that coming, but she's so excited about running her own bed-and-breakfast that I could only congratulate her. I don't know what brought this on and she'll be hard to replace, but I guess we'll figure things out. She plans to be here through Christmas and open her place after the first of the year."

"It'll be a big change for all of us."

"Yes, but everything changes." Her lips twisted ironically. "I've learned that since Brady came on the scene."

"Yeah, but Brady will make things better. Sharlene leaving will make things—"

"Different, but we'll adjust."

"I know. But…so many changes all at once."

"Most of them perpetrated by you," his daughter reminded him, affection in her eyes. He was glad she was coming to terms with this in spite of the lousy way he had handled things.

"I know. I know." He cleared his throat and met her gaze. "Zannie, before I go on my trip, I'm going to sign the papers with Brady. Milton Fines, you know, the attorney in town, is drawing up the papers now. Have 'em ready tomorrow."

Her face fell. "Tomorrow? Oh, I thought I'd have more time, that you'd wait until you got back, saw how things were working out with Brady and Eaglecrest—and me."

Her pain and disappointment were like a dagger in his heart. He sat forward, earnestly studying her face. "I know, honey, but it's not all bad. You're signing the papers, too."

"Me? Why?"

"Because you're going to own the other half, free and clear, like I told you. My original plan was for you and me to each own a quarter, but that's not fair to you. I won't own any part of Eaglecrest after tomorrow."

"What?"

He nodded and opened his hands wide. "Yup. When I come back, I'll be a hired hand, like I was fifty years ago. But with better pay," he added with a smile.

"I can't ask you to—"

"You're not. This is the right thing to do. I started this whole thing because we needed money, cash to keep the place going, and so you wouldn't have the full weight of the place on your shoulders when I'm gone. This way, you and Brady will have time to figure out how to forge your own path without any interference from me. That's another reason why it's a good idea for me to be gone for a little while. You two can figure out how to work together."

Zannah heaved a mighty sigh. "That might be easier said than done."

THE PAPERS WERE signed the next day, and Zannah found herself half owner of her family's ranch, along with a man she'd known for less than a month. They stood outside the attorney's office with Gus and Brady congratulating themselves and each other, and Zannah feeling as if her world had once again tilted on its axis.

It was one thing for her to insist that she needed to be fully informed about everything that happened at Eaglecrest and quite another to see that fulfilled and to become a full partner.

To make herself feel a little more normal, she called Phoebe to see how things were going. Her cousin reported that everything was fine and for Zannah to not hurry back. Brady called Chet, who reported the same thing.

She hung up, reflecting that none of this felt normal. She wasn't even wearing her usual boots and jeans, but at the insistence of her nieces and Sharlene, she had pulled a sundress from her closet, one she'd bought in town and never worn, as well as a pair of her favorite sandals. She glanced down and acknowledged that they would look much better if she ever took the time for a pedicure.

As for Brady, new jeans, a crisply ironed shirt in pale green with the sleeves rolled up and highly polished boots made him look like the tenderfoot he was, but Zannah had to admit that he looked pretty darned good.

In fact, Zannah admitted to herself, he always looked good. Even when he was participating in the down and dirty aspects of ranching, he looked—sexy. It was the only word that fit.

Standing here in the bright sun, she could see reddish highlights in his dark hair. As he lifted his hand to shield his eyes from the sun, she helplessly watched the way his forearm muscles flexed and relaxed.

The heat that washed through her had nothing to do with the warm day and everything to do with Brady—and the completely inappropriate thoughts she was having about her new business partner. She forced her attention back to her father.

Gus rubbed his hands together and rocked up onto his toes as he looked from one to the other of them.

"So, anybody interested in having some lunch? I'm buying." He grinned. "Be the last time for a while that I can buy you lunch."

"I don't know," she began. "I feel like I need to—"

"It's a special occasion, Zannah," Brady broke in. "Let's celebrate."

"Good. Good." Gus looked around. "Let's go to Sadie's, get some barbecue. Haven't had a piece of their apple pie in—well, I don't even remember."

They crossed the street to the oldest eating establishment in Raymond, founded in the

1920s. Sadie and Clay had long since passed away, but they had left their treasured recipes behind for Sadie's descendants to use.

The lunch crowd was beginning to thin out, but there were enough people who knew Gus and wanted to hear about his plans to look for the lost mine that he was quickly pulled away.

"Be right there, Zannah," he called over his shoulder. "Order me a beer, and the barbecue basket with sweet potato fries. Beef, not pork," he added.

Brady gazed after him doubtfully as they wound through the room to a table by the window.

Zannah glanced back to see what he was looking at, then stumbled awkwardly when he stepped over to hold her chair for her. "Um, sorry," she said. "Not used to wearing anything except boots."

Brady sat down opposite her and pulled two menus from the holder. He handed her one as he said, "I know what you mean. I'm two inches shorter today since I don't have manure caked on my boots."

Zannah laughed and decided not to be nervous about having lunch with him. Gus would be joining them momentarily, and hearing him talk about his plans would smooth over any awkwardness.

As for Brady. She stole a peek at him over the top of her menu. That green shirt he was wearing shouldn't make him look even sexier and more appealing than usual, but it did. She wondered how long it would take him to look like a real cowboy, like the men who had grown up on a ranch. It would take a lifetime, if he stayed that long, which she doubted.

He seemed to have shaved extra close that morning. His subtle, woodsy cologne had been teasing her all morning. She looked at his jaw, then at his lips. She had figured out that the odd little twist they gave occasionally wasn't a smirk as she'd first thought, but a nervous habit he didn't seem aware of. When he wasn't doing that, he had beautiful lips.

Not liking where her thoughts were leading her yet again, she quickly looked down at her menu. After they placed their orders, a silence fell between them, but it wasn't an awkward one. Zannah was busy thinking about what this partnership was going to mean for her, and she suspected he was thinking the same thing.

Brady frowned as he looked across the

room. "Do you think it's a good idea for him to be talking about this trip of his?"

"Why not? As soon as he told one person, the news flew through town on wings of gossip."

"I think we've seen what gold fever can do." He shrugged. "It's highly contagious."

Zannah glanced over to where her dad was entertaining a tableful of local men. "Oh, you mean you think that someone might follow him into the mountains and try to take the gold if he finds it?"

"It's possible." Brady answered slowly. He seemed to consider that for a moment, then said, "He probably owes money to some of those cattlemen—we owe money, that is."

Zannah glanced around. "No doubt, and some of them owe money to us." She nodded toward one of them, an older man who was leaning forward, listening intently to what Gus was saying. "Jake Billings, for example. Last year, one of his bulls, a mean old Brahmin, got loose and trampled part of our fence. Ordinarily, he would have fixed it, or paid to have it fixed, but he'd been sick, so he couldn't get it done. Dad and Chet took care of it, and I'm sure Jake doesn't even remember how it all came about." She met Brady's gaze. "And no one on Eaglecrest will ever remind him."

Brady nodded. "Point taken."

"He's known those men all of his life. They've pulled each other out of ditches, rounded up each other's cattle, rented out their balers during haying season, attended every important event in each other's families. No, there's no possibility that any of them will hurt him."

"And we have begun paying them back."

She frowned. "I hear a but in there."

"Nah, not about him, or them. Growing up the way I did, moving so often as my dad pursued his businesses, I never felt like part of a community."

"It's different here," she admitted. "As far as my dad is concerned, do you think we could stop him?" she asked. "Look at him. I haven't seen him this animated in…" Her voice trailed off. "More than ten years."

Brady gave her a swift glance, but she didn't say anything else, her thoughts turning back through the years. Belatedly, she recalled both of her parents talking about taking an extended trek into the mountains, spending days exploring. That was a plan that went by the wayside when her mother got sick, but it must be part of the reason he was doing this now.

As hard as it was for Zannah to understand this, to even believe it was happening, she could see that signing the papers, turning the operations of Eaglecrest over to her and Brady was giving Gus a new lease on life. Without the constant demands of the ranch and the college, he could pursue his own dreams.

And he deserved that.

Humbled by this realization, she looked up to see Brady watching her. He gave her a smile that said he understood what she was thinking, which was very disconcerting.

"So," Brady said slowly, his gaze on her as if assessing her reaction. "If this town is so important to you, and so is Eaglecrest, how did you end up in Las Vegas?"

"Roll of the dice," she quipped.

"No, really. It's an eight-hour drive from here."

"You asked me that before, and I thought I'd answered it."

"You did." Brady looked out the window,

his mouth turned down in a frown. "I guess I'm trying to understand your connection to the land, and how you could leave." He shook his head and glanced back at her. "I don't know."

It seemed important to him to understand this, so she said, "That's where Casey and Vanessa were. He's a botanist, and she's a soil scientist. I lived with them for a while—a big thing for a couple of newlyweds, but they welcomed me and I'll always be grateful. I needed to be away from here but with family." She smiled. "Then when Emma came along the next year, and Joelle a year later, I helped out, worked, went to school."

"Grieved," Brady added.

She shot him a swift glance. "Yes, it got better for a while. Then Casey and Vanessa got jobs in Phoenix and moved. I had my own place by then, of course, and I had made some good friends, but the joy had gone out of things, and my job—"

"Was killing you. Gus told me."

Zannah wanted to stop talking about this, but something about the way he leaned forward, those deep brown eyes of his compelling her to keep talking, made her go on.

"Yes, Vegas isn't an easy place. It's built on tourism, of course, but the tourists often don't seem to understand that it's people's hometown. It adds to the atmosphere of anything goes. People come there, thinking they'll strike it rich." She laughed ruefully and nodded to her dad. "Like with the Lost Teamsters Mine. They end up busted, homeless, dragging innocent children around with them. They're hopeless and helpless."

She paused. "There was one family with two little kids—" Her voice broke, and she cleared her throat. "They were so badly neglected they nearly died. Honestly, I'd seen worse, but somehow that was the one that broke me. However, I searched until I found a responsible relative to take them—a grandmother in Colorado who hadn't even known they existed."

Brady reached across the table and covered her hands with one of his. Her eyes full of tears, she looked up.

"Did you do your best for them?"

The warmth of his hand, of his expression, made the tears start down her cheeks.

"Yes, of course. Everything the law would allow."

"Then, that's all you can ask of yourself in any situation."

Nodding, she slipped her hands from beneath his and fumbled for a napkin from the holder.

"Do you think that your experiences there may have colored your reactions to Gus's decision to go look for the mine?"

"What?"

"Seeing so many people take a gamble and lose so badly must have affected the way you look at any type of gambling."

Zannah stared at him as the experiences of the past few weeks clicked through her mind.

"Yes. They must have. I hadn't thought about that." It was disconcerting to think that he understood that about her, and she'd had no idea. What else did he understand about her?

CHAPTER TEN

Zannah was grateful that the waitress chose that moment to bring their drink orders. Brady held up his glass of cola and gestured for her to lift her glass of iced tea. He seemed to see that she needed a change of subject.

"Here's to the beginning of a beautiful partnership."

Zannah clinked her glass against his as she said, "Even though it was unexpected."

"You never know. That might turn out to be the best thing about it."

She smiled and settled back in her chair. It was oddly pleasant to be sitting here like this with him, to be having a normal meal, not their usual testy confrontation. Later, she would probably regret what she'd told him, how she had made herself vulnerable, but not now.

"This is nice," Brady said.

"Yes, it's one of the longest-running businesses in town. It's always been popular."

"No, I mean being here with you, doing something out of the ordinary, having a meal and a conversation instead of having an argument about something with everyone on the ranch watching us."

She stared at him, wondering if he'd read her thoughts. It was odd that they were actually on the same wavelength.

"Try to remember it will always be that way," she answered. "Eaglecrest is its own small town."

"I'm coming to understand that. Tell me about this place," he said, looking around at the stamped-tin ceiling and the original artwork with Western themes, some of which were truly terrible.

He chuckled. "They should hire your aunt Stella to paint some better depictions of ranch life," he said, pointing to a drawing of a cow with outsize horns, a badly misshapen head and enormous eyes. "That one could turn a person into a vegetarian."

Zannah laughed, warmed that he thought her aunt's artwork was superior to any inside Sadie's. "Most of these were painted by one of Clay and Sadie's sons. Fortunately, he was better at operating a cattle-themed restaurant than he was at painting."

Brady smiled and went back to examining the décor—the photographs of rodeo cowboys with their shiny winners' buckles, soldiers from two world wars preparing to march off to battle and local parades of riders on horseback.

"You can see the whole history of the area in those photos," she said.

"Do you have any photos up here?"

"No."

"That's a shame."

He leaned over to examine the hardwood floor, which had long ago been deeply scorched with the brands of the local ranches. He pointed down and made a circular motion with his hand. "What about these brands? Is one of these yours? Ours?"

"Yes." She twisted in her chair and pointed across the room. "Over there, in front of that table for six, on the right hand side as you come in the front door and under the first east-facing window. When we came here as kids, Casey and I would race to see who could stand on all three of them first. We had to be sneaky about it, though, and pretend like we were taking a roundabout path to the bathroom, because if Mom caught us being disruptive, she would haul us outside."

Brady laughed. "She and my mom would have gotten along fine. So, the owners wanted people to brand the floor?"

"The story is that Sadie and Clay sent invitations to all the local outfits to bring in their branding irons when they were putting the finishing touches on the place. I think the goal was to make it so much a part of the community, it would always be here."

"Looks like they achieved that."

"This has become a community institution, and a meeting place." She nodded to a set of double doors across the room. "There's a large room that people can rent for get-togethers. Like I said, it's very popular. And the food helps," Zannah answered on a blissful sigh as the waitress brought their order, unloading juicy barbecue sandwiches that had the spicy meat overflowing the bun, fries and dishes of creamy coleslaw.

Gus finally managed to get away from his audience and joined them, eyeing the food with deep appreciation. "Yes, sir," he said, on a happy sigh. "This is turning out to be a really good day."

For the next half hour, they talked about the town of Raymond, Gus telling Brady some of the more notorious happenings from years past.

It helped her keep her mind off what she had told Brady. She rarely talked about herself, and certainly not to someone she didn't know very well, someone she didn't fully trust. Or did she? They may have serious disagreements about Eaglecrest, but she had no reason to think he would turn anything she had said against her. She found that comforting but unsettling, because it meant she was truly beginning to trust him.

After Gus paid for their lunch, they stood outside Sadie's, discussing the errands they needed to do before heading home.

"Good afternoon," a man's voice said. "How are things at Eaglecrest?"

They turned to see Lucas Fordham strolling toward them. While Gus greeted him and introduced Brady, Zannah said a polite hello, then held back, observing.

Lucas was a few years older than her. He and Casey had been friends growing up, but things had changed when they were in high school. Lucas's father had died, leaving him in charge of the family ranch and other holdings. It had meant long days of work for a boy who wasn't fully grown. He'd no longer had time to hang out with his friends, play a game of pickup basketball, go fishing or practice roping.

He had grown up hard and fast, and she thought it had made him ambitious, maybe even ruthless. He was usually all business, serious-minded and completely focused on the next thing he had to do. So he was often asked to participate in community projects, to serve on the city council or to head up some committee or other. As the mayor of Raymond, Nancy Fellowes, had said, there needed to be somebody who was willing to lead the hard decisions and say no if necessary.

Lucas was the person to do it. He wasn't an easy man, but she'd never heard of him being dishonest.

To be fair, she thought, the Fordhams had come within inches of losing their place altogether, and Lucas had been the one to save it. She doubted that the Fordham ranch ever had the kinds of financial problems that Eagle-crest was currently facing. Maybe his ruth-lessness was understandable, but she was wary of him nonetheless.

"I hear that you've got quite an extensive operation going on at your place," Brady said.

"True. We run cattle, and we have guests like you do, but with more entertainment options—zip line, rock climbing, ATVs, motocross."

Zannah bit her lip to keep from pointing out how some of those activities harmed the environment.

"Keeps people coming back year after year," Lucas continued. "'Course, the insurance on all that runs pretty high."

"Don't doubt that for a minute. Mind if I come over and see for myself?" Brady asked, earning a look of alarm from Zannah.

"You're welcome anytime. Be glad to show you around. Maybe you'd like to try a few of our activities for yourself."

"I would," Brady said. "I definitely would."

"Let me know when." Lucas shook hands all around and then headed toward the bank.

Zannah tried to tamp down her alarm, even as she hoped Brady wasn't going to get any ideas about new activities at Eaglecrest. If he did, she would have to find a way to deal with it. After all, they were partners now.

TWO DAYS LATER, Gus made his departure, riding Daisy and leading Honus, who was carefully packed with everything he thought he'd need for a few weeks.

Emma and Joelle stood and watched tearfully as he waved to the small crowd that had gathered outside the corral.

Zannah stepped up to place an arm around each of their shoulders. "Don't worry, girls," she assured them. "Grandpa will be back."

"We thought he'd change his mind and take us with him," Emma said.

"We were sure he wanted us to go with him," her sister added. "Won't he need someone to take care of him?"

"Make sure he comes back okay?" Emma's lip quivered.

Zannah gave them tight hugs as she tried to think of the best way to comfort her heartbroken nieces.

"No, this is his adventure. He wants to go on his own," she said, careful not to point out that having a couple of young girls along wouldn't be very helpful, because his first concern would be their safety and comfort.

"In fact, he needs to," Sharlene added.

Zannah turned to look at the older woman, who was watching Gus ride away. She was different lately, and it didn't seem to be strictly because of the inn she was buying. Sharlene had a look in her eyes that Zannah had seen several times lately, one of longing, but also of resignation. It was as if she wanted something but knew she couldn't have it, so she was forcing herself to move on.

Zannah admitted that she might be imagining that. She had been through so many upheavals lately that she might have completely lost her ability to understand those around her, even ones she'd known her whole life.

She wondered if Sharlene was regretting her decision to leave and open her own bed-and-breakfast. But she didn't think that was it. The housekeeper was clearly excited. She talked frequently about her plans and the expectations of the investors in her inn.

Zannah's mind returned to the same thoughts she'd been having since the day Brady Gallagher landed in her life. Everything was changing. The situation, and the people she knew and loved. The question was, could she change, too?

"Come on, girls," she said, shepherding them toward the corral. "I'll bet Phoebe needs our help."

BRADY FELT A bit like a sneak for making an appointment to talk to Lucas Fordham and view operations at his ranch without telling Zannah. She hadn't been too fond of many of his ideas, and he'd noticed that when they had met their neighbor in town, she hadn't said much but watched how the men interacted. He couldn't even begin to guess why. She was a puzzle to him, so he wasn't surprised that he spent so much time thinking about her.

As he drove over the cattle guard that separated the entrance to Lucas's ranch from the highway, he made a mental note to get serious about buying a vehicle better able to handle the realities of ranch life than this sporty car. He'd call his dad about it. He was sure Gallagher Motors could help him out.

His thoughts returned to Zannah. Talking without having an argument at Sadie's had been pleasant. More than pleasant, he thought with a smile. He'd learned some things about the restaurant, about the community and her pride in it.

Best of all, he'd learned some things about her. Important things about her background, her time away from Eaglecrest, how her time in Vegas had affected her. In a way, he felt like she'd given him a valuable gift that he would need to safeguard.

He'd expected some last-minute resistance from her regarding him buying into the ranch, making them full partners, but she had obviously been swayed by her dad's decision.

Turning the other half ownership over to her had been a wise move from Gus. Brady could only hope that everything would run more smoothly between them with the agreement signed, sealed and delivered.

He decided to quit thinking about her and focus on the task at hand. He'd called ahead and confirmed his appointment so he could pick Fordham's brain.

The driveway up to the ranch buildings was paved and well maintained, wide enough to accommodate two cattle trucks. It was a far cry from the one at Eaglecrest. Improving the road was at the top of his list of things to do.

The closer he got to the main house, the

more he straightened up and looked around with interest. Unlike Eaglecrest's guest cabins, this place seemed to be self-contained. The main building was more of a lodge than a home, two stories high with wings on each side, probably added on later to double the number of available guest rooms.

Beautifully lettered signs out front welcomed guests, pointing them to the parking area and giving directions to the various activities Fordham offered.

The building itself was painted white with trim and shutters of dark green, highlighted with touches of a dark gold. It looked welcoming but also businesslike. The cabins at Eaglecrest could only be described as cozy, he decided, and realized that the two ranches attracted a very different clientele.

The people who came to Eaglecrest wanted a slice of the Old West, a chance to experience something from the nation's past, a rapidly disappearing way of life. They loved the animals, the nights around the campfires and the simple camaraderie with the other guests.

A group of people in their twenties who were dressed for hiking passed Brady as he stepped from his car. He watched them head for a trail whose directional sign indicated a four-mile hike.

At Eaglecrest, he had found it interesting that many of the guests were older men who had, no doubt, grown up watching Western-themed dramas on television and were interested in experiencing that life but also wanted to return to a hot meal, a comfortable bed and functioning plumbing every night.

He would have to research the viability of developing more hiking trails around Eaglecrest, maybe even charging for groups to be led by an experienced guide.

From what he could see as he entered the lobby, this place offered all of that, but in a much more high-end atmosphere. He told the receptionist that he was there to meet with Lucas and was invited to have a complimentary beverage and freshly baked cookie while he waited.

He took her up on the offer and munched on a chocolate chip one as he perused the brochures neatly displayed nearby. They all advertised additional adventures available to the guests. Zip-lining, rock climbing and motocross racing were offered, along with a list of prices.

Brady's eyebrows shot up when he realized how much the guests were being charged for these activities. Lucas Fordham was no slouch when it came to developing additional income streams.

Yup, time for Eaglecrest to follow Fordham's example.

"Good morning, Brady," Lucas said, reaching out to shake hands. "Did Gus get off for his gold-hunting trip?"

"Yes, he did."

Lucas tilted his head. "How is Zannah handling all of this?"

"She's adjusting," Brady answered, then felt disloyal for even discussing it with someone outside Eaglecrest. "Um, I'm surprised that so many people know what's going on. I mean, apart from Gus telling people he's going to look for that old mine." He shook his head. "I still can't believe he said so much."

Lucas shrugged. "It's a small town. Even if he'd kept quiet, people would still know somehow. I've lived here my whole life, and it never ceases to amaze me." He smiled and glanced around, obviously proud of his surroundings. "Part of the charm, I guess. So, what can I show you?"

"Everything. I'd like to know how you run the various experiences you have for your guests, and, frankly, how well it pays."

"Sure. Let's go this way."

Brady ran a critical eye over the all-terrain vehicles Lucas led them to, noting how clean and polished they looked even though they were strictly functional. He thought about the old four-wheeler he'd put back into working order. Repairing it had been far cheaper than buying a new one, but he wondered if it also advertised the fact that they didn't have the cash flow they needed.

Oh, yes, he thought. This place was very different than Eaglecrest.

Lucas talked about the improvements that had been made over the years. Like Zannah's family, his had been in the area for nearly one hundred years, but they had always focused on raising and selling cattle until Lucas had taken over the business. He quickly realized they were leaving too much money on the table by not offering adventures that would take advantage of the unique area.

"People want to feel like they've accomplished something, even if they're only supposed to be on vacation," he said as they reached the top of the mesa where the zip line was located.

"I'm seeing that they like to challenge themselves," Brady said. "Face danger and prove they're not cowards."

"Yup, that's pretty much it, but they like to have fun, too." He pointed to the zip line, where two young men waited to assist the customers. "Care to try it?"

"Sure."

"I'll drive around and meet you at the other end."

Even as the attendants helped him into the gear, checking and rechecking the safety harness, Brady could feel his excitement growing. His mind clicked over possible locations for this kind of thing, even as he wondered if there was enough business to maintain two zip lines in this area. When he had talked to Fordham on the phone, he'd made it clear that he was only fact-finding, which the other man seemed to understand, stating that he was proud of his operation and didn't mind showing it off. Brady didn't want to undercut Fordham's prices, but he knew this was what people wanted. This was the kind of thing they needed to be offering their guests.

If they could afford the insurance.

Once he had signed a waiver, and was safely strapped in, he was released and sent sailing through the air. He couldn't resist a shout of joy at the sheer exhilaration of it, the sense of freedom. Even though the trip only lasted a few minutes—and he grew a little alarmed when the ground seemed to be rushing up to meet him—he slid easily into the landing area, where two more people waited to help him out of the harness.

Lucas hadn't arrived yet, so Brady had time to ask the teenagers manning the zip line about the kinds of guests who used it. They responded that it was mostly kids and families who liked a thrill.

Brady didn't know what kinds of additional exciting activities Eaglecrest could offer, but he knew it had to be unique.

Lucas drove up a few minutes later. "So, what do you think, Brady?"

"I think I'd like to do that every day. I can see the appeal. So," he went on slowly, making a circular motion with his hand to indicate the zip line venture. "If you don't mind my asking, how much does this whole adventure cost? Not only the customers, but you, too."

"I barely break even," Lucas admitted. "But it brings in people who want the other experiences, as well. Groups of locals come over for the zip line, families celebrating birthdays, church groups, even corporate clients who bring people over from Tucson for a day of team building—you know, the kind where you have to depend on your team members to catch you as you fall backward, things like that."

Brady nodded. He'd heard of those, had even participated in a few, but not many. Maybe because he'd always worked with his family. He knew he could trust them. Maybe he and Zannah should try something like that. He liked the idea of catching her if she fell.

"I've thought for a long time that golf would do well here," Lucas went on, "but I'm not willing to give up rangeland to build a course. Might work over at Eaglecrest, though. They've got more available acreage than I do."

The two men visited the other attractions, then came back to the main lodge. As they shook hands and said goodbye, Lucas said, "Hey, would you be interested in joining some of us for poker? You'd get to know some of the locals."

"Sure," Brady said, pleased and surprised. It was a way for him to begin being part of the community. His little guest cabin already felt like home. "I'd like that."

As he drove away, his mind was busily turning over ideas for Eaglecrest.

Now all he had to do was convince Zannah to give some of them a try. He paused as he was climbing into his car. Perhaps he should seriously consider doing a trust exercise with her.

ZANNAH LOOKED UP from the computer screen where she had been studying facts and figures to see Brady strolling in the door. There was something about his manner that made her eye him warily.

She could almost hear the jet engine backwash as ideas raced through his mind. She was so certain of what his next words would be that she didn't even congratulate herself when they came.

"Hey, Zannah, I have an idea," he said, taking off his hat and hanging it on the hat rack before sitting down in a chair facing her.

"Despite the fact that those are words sure to strike terror into my heart, I'll do the polite thing and ask you to tell me all about it." She folded her hands on top of the desk and made a big show of listening attentively.

"Smarty-pants," he murmured, but she could see him fighting a smile. "Now that we're full partners, I think we need to participate in some trust-building exercises."

"Trust building?" she asked in a flat tone.

"Sure," he said, sitting forward and warming to his subject. "It's when a group of co-workers or, say, you and your partner get together to complete a series of tasks, depending on each other for help. We've done this any number of times with the employees at the various Gallagher companies."

"I know what it is, Brady. Social workers often participate in that type of thing. I'm trying to figure out why we need to do them." She picked up a pencil from the desk and began turning it end over end as she listened.

"To build trust." He said each word slowly, obviously to help them sink in.

She used the pencil to point to herself, then to him. "You mean, between the two of us?"

"Yes, and every other employee. We can divide them into two groups," he said, warming to his subject. "One group will cover the evening's activities while the other one takes part. Then, the next night, we'll switch. As the bosses here, we'll have to work both nights."

When he paused, she asked, "Is this where I'm supposed to applaud?"

He ignored that, obviously too caught up in what he was saying. "Of course, we'll have to pay them for their time."

"That should get everyone on board," she conceded, feeling a bit ashamed of herself for scoffing at him when she hadn't even heard him out. "But it sounds like a huge amount of coordinating. What kind of activities are we talking about here?"

"Oh, you know, walking over hot coals—" *"What?"*

His expression was pure innocence as he went on. "It's only for a few feet—"

"Brady," she said, exasperated. "Be serious. Are you sure this is necessary?"

He spread his hand wide as he said, "Why not? It can't hurt, and it might help."

"Help what? Help who?"

"All of us. I think it would help everyone to get off on the right foot together."

"All the other employees have worked together for years. They're already on the right foot. They all pretty much grew up together, know each other, trust each other."

"That means I'm the only wild card. I didn't grow up here, and they don't know me yet, so they haven't had time to learn to trust me. If I'm going to be here, work here as one of their bosses, they need to trust me as much as they trusted Gus, as much as they trust you." He shrugged one shoulder. "Frankly, Zannah, I think it's time for you to stop looking at me as the enemy."

Embarrassment flushed Zannah's face pink. "Oh, of course. That makes sense."

She glanced at the bookkeeping program she'd been updating. With Brady's infusion of fresh cash, she was finally able to achieve some measure of balance in the books.

She dropped the pencil on the desk and sat up straight as she asked, "What do you have in mind?"

"Some group activities, some between pairs who work together. And I think we need to start right now."

"Has it ever occurred to you that maybe you think too much?"

"'Course not. Thinking things through is

better than going by feelings or knee-jerk reactions."

"Okay, what do you want to try?"

"Trust fall, where one person falls backward into the waiting arms of their partner.
A blindfold walk where one person has to
depend on another to guide them through an
obstacle course. That sort of thing."

Zannah raised one eyebrow at him. "Do
you honestly think you're going to get Chet
and Juan to do something like that?"

"Won't know till we try." He stood up.
"There's one activity that you and I need to
try right now."

"Does it involve both of us getting back
to work?"

"In a minute."

He dragged his chair around to her side
of the desk and indicated she should scoot
her chair away from the desk and face him.
"We're going to look into each other's eyes
for sixty seconds."

Zannah was unable to hide her alarm.
"Stare into—?"

"Oh, come on. Not like that. Don't look so
much like we're going to chase each other
around the office with fire axes."

"That might be easier," she answered.

"I don't know what you're so worried about." He sat back with his hands relaxed on the arms of the chair, tilted his head to the side and regarded her with a puzzled half smile.

What was she worried about? Him, obviously. Seeing him every day, several times a day, often when they were at odds, rarely on the same page, made her feel out of stride, almost as if she were riding a horse that had suddenly gone lame. She only wanted to get back in her own comfort zone.

"Never mind," she said hastily. "What does this actually accomplish?"

"It really helps you to understand someone. My mom used to make my brothers and me do this whenever we got into an argument."

"Did it work?"

"Heck, yeah. There's nothing worse than having to sit and stare into the eyes of one of your brothers as they're beaming twin lasers of fury into yours. Makes sixty seconds seem like a lifetime."

"And did it help you to understand your brothers?"

"I am the middle brother, after all. Mostly it

helped me figure out how to get what I wanted from them without making them mad."

"That is so you," she marveled.

"Come on." He set the timer on his phone and placed it on the desk, then scooted up until they were knee to knee. He reached out both hands, palm up, encouraging her to offer hers.

Zannah had a fleeting memory of touching his hand when he'd helped her up once, a few weeks ago. His hands had been warm and smooth. At Sadie's, his hands had been reassuring. For some reason, her heart fluttered anxiously. Telling herself she was being silly, she placed her hands in his.

She immediately realized once again that her hands felt work-roughened and harsh against his smooth palms and tried to pull away.

"Come on, Zannah. We can do this for sixty seconds."

Easy for you to say, she thought in dismay.

"Quit wasting time. Look at me."

At any other time, she would have taken exception to his bossy tone, but she reminded herself that she had agreed to this. After all, it was only for a minute. She could do this. Once she had decided that, she settled in, meeting his gaze with her own after he started the timer.

Her first realization was that she had been wrong about the color of his eyes. They weren't strictly brown, even though they appeared to be. The irises were almost black around the outer edge, but closer toward the pupil, there was an array of yellow-gold and light brown.

No, she thought dreamily, the intriguing effect was a combination of those colors. It was really quite beautiful. Why hadn't she ever noticed it before? As she watched, that array seemed to spark outward as if he'd seen something pleasing to him, but she quickly decided it was her imagination.

She noticed the beating of her own heart, and the unaccustomed warm feeling that was sifting through her.

She had felt like this before, she assured herself. After all, she'd had male friends her entire life, several boyfriends. This was no different than that. Not at all.

Sitting like this, so close together, focusing on each other, with her hands in his, her total attention on his eyes, should have made her feel panicky, ready to jump up and sprint for the door.

Instead, she was…content, she decided. Did that mean she trusted him?

When the timer sounded, she pulled her hands away, reached up to brush her hair away from her face, adjusted her collar, then pushed her chair back, ready to return to the computer.

"That was a really long minute," she said.

"I set it for two. I knew it would take you a while to settle into it."

"Oh, for heaven's sake," she protested. "That was sneaky."

"No, that was strategy." He stood up and pulled his chair around to the other side of the desk before he grabbed his hat and headed for the door. "And that is something you need to be able to trust your partner to do."

CHAPTER ELEVEN

STRATEGY, BRADY THOUGHT as he loped out the door. Exactly what had he been strategizing? He'd done that identical exercise dozens of times over the years. Never had he felt the jolt of awareness he'd experienced with Zannah. He had to get himself under control, because this partnership would never work if he was more interested in her as a woman than he was as a partner.

He was a fine one to talk about trust, he thought in annoyance. Ordinarily, if he saw a woman who interested him, he would have pursued her, asked her out to see where things went.

But this was different. He'd been uneasy about Gus's plan to keep their agreement a secret. The challenge from his dad had been to find a business different from any he'd worked in before. He should have remembered that didn't mean to throw good business practices out the window.

All their subterfuge had done was to give Zannah, an already skittish partner, even less reason to trust him.

The staring-into-each-other's-eyes exercise probably hadn't helped. While she had been looking at him, trying to find a reason to trust him, he'd been thinking very different thoughts, ones that should make him blush and would almost certainly have made her take a swing at him.

He had to keep his mind on his task, he decided, and headed toward the main house where he would get Sharlene and Chet to help him figure out a schedule for the team building he was planning. He had begun to make headway with the staff, especially when he had bought drinks for them one evening, then sat around talking about the ranch.

Piece of cake, he thought. Only had to keep his mind on business.

"Honus, Daisy, you two have the right idea about sleeping standing up. I don't remember the ground being this hard."

Because no one but the horses was listening, and they wouldn't tell anyone if he wasn't tough, Gus followed his complaint to his animals with a loud groan as he sat up and pushed his sleeping bag down so he could rest his elbows on his knees and rub his face with both hands.

He looked around, bleary-eyed, at his camping spot. He'd remembered it from years ago when he and Esther had been young, before the kids had come along. They'd gone camping and found this place where wind had eroded an overhanging cliff to provide shelter while also depositing sand that made a softer bed than the usual hard ground. He had even been careful to scoop out a depression in the sand to give support to his hips.

"Well, it must have been softer forty years ago," he muttered to his equine audience, who couldn't have cared less about his discomfort. He'd managed to find them a patch of grass near a trickling stream. Summer heat would dry it up in the next few weeks, but for now, it was perfect for them.

"I should have cut some grass for my bed. Might have helped."

He rubbed some warmth back into his legs

and hauled himself to his feet, then stretched, popping several stiff joints.

This was a heck of a lot harder than it had been the last time he'd been out camping by himself.

Shame settled on him. That had been when Esther was dying. Some cattle had wandered far from the herd, into the foothills, and he'd gone after them. Someone else could have done it. Chet had been a young hand then, but experienced with cattle. He would have been happy to locate the animals and probably would have brought them back in record time. But Gus had seen it as an escape from a situation he couldn't fix—a position he'd rarely been in since the miserable childhood he and Stella had escaped.

Feeling helpless had made him stupid. After a few days in the mountains, he'd gone home, been there for her and Zannah. Still, after all this time, the shame lingered.

"So," he said, pulling his mind away from an old mistake he couldn't correct, and still addressing his horses. "Either of you two interested in some coffee? No? Your loss."

Moving upstream from them, he filled his coffeepot and built a fire to get the water boiling even as he tried not to think longingly of how easy it was at home to walk into the ranch kitchen and pour himself a cup of the coffee the cook always kept freshly made— along with warm cinnamon rolls, the source of several of the extra pounds that now circled his middle.

There had been a time when he would have crouched down beside the fire to have his coffee as he contemplated the day ahead. Those days were long gone, though. His knees couldn't take that kind of punishment.

He opened up his lightweight folding chair, wrapped a blanket around himself and sat down to wait for his hot brew to be ready.

Slipping Henry Stackhouse's old maps and charts from their waterproof case, he chose the one that showed the canyon where he was camped and studied it yet again, his mind mulling over every possible route, every obstacle he might encounter on the way to where he wanted to go.

He knew he would have a long, tough day ahead, but he was convinced he was on the right trail. At least it was the right place to make a good start. He wondered fleetingly how many times Henry had thought the same thing.

The difference between him and his late friend was that he wouldn't make this search his life's quest. He would be smart about it, do his best and go home when he was ready. The difference between him and Henry was that he wouldn't let it consume his mind, take over his life.

Henry had always been a loner. He'd never married and didn't have much family to speak of. He'd been an expert electrician and handyman, able to earn enough money to finance his gold-hunting trips, which had taken him all over the West until he'd settled on his search for the Lost Teamsters Mine about ten years ago. That was when his obsession had really begun.

Gus planned to stay interested in the quest but to avoid obsession.

Still, he liked to imagine returning to Eaglecrest with the gold so many had looked for and no one else had found.

Gus laughed at himself. Nothing in his harsh upbringing or in his lifetime of back-breaking labor had been a preparation for the kinds of fanciful thoughts he was having now. Visions of the old treasure filled his mind.

Maybe Zannah was right. Maybe he did have gold fever.

Unbidden, Sharlene's words came back to him, telling him he already had a treasure in his ranch, his family. In her.

Uncomfortable at the memory, he stood and checked on his coffee, then poured himself a cup and sat back down to wait for the boiling brew to be cool enough to drink.

He tried to distract himself with memories of long-ago camping trips when he and Esther and their children had enjoyed fishing, cooking out, spending nights around the campfire where Esther would tell and retell all the family stories that the kids treasured. His family had no such stories, but he'd come to feel a part of her family.

And just like that, his thoughts circled back to Sharlene.

In all the years he'd known her, she had been a faithful friend to Esther, and to him. She had been steady, reliable, never a surprise, never a source of dishonesty or, worse, drama, as some other employees had been. Everything he'd asked of her she'd done, often with discussions and suggestions that made his idea even better, more workable.

She'd been a real partner, someone who hadn't been afraid to tell him what she thought, rein him in when necessary, even spark his annoyance.

Gus raised his cup but paused with the coffee halfway to his lips as the thought struck him that, exactly as Esther had, what Sharlene had shown him all these years was what love was supposed to look like.

"So, WHAT DO you think now?" Zannah asked.

Brady lifted the ice pack from his face and said, "I think, given time, I might recover the sight in my left eye."

"I was asking Sharlene."

Brady grunted and replaced the only thing that was giving him any comfort. He wished he knew which was worse, the pain or the humiliation.

"We'll know more when the swelling goes down," Sharlene said, giving his arm a reassuring pat. "But I still think you should have gone to urgent care."

"I'll be okay."

"Are you trying to be a tough guy, Brady?"

Zannah asked, not for the first time. "'Cause even the fiercest, most competitive bull riders I've ever seen would know to go to the doctor after a spill like you had." She paused. "But most of the bull riders I've seen manage to land on their butts or their feet, not their faces."

If Brady could see her, he knew she would probably be biting her lip, trying not to laugh.

"You're going to have a really big shiner tomorrow," Emma said. She reached out to pat his hand where it lay on the cover.

The two little girls had followed the women into his cabin and were offering him sympathy. They were apparently enthralled by his injuries.

"I never saw anyone fall that hard on his face," her sister added. "I'm glad you didn't squash your nose."

"That makes two of us." Brady didn't think there were enough painkillers on the ranch to make him feel better. And the only way to make him feel less stupid was to stay hidden for the next few years.

He was lying across his bed, feet propped up, ice pack on his face, family gathered around. Sharlene and the little girls were observing him with suitable compassion.

Before he'd closed his eyes in self-defense, he'd seen that Zannah looked like she wanted to collapse into laughter. Another reason he was grateful for the ice pack. He wouldn't have to look at her growing amusement at his expense.

"Are you gonna do this again tomorrow night?" Joelle asked. "The second group didn't get to see what happened. They were working. Did you know you were actually flying through the air for a minute there? It was awesome."

"So glad you enjoyed it," he mumbled, peeking out with his one good eye.

Emma piped up. "It was even better than the time Breckin Dailey told Keegan Vasquez that she could fly and she would tell him the magic word and he could fly off the top of the jungle gym."

"What happened?" Zannah asked.

Joelle took up the story. "He fell on his face, but he mostly landed on the rubber mats underneath so he wasn't hurt too bad, but he did kinda squash his nose. It got okay later, though. You look a lot worse than he did, Brady."

Brady held up one scraped-up hand and tried to form a victory fist to pump the air as he said, "Yay me."

He couldn't see his hand, but he thought it probably looked more like a claw.

If it was possible, he would feel sorry for himself, but he suspected he'd broken his self-pity bone tonight.

Sharlene stood up, snapped the first aid kit shut and handed it to Zannah. "I think you might as well keep this in here. He seems to need it more than anyone else."

He heard Zannah snicker. "The good news is that when I took his boots and socks off, I could see that all his blisters have healed."

"I'm right here, you know," he complained.

"Come on, girls," Sharlene said, shooing them toward the door. "Let's leave Brady alone to recover."

"Okay," Emma said. "We need to call Mom and Dad anyway and tell them what happened. They're totally not gonna believe this. Can we use your phone, Aunt Zee?"

"Yes." She handed it over.

"'Course, if they'd let us have our own

phones, we wouldn't need to use yours," Joelle said.

"I'll be sure to tell them that," Zannah answered.

"Do you think Grandpa will call?" Joelle added. "I can't wait to tell him."

"Maybe," Sharlene answered. "But he might be too busy treasure hunting."

They went out and shut the door, leaving Brady alone with the person who seemed to be enjoying this the most.

After several seconds of silence, he lifted the ice pack again to look at her as he said, "So how long before you say 'I told you so'?"

She made a big show of looking at her watch. "I think I'm there right now. I told you so."

"It wasn't all bad."

"No, it wasn't. Everyone liked the trust fall, especially Juan and the waitstaff. They ended up rolling in the hay and having a hay fight."

"Yeah, that looked fun."

Zannah pulled a chair over to the side of the bed and sat down. "The obstacle course was good. Trusting them to lead each other, blindfolded, around cups of water set out on the barn floor was a good activity."

"And enough water got spilled that that the floor actually got an unexpected mopping."

"But—"

Brady replaced the ice pack. He knew he'd need it to get through the next part of the discussion. "Okay, I admit that that last activity I dreamed up probably went too far."

"Had you ever actually seen that done before?"

"Well, no."

"A race to see which team could inoculate the most calves, the fastest? Something you'd never, ever done before?"

"I may have overestimated my abilities."

"Thank goodness Chet and Juan were there to pull you out of the way when that mama cow took exception to you messing with her baby."

"I thought the gate was latched."

"It was, until she hit it at a run and headed straight for you. I'm glad she only knocked you down and didn't trample you."

"Me, too." Once again, he lifted the ice pack so he could look at her. "I would ask if you think our staff will still respect me, but I don't think they ever did."

Zannah went very still. Her gaze met his,

then dropped away. "They know you're trying, Brady." She stood up quickly and glanced around. She spied his cell phone on the dresser and brought it to him. "If you've got everything, I'll be going. Call me if you need anything."

"Sure. I will. Thanks, Zannah."

He watched her go, then lay down again. The heck of it was that he'd been trying to impress her. He should have stuck with trust falls. He knew how to fall.

Speaking of falling, he thought ruefully. In spite of his determination to not get romantically involved with his new business partner, he knew himself well enough to know he was falling for Zannah. It wasn't simply her looks—those golden-brown eyes and that curly hair combined with her pretty face were reason enough, but her independence, strength and dedication to her family were equally attractive.

The staring-into-each-other's-eyes activity had solidified things for him.

He was sunk.

He knew how she felt about him, though. She didn't want him here. He'd been secretly entertaining the fantasy of staying here even after he'd fulfilled the terms of the wager, but he had to put that out of his mind.

"ZANNAH, I REALIZE my last idea didn't work out very well, but Juan and I have a new one that I think will be a big attraction."

"But we're almost fully booked for the summer, Brady. How will we accommodate more purple— Oh, sorry." Juan squinted at the script Brady had written out for him. "More *people*." He lowered the paper to frown at his boss. "You've got terrible handwriting, Brady."

"You sound like my third-grade teacher."

The two of them were in the barn discussing last night's fiasco and trying to come up with a new moneymaking idea.

Brady indicated the lines he'd written, trying to anticipate Zannah's objections. "What do you think?"

"I think with you looking like a disaster victim, she's sure to go for this. Do you think you could try looking a little more pitiful?"

"Uh, yeah, I guess." Brady tried to arrange his battered features into an expression guaranteed to elicit sympathy, even pity.

"Nah." Juan stepped up to look at him.

"Now you look like someone she wouldn't want to meet in a dark alley."

"Well, maybe that will work in my favor. Come on."

Juan shook his head. "I've got to go repair the corral fence, remember? That calf did a pretty good job of taking it down." He headed out with a wave. "See you later."

Brady gave the fleeing man a dark look, then stretched gingerly, testing out the parts of him that were bruised the worst. It really wasn't as bad as he'd thought it would be. A hot morning shower had gone a long way toward making him feel better, but he was too stiff to pull on his boots. In his old sneakers, he probably wouldn't go around the horses today.

Also, since his face had taken most of the impact, the rest of him was in pretty good shape. The scrapes had already begun to scab over, and he was a fast healer. A lifetime of adventures with his brothers had taught him that.

He started from the barn, but a soft whinny from Belinda's stall had him stopping to talk to her. She put her head over the stall door and looked at him.

"Yeah, I know it's bad, much worse than when you dumped me," he said, reaching up to rub his hand along her jaw. "I apologize for filling your saddle blanket with burrs. I promise it wasn't on purpose."

She whinnied again.

"I'm going to take that as an acceptance of my apology," Brady said, rubbing both sides of her jaw. "So, you want to be friends?"

When she dipped her nose down and whinnied again, he laughed, thanked her and walked out feeling as if he'd passed a big milestone.

He headed out to find some breakfast, and to locate Zannah. All the while, his mind was clicking over the string of arguments she would have against his new idea.

On his way across the yard, he was stopped by everyone who had seen or heard about last night's debacle. Most people sympathized. Some flat-out laughed.

He decided not to let it bother him, because he had figured out a long time ago that being the boss meant looking ridiculous sometimes—although maybe not this ridiculous.

Right now, he had the new challenge of convincing a partner who had, so far, liked few of his plans, that this one was spectacular.

He walked into the office, where Zannah was once again seated at the computer.

She got to her feet when she saw who it was.

"Brady, how are you?" She came around the desk and stood looking closely at his face.

"I'll heal," he said with a shrug. "I want to talk to you about a new idea that Juan and I have come up with."

"Already this morning?" she asked in alarm. "Please tell me it's not something induced by painkillers."

"Have a little faith, will ya?"

She answered by leveling a steady look at him.

"Okay, I admit that last night's idea didn't work out very well, but this one is surefire."

With the expression of someone who was about to take some really bad medicine, Zannah said, "Okay, let's hear it." She sat down, and he sat opposite her.

Her quick agreement surprised him a little, but he didn't waste any time before plunging in.

"I paid a visit to Fordham's place—"

"You did? Without telling me?"

"I wasn't going to ask your permission," he answered testily, but her hurt look had him contritely mumbling, "I'm sorry. I didn't mean that the way it sounded."

When she didn't respond, he went on, "Fordham invited me, remember?"

"For what purpose?"

Frustrated, Brady shrugged. "I don't know, trying to be a good neighbor, make me feel welcome? Maybe he recognized another businessman with similar interests, someone who might benefit from his expertise."

Zannah held up her hand. "I guarantee you he's not that altruistic."

"Maybe not, but he knows how to make a person feel welcome."

Her gaze darted away from him, but again, she didn't respond.

He forged ahead. "He's got activities going on that appeal to a much wider clientele than only their guests. To the locals, as well."

"I know that. He's also richer than the Raymond City Bank. In fact, he *owns* the Raymond City Bank."

"So he's got cash flow we don't have. Anyway, we need to come up with unusual attractions." He paused and gave a self-deprecating smile. "I mean other than watching a newbie land on his face."

She smiled. "What do you have in mind?"

"Fordham suggested golf, which the surveyors also mentioned."

"But that would cost millions." She shook her head. "There aren't that many golfers around here. Maybe because there are so few golf courses. If we developed one—" She held up a palm. "And please notice that I'm not objecting to this, only asking questions and bringing up important points."

"Good. That's what partners are supposed to do."

"But we would have to give up hundreds of acres of rangeland to make it feasible. And, like I said, it would cost millions."

"Which we don't have," he agreed. "But golf on horseback would be cheap."

She stared at him. "Golf on—"

"Horseback. Yeah."

Brady couldn't help himself. He grinned and nodded. "Great idea, huh? We've got the land. Probably won't need more than twenty acres."

He paused, waiting for her response. She only stared at him with a look of dawning alarm. Before she could begin forming objections, he forged ahead.

"So, we've got the land. We've got the

horses. All we need are some stock tanks, and we'll be in business."

"Stock tanks?" she asked in a strangled voice.

"Yeah. That's where the players will make a hole in one."

"You mean with actual golf balls?"

"Right, and golf clubs."

"Swung from horseback?"

"Right," he said triumphantly, thrilled that she was picking up on this brilliant scheme so quickly.

"Brady," she marveled. "You have a fascinating attraction to the principle of Never Gonna Happen."

"If you'd listen—"

"I have listened, because that's what partners do, but partners also try to talk each other out of harebrained notions."

"You haven't even heard the whole thing yet."

She threw her hands wide. "I don't need to. I've got a mental image of hard objects flying around, knocking out teeth, both human and equine."

"Well, there is that risk," he conceded.

"Our insurance fees will skyrocket."

"Maybe. Maybe not. Fordham has people

sign waivers, but I know that isn't a guarantee against a lawsuit."

Zannah sat back and stared at him. "Golf clubs, golf balls—"

"Not that expensive," he broke in. "Besides, I'll bet if we go to some thrift stores around retirement communities in Tucson and Phoenix, we could pick some up for a song. It's the price of doing business."

"Well, we're not *doing* this business."

They stared at each other. Her expression was one of amazement and resistance. He figured his was morphing into complete stubbornness.

Maybe they should both return to their corners before the next round, he thought.

He gestured toward the desk chair, even went around the desk and pulled it out for her. "Here. Sit down."

She did so, giving him a wary look. He returned to where he'd been sitting.

"How about if we both take a breath?" he asked.

"So you can try some new tactic on me?"

"Well, yeah, since the last one didn't work."

She took a deep breath and said, "I have

the feeling you have more to tell me. What else will this project need?"

"Horses—"

"Which we already have." The thoughtful look on her face gave him a spark of hope.

"You'll need someone to design the course."

"My dad knows a guy."

"You've already discussed this with your father?"

"Yeah, last night. My face hurt so bad, I called him up to distract myself."

"Oh, of course," Zannah said immediately, looking so sympathetic, Brady felt guilty for using his pain to his advantage. On the other hand, this tactic was avoiding their usual argument.

"And what were his thoughts?" she asked.

"He says it sounds like a moneymaker." He dragged a chair around the desk so he could sit beside her. "I found some videos online. Look, I'll show you."

Within minutes, they were watching the films he'd found last night of cowboy golf in action.

What he'd thought would be informational and instructional, she only found alarming.

"Oh, my gosh," she said in a strangled voice. "That looks really dangerous." She turned to him until they sat knee to knee. In spite of her worried look, he thought once again about how much he enjoyed being this close to her. His gaze fell to her lips, which pushed out, then pulled in as she thought things over.

"Dangerous, and still really expensive," she added. "Can you get together a list of costs, and maybe a price list of what we might charge, as well as an estimate on how much the insurance would be?"

It took Brady a second to recall what they were talking about.

"Sure," he said, scooting away. He got up and put his chair back in place before heading for the door.

"And, Brady? See if there's such a thing as protective face gear for people and horses playing golf together." She gave him a look that edged on dismay. "Or maybe if this catches on, inventing such a thing could be your next business."

CHAPTER TWELVE

"HAVE YOU FOUND the gold yet, Grandpa? Are you at the mine?" Joelle asked, attempting to look behind what she could see of him on the screen to examine the terrain. Emma wanted to get in on the action and tried turning the phone toward herself so she could see, too, but her sister held on tight. After a brief scuffle, Joelle triumphed.

They had told Gus about Brady's accident as soon as the call came through, with much hilarity at Brady's expense. Now they were moving on to what was really on their minds.

Zannah reached out steadying hands to pry them apart as Gus answered.

"Not yet, honey, but I know I'm in the right area," Gus responded. "This place has all the markers that Henry Stackhouse found and recorded before he died."

Zannah frowned. She wished he wouldn't

mention death while balancing on top of a peak and talking to two little girls.

He held up his phone. "See that shallow cave opening? I think that's the place I'm looking for. It's full of debris that I think fell down from inside when there was a landslide farther up the mountain. Same thing at Two Horse Canyon, so I'm checking both places."

"Are you on top of a mountain?" Emma asked.

"Not on top, but I had to climb this far to get data." He turned the cell phone away from himself and slowly panned the area so they could see for themselves. "It's called Anvil Peak because it flattens out on top, maybe because of the cave-in."

"Awesome," marveled the two who had no idea what an anvil was.

"Grandpa, do you need our help?" Emma asked. "We could come help you."

"No, grandgirls, I'm fine on my own. You're needed at the ranch. I'm sure Zannah and Sharlene can't get along without you. Right, Zannie? You might have to rescue Brady if he falls and scrapes his face again."

"That's right. Can't do without these two," Zannah answered as she looked over the girls' shoulders, trying to see his face, make sure he was okay. He looked the same as ever, maybe a little happier.

The girls protested, but he was adamant and pointedly changed the subject. "Zannah, how are things going? How is Sharlene? She's still there, isn't she?"

As soon as the conversation turned to adult topics, the disappointed girls headed outside, no doubt looking for adventure.

Zannah called after them, "Emma, Joelle, don't go too far. Remember, we're going into town with Sharlene so she can show us her new inn." To her dad, she said, "And then I've got four friends from Las Vegas checking in this afternoon. We're having a bachelorette party for one of them."

She had the fleeting thought that she was going to have to talk to the girls again about running inside the house, and about their persistent notion that Gus simply couldn't find the gold without their help. Not for the first time, she wished he'd never started this.

"Zannie," Gus said. "Sharlene's still there, right?"

Bringing her attention back to the phone call, she answered, "Of course Sharlene's here, and she's doing fine. Taking some time off every day to go into town and work on her project. She's very excited about it. We're going with her today to see how things at her inn are shaping up."

He frowned. "Well, as long as she's not neglecting her work."

"When has she ever neglected her work?"

When he shrugged, she said, "Everything's fine here. Don't worry."

"I'm not. I turned the place over to you and Brady, and I'm not taking control back again, but of course I care about the place and everyone there."

Zannah couldn't help thinking there was longing in his voice, but he hung up a few minutes later without asking any more about Eaglecrest. Zannah didn't mention the cowboy golf course that Brady and his new sidekick Juan had begun planning. If it didn't work out, there might not be a reason to bring it up.

She sat in the girls' room, holding her phone and thinking about the conversation. It sounded as if he missed everyone, but there was more than that. As if he had let something go, or left something behind he'd meant to bring with him.

He did seem happy and engaged in what he was doing, though, so she had to let it go. She had plenty of her own issues to think about.

Brady Gallagher was the main one.

Although she had seen him last night when his wounds were fresh, she had been shocked at the state of his face this morning. He said he was okay and would heal fast, but seeing him with scrapes and scabs on his face had made her want to weep—a reaction she certainly hadn't expected. It made her ashamed of how she'd barely been able to contain her laughter when he'd face-planted in the corral.

This morning she had wanted to soothe him and had a disturbing desire to kiss away his hurt. Her face burned at the thought, because she knew he certainly wouldn't welcome such a thing.

Of all the incidents that had happened in the past few weeks, all the changes Gus and Brady had brought about, Brady himself was the biggest one. Having him at Eaglecrest, making changes, making plans, dragging her along with them, had her mind whirling and her emotions in turmoil.

"Too many emotions," she murmured, staring down at the brightly patterned rug at her feet. "Emotions bring romantic feelings, or maybe it's vice versa."

Whichever way she looked at it, the feelings she was having were all centered around Brady, and they included frustration, humor, exasperation and a kind of admiring awe that he could come up with so many plans and notions to pursue. The problem was that she didn't know how many of them he would see to completion while he was here.

When would he leave, and what would he leave unfinished? It had never been a secret that there was a time limit on the challenge he and his brothers had been presented by their dad—major progress in six months, and a turnaround in a year.

What was going to happen when his time was up? Winner or loser, would he stay? She doubted it. He loved change too much, loved learning new things, figuring out a way to make them profitable, then moving on to the next new thing. He seemed to be enthralled with what her mother used to call TYNT and NYNT—this year's new thing and next year's new thing. She didn't understand that kind of mind-set, chasing after every shiny new object that seemed to draw him. It didn't make for a stable life, and certainly not for long-term relationships.

Had he ever had any long-term relationships, other than those with his family? He talked about his parents and his brothers with affection, so she knew they must be a strong family unit. That was probably why they all seemed to think alike about the way they did business.

Suddenly stifled by the warm room, Zannah stood, slipped her phone into her pocket and headed outside to clear her head. She grabbed her hat as she went, trotting down the front steps as if she was running away from something.

She checked in with Chet and Phoebe, saw that her nieces were playing a game with some of the younger guests and that the remainder of their guests were engaged in activities and having fun, then took a walk to the corral to see Juan's progress on the repairs.

She looped her arm over the top rung of the fence and watched him absently as her thoughts circled back to Brady.

Would he stay? If he stayed, would he continue to come up with new schemes? Would he work at becoming a real cattleman, settle into everyday life on Eaglecrest?

Or would he leave? Worse, would he decide he'd had enough of ranch life and sell his half? If so, whom would he sell to? She would love to buy him out, but she certainly didn't have the money.

What if he sold to someone like Lucas Fordham? Or Fordham himself. It was certain that their neighbor would be there, checkbook in hand, ready to buy in so he could get the river access he craved.

The agreement between Brady, Gus and herself had stated that she or Brady could sell whenever they wanted to. There had been so many details in the agreement that she hadn't focused on that one. She wished she had, because Brady could sell at any time after he had either won or lost the challenge. She didn't know if he would consult her or not. She hated the uncertainty.

She couldn't continue to speculate like this. She needed answers. Turning away from the fence, she ran right into Brady.

His hands shot out to catch her as he asked, "What's the hurry?"

Zannah fell back a pace and started to answer, but he rushed ahead. "Listen, I need you to come with me."

"Well, what's *your* hurry?"

"I'm pretty sure I've got this golf course figured out. Come on." He scooped up her hand and tugged her with him. "Juan and I were drawing up plans this morning. Apparently I think better when I'm a little banged up."

Behind them, she could hear Juan chuckling. She twisted her hand out of Brady's grip, but he barely seemed to notice.

He went on, "I've saddled our horses. We'll have to go on horseback so you can get the full impact."

"Exactly where are we going?" she asked as they loped across to where Buttercream and Trina waited. "Full impact of what? And don't forget my friends are coming for a bachelorette party. I've got to finish getting things ready."

"And I'm in charge of the guests tonight. Yeah, I know."

Brady was moving at such a headlong clip that, for a moment, she thought he was going to try to boost her into the saddle to get them going faster.

"We're going to that north pasture on the other side of the road. I've been all over this place and I think it's perfect. Level ground, big enough for as many as six stock tanks, plenty of room for horses and riders to maneuver."

"And swing golf clubs, I'm guessing."

"Right."

"But that's prime grazing land, Brady. Didn't Juan tell you that?"

He shook his head. "We didn't actually talk about it. I remembered that pasture, and it seems perfect. It is perfect," he repeated, probably because he thought she hadn't caught on the first time.

"It's prime grazing land." Two could play this game of repetition. Besides, her point was actually more valid than his.

"They can't be on it all the time, can they? Besides, how much of it do they use?"

"They eat the grass until it's gone, then we move them somewhere else so the grass can grow back."

"That means we can use it for cowboy golf when the cattle aren't on it. Right?" Brady threw a hand out in a sweeping gesture. "And it has the advantage of being close to the main house and all the activities there, so people can watch cowboy golf, too. It's a win-win."

Her dismay grew. She hadn't even thought about the possibility of spectators. He was so enthralled with this idea that maybe not knowing the hazards was a blessing for him.

"Brady, I still think the whole plan of horses, riders, golf clubs and flying balls is a disaster on the hoof. I had friends in Las Vegas who lived right on a golf course. They thought they would love it, but they had so many broken windows and holes pounded into their walls that they were nervous wrecks. They finally sold up and moved away."

He waved a hand at her. "Yeah, yeah, I hear you, but we can build a seating area with a net in front of it for spectators."

They were moving along at a pretty fast clip, but she glanced over to see the eagerness in his face. This was really important to him, but she had to burst his bubble.

"But all of that aside, the biggest problem with the pasture you want to use is that horses and people running over it for even part of the summer wouldn't exactly encourage the grass to grow, and we have to have the grass. Remember, cattle are sold by weight. We can't sell underfed, skinny cattle."

Brady pulled Buttercream up and sat staring ahead.

He had stopped so suddenly that Zannah dashed past and had to circle back to him.

He was deep in thought, then leaned forward and rested his forearms on the saddle horn as he said, "Let's put all your other objections aside for a minute. Do you have a better idea for a location?"

Zannah had the feeling she was watching a man seeing his fondest dream die an early death. She would feel sorry for him if she didn't know he would have a new dream in about five minutes.

She decided to be happy and honored that he was asking her opinion rather than rushing ahead for once. Briefly, she considered suggesting he forget the whole scheme, but looking at his battered features, she felt a warm glow.

She had to admire his tenacity. Even when he was down, he was never out. He was the living embodiment of the motto Never Say Die.

"There's a parcel about a mile from here, one we've never developed for grazing. It's not flat, though. It would have to be graded and leveled, I think, for your purposes. Our purposes," she added, earning a big smile from him, then amended it. "Our potential purposes."

"Lead the way," he said with a dramatic wave of his hand.

Laughing, she headed Trina to the west.

Once they got there, they dismounted and walked the ground. It was as rocky and unappealing as she remembered.

"Do you see what I mean?" she asked. "My grandfather thought that since this area is the lowest in elevation, a flood had scoured it out long ago, leaving nothing but rocks. It would take a massive amount of work."

"I'm not looking for this to be easy."

"Nothing has been lately," she pointed out. "Why should this be any different?"

Brady must have decided to ignore her lack of enthusiasm—a habit she knew she needed to change.

She cleared her throat and changed her tone of voice. "Do you have any ideas about how we would go about getting this ready for golfers?"

He shrugged one shoulder. "Like you said, we'd have to clear it, get these boulders out of here, grade and level it." He paused, looking into the distance as his thoughts formed. "We'd have to top it with something softer, like sawdust."

"Won't that get tossed up by hooves, clubs and golf balls?"

"Oh, yeah, I guess so. Do you have any ideas?"

"I would suggest artificial turf, but that really would cost a fortune."

"And can horses even run on it?"

"I could check, maybe find out what it would cost."

Brady turned to her with a smile that lit up his whole face and warmed her clear down to her toes.

"Hey, that would be great," he said. "Thanks. It's almost like we're starting to work as a team here."

She loved how delighted he was but couldn't resist saying, "Don't get too used to it. You only like it because I'm supporting your idea."

"Ah, Zannah, don't ruin it for me."

Laughing, he reached an arm out as if to hug her, but she teasingly ducked away. She stumbled, and his arm hooked her around the waist, reeling her in and bringing her around to face him.

Her hat fell off and she made a grab for it, but it tumbled to the ground. Her breath caught on a laugh. He grinned at her, but it faded as he looked down at her.

His eyes were alight as if he was seeing something that pleased him, but his expression grew solemn as he studied her face.

Zannah did the same, her focus going from his eyes to his lips, then back again. Even when he'd had them do the staring-into-each-other's-eyes exercise, she'd only actually been this close to him, been in his arms, one other time. And she hadn't truly noticed that his lashes were dark, thick and lush around his eyes. She thought if she ran a fingertip across them, they would be as soft and supple as a fine-tipped painter's brush.

Swallowing hard, she also realized that she'd never had such thoughts about a man's lashes.

Brady, usually smiling and upbeat, was very solemn as he looked at her. "Zannah, I'm going to—"

She didn't give him a chance to finish but placed her hand at the back of his neck and pulled his lips down to hers.

They were softer than she expected, warm and delicious. He seemed stunned at first, but then he pulled her more fully into his arms and met her fervent kisses with his own.

Her fingers skimmed over the scrapes on his face, and she pulled her lips from his to place light kisses on them.

"Zannah," Brady said in a strangled voice. "What are you doing?"

"Making it all better."

He cleared his throat. "I think this will only make things more complicated."

Dazed, she drew back and blinked up at him. The gentle look in his eyes jolted her into stepping back. She felt heat washing over her face.

"Oh, Brady. I'm sorry. When you caught me, I—" She gulped. "You probably shouldn't have caught me."

He smiled. "Next time, I'll let you fall."

"That's a better plan."

She stepped back and tried to quell the embarrassment washing over her. What had she been thinking?

Brady stooped to pick up her hat. He made a point of examining it and dusting it off carefully, giving her a minute to compose herself.

Taking a deep breath, she cast around for a change of subject.

"So, once we get this leveled, graded and

cleared, and can begin using it, how much do you think we should charge? Will it be part of guests' regular fee, or extra? And if local people want to come out and try it, how much will that be? Will we factor in the additional costs to our insurance?"

Brady walked a few feet away, then turned and strode back and forth, covering more ground with each pass. She knew he liked to pace while he thought, so she waited.

"It will have to be free at first."

"Free? I thought the idea was to add another income stream. We can't do that if it's free."

"We have to see if people enjoy it before we can figure out how much to charge. It's called a loss leader. Take a financial hit up front and make it up later."

"I really don't like the idea of going to all this work and expense and not knowing if it will pay off." She put up a hand, palm out, to stop him from saying what she knew was coming. "And, yes, I know what you're going to say. It's the cost of doing business."

Brady gave her an admiring look. "Now you're catching on, partner."

She laughed and turned to face the big, open area before them. "So, tell me how you think this course will work. You said we'll need six stock tanks?"

"Yes, it's something like golf in that the players have to get the ball into a tank."

Zannah frowned. "Where's the challenge in that? Stock tanks are a lot bigger than a hole in a golf course. Even the worst player can't possibly miss."

"But they're not in the ground. I think we'll get the ones that are at least two feet tall so it's more of a challenge. Fill some of them with water, turn others into sand traps. When we get it set up, I'm going to invite my brothers to come and try it out. They both like golf and think they're pretty good."

"Uh-oh. I see brotherly competition heating up." Zannah paused. "Wait a minute. I thought you and your brothers were all keeping your projects secret from each other."

Brady shook his head. "Not completely. I've told them all about this place. I'm not as secretive as they are."

"And are you thinking that once they've seen everything you're accomplishing here at Eaglecrest, they'll throw in the towel and let you win?"

Brady wagged his head from side to side.

"Well…not really. I guess I didn't tell you all the details of the challenge my dad gave us."

She leveled a steady look at him as she crossed her arms at her waist. "Can't say that I'm surprised. What other little nugget of information do I need to know—partner?"

"Finding a business in some branch of the entertainment industry and turning it around, making it profitable, is only part of it. The other part is that one of us also has to have the best, most sustainable plan to ensure the financial health of the project for many years into the future. When Dad is satisfied with that, along with all of the other details, he'll decide the winner and fund our next project."

"You mean, after you're long gone from the area, taking the profits with you?"

"No! Zannah, we're not corporate raiders." He looked deeply annoyed. "My family has never done business that way, and my father trained us to never do that, either. This whole plan came about because Dad was seeing too many businesses that went under, and the main reason was that, even with an influx of cash and a solid business plan, there was no long-term vision. Planning was needed, not only years down the road, but decades."

"I see." Zannah thought about that for a minute. "I've learned more in the past few weeks about business than I thought my brain could hold, but I don't see how golf on horseback is going to sustain us long-term."

"Me neither," he admitted. "This is for fun. I've got something else in the works."

She looked him right in the eye. "And you'll tell me about it when?"

He gave another little shrug, but he didn't quite meet her gaze. "As soon as I know it will work. There are some details to handle first."

Disappointed, Zannah said, "That's all you'll tell me right now, partner?"

"It's better to keep it to myself for right now."

"Why?"

"Because it's big."

She shook her head. "I thought you understood how much I hate being kept in the dark."

He started to speak, but she walked over and picked up Trina's reins. As she swung into the saddle and turned toward home, she thought about the kiss they'd shared, the one she had instigated. The closeness they had felt for a little while had dissipated as quickly as dew meeting the morning sun. It was nothing more substantial than that.

CHAPTER THIRTEEN

"AND WE'RE TAKING down the walls between this room and the next one to have one much larger one, and a bigger sitting area," Sharlene explained. "Can you believe we found the original hardwood floor underneath? And it is quarter-sawn golden maple in the bird's nest pattern. It was beneath green shag carpeting and four layers of linoleum."

"But the joke was on all those people who kept adding layers," a voice said from nearby. A tall man Zannah didn't know walked in to join them. "The bottom layer had never been glued, only tacked down."

Sharlene glanced over her shoulder and smiled as she finished. "That's right. The original floor was down there, filthy but virtually untouched. Refinishing this floor is going to be a breeze."

The newcomer was slim and distinguished looking, with hair graying at the temples and an easy smile. Zannah thought he was about Sharlene's age.

With a big smile, Sharlene walked over and took his arm, drawing him forward.

"This is Jeff Denton, the Realtor who's been such a big part of this project. When he learned that Lucas was interested in selling, he got a bunch of us together to make this happen."

She introduced Zannah and the girls. The whole time Sharlene and Jeff were talking about the ideas they had for the inn, they sprinkled compliments for each other into the conversation, pointing out how one or the other of them had brought in people who had necessary good ideas and skills.

They talked about how the building had originally been a hotel, then transitioned from that to a boardinghouse, getting more and more run-down over the years. The investors had decided to rename it the San Ramon Inn.

Zannah could barely keep her mouth from dropping slack in amazement as the years seemed to drop away from her lifelong friend. At one point, when they all went upstairs to see the progress, Jeff commented on the cleverness of Sharlene's ideas for bathroom redesigns and Sharlene actually blushed.

Try as she might, Zannah couldn't recall that ever happening before, and she had known Sharlene since birth. There was a whole lot more going on here than remodeling an old house into an upscale inn. Sharlene appeared to be getting a remodel, too.

Zannah felt a little ashamed that she had been so involved in her own issues with the ranch and Brady that she hadn't given Sharlene as much thought as she should have. Beyond thinking of ways to fill her job at Eaglecrest, she hadn't really considered what would happen next, but this was huge for Sharlene. She was starting an entirely new life. Zannah felt immensely proud of her.

When they were back in the car and headed home, Emma asked, "Is Sharlene gonna marry that guy?"

"No, of course not." Zannah's gaze shot to the rearview mirror so she could see her niece's face. Emma was staring up into the sky, a faraway look in her eyes.

"He really likes her," Joelle added. "He said nice things about her."

"Well, he's a nice man, and…and they're friends."

"Grandpa never says nice things about her."

"Well, he certainly never says mean things to her," Zannah insisted.

"No, but when you're friends with someone, especially for a long, long time, you need to say nice things."

"I'm sure he thinks them," Zannah answered, wondering where in the world all of this was coming from.

"He needs to say them."

Since they were absolutely right, and she didn't want to talk about this anymore, Zannah asked, "Who wants ice cream?"

Gus moved restlessly around his camp, rechecking his horses, who were peacefully grazing and probably wishing he would leave them the heck alone.

He still had daylight, so he could read the book he'd brought. It was about lucky precious-metal strikes in the West. Or he could go back to what he'd been doing for months, which was studying Henry's old maps. Usually they were endlessly fascinating to him, but not tonight.

The only thing he could think of was Sharlene.

What was she doing? Was she at the inn she

was abandoning him for? *Them* for, he corrected himself. He didn't know who all was involved in this project, but he had a mental picture of her working with them then heading over to Sadie's for a bite to eat, just a big, happy bunch of friends.

She used to be in her little house every night. When Esther was alive, the two of them would work on sewing projects together. They were together many evenings making curtains and matching bedspreads for the cabins, kids' clothes for the community clothing bank, or any number of other projects.

It hadn't occurred to him until this minute to wonder what she'd done with her evenings since Esther had died. He knew she'd grieved for her best friend, her sewing and decorating partner.

He could see now that the big change he had decided to make had pushed her into making one of her own.

But she'd said she loved him, had for years. She hadn't told him earlier, but he had to wonder if it would have made any difference if she had. Probably not. He was starting a new life, and so was she. He had to accept that.

Gus took another turn around his camp, poked up his fire, added more wood, then sat down again. He considered drinking another cup of coffee, but knew he was already going to be awake well into the night. He couldn't seem to let go of what was on his mind—had been on his mind for days now.

Maybe Sharlene wasn't out with friends. Maybe she was on a date with that guy. What was his name? Jeff something. He should have looked the guy up before he'd left, found out his intentions.

Gus had seen him, and thinking back, he realized that he was probably a little too slick. He already knew he wouldn't like the guy if he met him. Sitting back, he thought about that for a minute. He had friends in Raymond that he could call to ask about this Jeff, but Sharlene would probably hear about it and be mad at him.

But how could she be mad at him? Hadn't she said she loved him? That meant she wouldn't stay mad at him for very long.

He called Zannah, who answered on the first ring.

"Hi, Dad," she said breathlessly. "I can't really talk now. The girls and I got back from seeing Sharlene's place only a minute ago and I've got to get ready. My friends will be here soon."

"How is Sharlene's place?"

"It's going to be wonderful. She's so excited." Zannah chuckled. "I think a big part of it is that Realtor who's involved, though. His name's Jeff Denton, and I think she really likes him."

Cold swept through Gus. "She does, huh?"

"Yeah, they're so sweet together. She was really down in the dumps around here, but now she's cheered up."

"She has?"

"Yes. Listen, can you call back tomorrow? I've got to get ready."

"Sure, honey. Goodbye." He ended the call and stood staring at the rocks around him on the windswept peak. The guy's name was Denton and he and Sharlene were so sweet together.

ZANNAH SHOULD HAVE pushed Brady about the idea he had percolating for long-term financial growth. She fretted over it when they returned to Eaglecrest and got her nieces settled in their own room with books to read. She had told them the bachelorette party was only grown-ups. If she was truly lucky, they might actually listen.

The call from Gus slowed her down some, but she didn't have time to think about the odd call or the flat tone of Gus's voice.

She hurried to her room to shower and change, her thoughts circling back to Brady. There wasn't time to deal with it right now, though. She was excited about her friends coming, and she didn't have the time or extra energy to track him down to see what he had in mind. She didn't like not knowing, and she hated that he didn't come right out with it. It made her feel as if any progress they had made toward trust was once again snatched away from her.

And why was it that she was supposed to trust him, but he didn't seem willing to do the same thing?

She made a conscious effort to push it away. She wasn't going to let it ruin the next couple of days.

Zannah picked out sandals and a turquoise sundress with a wildly patterned belt, brushed her hair out so that it fell around her shoulders, then stood back to look at herself.

She had to smile. When she had left her job

in Vegas, she had promised herself that she would never again scrape her hair up into a bun or pull it back in a severe twist simply to keep it out of her way.

However, she had done exactly that when she got back home, braiding her hair or pulling it into a ponytail so she wouldn't have to bother with it.

By the time she arrived downstairs, camera in hand, her friends were driving up to the entrance. She was soon swept up in the excitement of seeing them again.

BRADY STOOD OUT of sight of Zannah's guests, watching her interact with the newcomers. He'd been invited to play poker over at Fordham's, and he needed to get going, but the opportunity to linger and watch Zannah with her friends was too tempting.

This was a different Zannah than the one he saw every day at Eaglecrest. She was free to relax, chat with her friends and Phoebe, eat an actual meal and drink a little wine.

They had commandeered the screened-in terrace that ran the full length of the back of the house, had even closed the doors into the dining room so they wouldn't be disturbed.

Though he'd been to many bachelor parties, he wasn't too familiar with the female version. These women were having fun but were much more restrained than what he usually saw with men. They appeared to be more interested in visiting than in drinking.

And he was lurking in the nearly empty dining room like a stalker.

Turning away, he was almost run over by Emma and Joelle, who had somehow managed to find themselves some party finery consisting of rhinestone tiaras and feather boas.

"Hi, Brady," Joelle said. "We're going to the party."

He was surprised they were invited, but they zipped past him and he received his answer with the surprised look on their aunt's face when the girls whirled through the door.

"This is better than a stage play," he murmured, fascinated by the way she was obviously trying to be firm, yet not hurt their feelings.

He leaned against the wall and crossed his arms over his chest as he watched.

One of Zannah's friends unobtrusively placed a couple of vases of flowers in front of the pile of gifts, and he wondered how many not-little-girl-appropriate items were among them. The other women rallied around, got the girls some food and cups of soft drinks, and included them in the conversation.

It was easy to see who the bride was, because she had a hot-pink veil on her head. It was interesting that she wasn't the center of attention, though. Zannah was. Maybe it was because they hadn't seen each other in a long time, but all the guests seemed to gravitate toward her, sitting by her, moving away, coming back. She gave each of them her undivided attention, probably asking questions, but also listening in that way she had, tilting her head slightly and squinting her right eye a tiny bit.

They were all drawn to her. As he was.

"This is wrong," he muttered, straightening away from the wall and heading outside. "I've got to get to that poker game."

As he walked toward his cabin, he was shaken by the thoughts that were forming, the certainty that Zannah had become far more important to him than he realized.

And that kiss! It was true that she had initiated it, but he had been a willing and eager participant.

When she had kissed the scrapes on his face, he'd been overwhelmed with tenderness and a fierce desire to grab her and hold on, but he was afraid it would terrify her. He knew her well enough now to understand that she was a combination of strength and vulnerability. He wouldn't do anything to jeopardize either of those qualities.

Everything they had been through since his arrival, every talk, every argument, flew through his mind. The certainty of his plan to win his dad's challenge, the straight-line path to finish up here and move on, suddenly seemed far less appealing.

Oh, who was he kidding? He'd known for days that he was falling for her.

He stopped with his hand on the doorknob as the realization overtook him—he didn't want to leave Eaglecrest. He didn't want to leave her.

"BRADY, IS SOMETHING WRONG?" Zannah looked at him with concern. "You've hardly said a word all morning." She smiled faintly. "Did you lose at poker?"

"Not too badly. You're right, though. Lucas Fordham is kind of a shark."

They were standing by the corral, waiting for her friends who had insisted they wanted to go horseback riding, although she knew at least two of them would be the worse for wear due to the amount of wine they'd drunk the night before.

Her nieces were there, fairly dancing with excitement as they waited for the women to arrive. Zannah had quickly realized last night that there was no point in trying to keep them away from the festivities. The girls were too enthralled with her friends. Two of them, Abby and Sarah, were her colleagues from her old job, and two, Sandrine and Violette, had lived in her apartment building. They were showgirls who had started a dance and exercise class all of the others had joined. They were great fun and never looked less than gorgeous.

However, due to the nature of their jobs, they weren't usually up this early, and none of them had much experience on horseback. This might be a short ride.

Emma and Joelle were getting tired of waiting. She had given them her phone so they could play some games.

"Are you okay?" She studied Brady's face, which was healing nicely. "You seem a million miles away."

"Not that far. Over on the main road." He pulled a piece of paper from his pocket and unfolded it before handing it to her. "I was going to wait to show this to you, but I need to make some calls today about it. We received all the bids for the repair work that's needed." He looked grim as he added, "I compiled them into one spreadsheet—lowest bidder at the top—but it's a moot point since, top to bottom, there's only a few dollars' worth of difference."

Alarmed, Zannah scanned the paper. She gulped as she stared at it. "Seriously?" she asked in a weak voice. "This isn't a misprint?"

"Don't I wish. Repairs will be much more extensive than repaving. All the contractors say we have to scrape it down to the base and basically start again, not to mention building new bridges over the two washes the road crosses. If we do it right, though, we'll probably never have to do it again."

When she didn't respond, he went on, "I didn't want to show this to you until after your friends left, but the surveyors we used recommended Olsen Construction. They can start next week."

Zannah's stunned brain tried to take in

what he was saying even as she looked at the numbers and tried to balance them with what was in their bank account. Not even close.

"We can't afford this."

"We can't afford *not* to do it, Zannah. The old road we're using can't handle the traffic, and it's in even more danger of washing out with every rainstorm. The monsoon season is only beginning, which means we could be completely cut off."

"I… I know. I get that, but…wow, this is huge."

"Yes, but we have to also think about safety. What if we had a disaster, like fire or a medical need? Emergency vehicles couldn't get in here."

Brady propped his forearms on the top rail of the corral and ran his thumb across his chin.

She appreciated that he was giving her a minute to think, but she couldn't seem to get past the enormous numbers.

"Will we have to get a loan?"

"Maybe short-term." He turned to look at her. "I've got something else in mind."

"You mentioned that yesterday. What is it, exactly?"

Before he could answer, her phone rang,

and Joelle called out, "Aunt Zee, it's Grandpa again." She touched the green button and asked eagerly, "Grandpa, did you find the treasure yet?"

"No, but I know I'm in the right place," Gus answered. Joelle put the phone on speaker, and his voice boomed out, "Where's Zannah?"

"Here I am," she called out, then gave Brady a regretful look.

"I'll catch you later," he said, then glanced over his shoulder as he heard her friends approaching. "I'll take care of them."

"Thanks." Feeling frazzled, she hurried to the phone, but Joelle and Emma were peppering their grandfather with questions.

"No, you can't join me, girls, but if you'll look in my room, on top of my desk, you can see a map of exactly where I am, on Anvil Peak. That way, you'll see where I am the next time I call. Sorry I didn't think of that sooner."

Neither of them seemed to like the idea of looking on a map instead of going to help him, but they grudgingly agreed, talked for a few more minutes and handed the phone to Zannah.

She glanced up and experienced a moment of humor as she saw Brady surrounded by her friends, including Sandrine and Violette, who wore jeans the way they were intended to be worn.

"So you're her new partner, right?" the one named Sarah asked him.

"That's right." Brady looked at the half circle of women before him. A couple of sets of eyes were decidedly bloodshot, but all were laser focused on him. He was grateful they didn't comment on his still banged-up face.

"This place means everything to her," a statuesque blonde pointed out. He didn't know her name at all but thought Ms. Gorgeous would fit both her and her friend. They looked as if they wouldn't put up with any nonsense. Good thing he didn't plan to give them any.

"Yes, it does."

"She's a really strong woman. She had to be, with what she went through."

"Yes," he agreed, wondering where they were going with this. "Her mother's death—"

"That was only the start." The one named Abby, who was still wearing her veil, stepped forward. "She went through years of torture in her job. It's the kind where you have to work hard to separate yourself from it, but she was stubborn, so she stuck it out long after she should have left."

"Not stubborn," he found himself saying. "Maybe conscientious?"

All four women exchanged pleased smiles.

"And this place means everything to her," Abby added.

"I know." He looked from one to the other of them and decided they weren't exactly suspicious. More like cautious. She was lucky to have friends like these. "It's her refuge." He hadn't even known he understood that until he said it out loud.

The women's smiles went even broader and were filled with satisfaction.

"He gets it," another of the majestic ones said. "She'll be all right."

To his complete amazement, she gently patted his cheek as if he was a toddler, then turned toward the saddled horses and asked, "So how do we get on these beasts?"

To his relief, Juan arrived right then, and he was more than happy to help these beautiful ladies. Zannah ended her call and returned to the group, but there was no time for them to resume their talk. He knew it would have to wait until after her friends left.

He had a few more clues as to what her work life had been like in Vegas. He was deeply grateful that these women had been there to support her, and then wondered when or if he'd ever had a thought like that about a colleague.

Once the group left on their trail ride, he returned to the office and the tough decision they needed to make. An uneasy feeling was growing that it would either make or break them.

"WE HAD MAP-READING in class last year," Emma informed her little sister. "Mrs. Gomez said we can't always depend on GPS and phones. She even taught us how to use a real compass. It's called orienteering. She talked about it for *days*, and we had all kinds of activities and then we had a test."

They were standing in their room, staring down at the map their grandfather had told them about. Joelle frowned at the squiggly lines she still didn't understand. She gave her sister a dubious look. Emma was always so sure of herself, so full of ideas that sometimes got them into trouble.

"So, with the map and a compass, we can find Grandpa?"

"Yes." She pointed. "See, here's Anvil Peak, and here's Two Horse Canyon. He's in one of those places and he needs our help."

"Do you have a compass?"

"No, but I'm sure we can get one. I'll bet there's one in Grandpa's room or his office. He would want us to use it," she said with complete confidence.

"But we'll get in big trouble."

"Not if we help him find the gold. Then everybody will be too happy to be mad at us."

"Are you sure?"

Emma clapped her hands onto her hips and faced her little sister. "Listen, Jo. We've heard Zannah and Brady and Grandpa talking about money like a million times. If they had the gold, they'd never have to worry again. I'll bet they would even share with Mom and Dad." She paused, obviously liking that idea. "We could get a pool."

She started to fold up the map, then stopped and looked up like a great idea had hit her. Uh-oh. Joelle knew that look all too well.

"What?"

"We could be famous," Emma said in a reverent tone.

"We could? How?" This was beginning to sound a little bit better.

"We can make a video. We can film our whole trip, especially the part about us finding the gold, then we can put it online. I bet we could have our own channel and everything."

"Do you think Mom and Dad will let us?"

"Sure, we'll be rich. You want to be rich, don't you?"

Joelle thought about that. "I didn't know we were poor."

"We're not, but finding the gold, helping Grandpa find it, will mean we won't ever *be* poor, and Eaglecrest will be here forever."

Joelle loved the ranch so that statement sent her over the edge of agreement. "Okay. What do we need to do?"

ZANNAH WATCHED AS her friends drove away. They'd all had a wonderful time, but now she was exhausted. She waved until they were out of sight down the bumpy road and then went to sit on one of the porch chairs.

Eagerly, she looked at her camera, flipping through her photos, delighting in the candid shots, decided which ones she would send to her friends to solidify their memories of the weekend.

Emma and Joelle had skipped away, saying they were going to help Juan in the stables and corrals. Zannah was thrilled that they were actually volunteering to help out, though she doubted it would last very long. They would tire out and return to their room, probably to study the map their grandfather had pointed them to and dream of how they would spend the gold when he found it.

She smiled. That was one of the best things about those two—they had absolute faith in their grandpa.

Leaning forward, she propped her chin on her hand and gazed the way her friends had gone.

That road.

She drew in a long breath and then released it. Brady was right. Even with the basic maintenance that needed to be done, this road couldn't stand up to the amount of traffic that needed to use it every day.

Getting a loan and raising their fees would help short-term to cover the cost of the repairs, but it wouldn't be enough. Brady had said that he had an idea of what to do. She only hoped she liked the idea.

She would have to talk to him about it, but right now, there was maintenance to be done on some of the empty cabins. Sitting for a few more minutes, she planned her day, then got up to locate her toolbox and get started on loose curtain rods and leaky faucets.

By late morning, she had finished her chores, so she went to find Brady.

"Oh, hey, Zannah," he said when she walked in. Looking up from the computer screen, he rubbed his eyes, then his face and stood up to stretch. "Did your friends get off okay?"

"Yes." She picked up a pile of neglected mail and began sorting through it but paused to watch as he twisted from one side to the other, then lifted his arms above his head as far as he could. The front of his shirt pulled up, exposing a hairy tummy and belly button. Then he lowered his arms and began rolling up his sleeves with quick, efficient tucks of his fingers.

It was such an unconsciously masculine gesture, Zannah found herself mesmerized. She had a vivid recollection of how those arms had felt around her. And she had a soul-searing memory of what it had been like to kiss him. She knew she should feel embarrassed about it, but she didn't. In fact, she wanted to do it again.

When Brady finished stretching, he placed his hands at his waist and stood staring down at the screen.

He seemed to have forgotten she was there, but that was okay, because it gave her a minute to study him.

She had been looking at him for weeks now. Every day he'd been here, they had talked. Sometimes they came to an agreement, but more often not. He was determined to make her see things his way, and she was equally determined to have him see hers. Most of the time they were able to come to a solution that worked for both of them but, best of all, worked for Eaglecrest and its future.

Compromise was becoming a way of life for her. For them. It was something she hadn't expected when he had first arrived, her reluctance made even tougher by the way her dad had brought him there.

She admitted compromise was a good thing, and it was such a surprise that it had come about so quickly.

After all, compromise was something you

did with someone you respected—or with someone you loved.

Loved?

That thought jolted her so much that the mail in her hand slid to the floor.

When she stooped to pick it up, Brady came around the desk to help her.

"Hey, butterfingers," he teased, crouching beside her. His smile faded when she looked and met his gaze. He must have seen the stunned look in her eyes because he immediately asked, "Hey, are you okay?"

"Uh, um, yes—"

Urging her to her feet, he said, "Forget the mail. Come sit down."

She felt too weak-kneed to argue, so she leaned on him as he helped her to the chair, then turned to the small refrigerator in the corner and grabbed a bottle of water.

As he twisted off the cap, he said, "Too much partying, maybe? I'll bet you're dehydrated."

She took the bottle and drank deeply. She knew being well hydrated was necessary for brain function, and hers had obviously short-circuited.

Love? That wasn't possible. He wasn't going

to stay. She knew that, so how could she have allowed her heart to make such a foolish mistake?

"Better?" he asked, sitting on the edge of the desk.

"Yes. Thanks." She drank some more, then set the bottle down beside her. She couldn't think about this right now. They had ranch business to discuss.

Straightening, she cleared her throat and said, "Okay, what is your idea for funding the road?"

He gazed at her for a few seconds before answering, but finally, he gave her a faint smile that seemed almost sympathetic.

"We need to sell off part of the ranch. Maybe a large part."

CHAPTER FOURTEEN

"SELL—? ABSOLUTELY NOT. Are you crazy?"

The shock on her face made him feel sick to his stomach, but he ignored it and tried to sound businesslike and reassuring.

"It's the only way, Zannah."

"No. We're already selling off Hawk's Eye Mesa as homes for the rich and famous. What more do you want?"

"It's not what I want, Zannah. It's what will ensure the long-term financial health of the ranch."

"Oh, yeah, so you can win the bet with your brothers."

Hurt warred with anger in her face. He reached out a hand to her, but she drew away. So he went around the desk and grabbed a handful of papers he'd printed out. He rolled his chair around, then sat facing her. She scooted back. He knew it was personal, but he tried not to take it that way.

"Here are the bids from the road contractors. You can see for yourself that rebuilding the main road and repairing the old one is going to put us so far into the red that we won't get out in our lifetimes."

"Oh, that's an exaggeration," she snapped.

"Even if we raise prices at the cowboy college, charge more for our cabins, offer more events." He pointed toward the main house. "More events like bachelorette weekends, maybe even with spa treatments, it will be years before we can dig ourselves out of the financial hole."

She shook her head. "Bachelorette weekends? Spa treatments?"

"Those are only examples. We have to grow the business. A business that's not growing is actually failing, which is what Eaglecrest has been doing for quite some time now. We have to turn things around, and selling part of the ranch will do that, establishing financial health for decades."

"Who do you plan to sell to? Your new friend Lucas Fordham?" Angry tears stood in her eyes. It didn't matter if they were from hurt or fury. The effect was the same—they served to close her mind.

"Only if he wants a one- or two-acre ranch-ette."

"What?"

"Along with developing high-end vacation homes on Hawk's Eye Mesa, we can divide many acres not used for grazing into sites for more modestly priced homes."

"But developing all of that will cost us even more."

"Initially, yes. But our initial outlay will soon be covered by sales. The more reasonably priced our sites are, the faster our sales will grow. If we also offer home maintenance and security, we'll have another income stream."

The color that had washed out of her face was beginning to come back. Red stained her cheeks as her indignation grew. She swept more tears from her cheeks. "Maintenance? Security? You're talking about winter visitors, aren't you?"

"Retirees want to spend their winters in warmer places like this, and think what a boon it would be to the town of Raymond to have more visitors every year."

Zannah propped her elbow on the chair

arm and put her face in her hand, covering her eyes.

He'd known this would be a shock to her, and he'd spent half the night trying to think of the best way to tell her. Every other discussion—argument—they'd had was tough, but this was worse.

This was different because of how much he cared for her, how concerned he was about how this would affect her.

"You can't sell off any part of Eaglecrest, Brady," she said, lifting a stricken face to him. "You can't!"

He leaned forward and gently asked, "Do you have a better solution?"

"I don't know," she choked out. "But there has to be one."

"What is it you're so afraid of?"

Tears ran down her face as she said, "You're putting everything at risk. It's all I have left of my mother and you're going to lose it, give it away to strangers, people who didn't even know her—"

"No, Zannah."

Full of pity and sorrow, he tried to pull her into his arms, to comfort her.

She jerked away. "You don't understand.

You've never been rooted in a place the way I am. Your parents are together and well and happy, and so are your brothers. They're always there for you. They're your security. My mother is gone. My father is traipsing around the mountains looking for gold. This ranch is my security."

"And it will continue to be if we do this."

She surged to her feet and stood facing him, hands clenched at her sides. "You lied to me. You said you weren't a corporate raider, but that's exactly what you are—someone who sweeps in and buys a company then sells off its best assets and moves on, destroying what someone else was trying to build."

"That's not true." Being unfairly accused like this was infuriating. "My family and I always try to build, not destroy."

"So why have you decided to change your way of doing business by destroying Eaglecrest?"

"It's not like that."

Standing up, he crossed the room and pulled a large portfolio out from behind the bookcase. "I took the liberty—"

"Oh, I have no doubt that you did."

"—of talking to some contractors about

this idea. They worked up some renderings for the architecture and the landscaping."

"Which you hid from me." Her lips pressed together angrily as she pointed a shaking finger at the bookcase.

"I didn't hide them. That was the only place to store something this big." He proved his point by untying the tapes that held the two sides together and opening it on top of the desk.

He chose the one that he thought best depicted what he had in mind. The example was typical of the Southwestern style, with adobe brick and brightly colored tiles around the doors and windows. It was built around an inviting patio with a center fountain.

She gazed at him, trembling as she choked out, "I can't believe you did this behind my back. I can't believe you've gone this far with it and didn't even mention it to me."

He dropped the paper onto the desktop in frustration. "I thought it would be easier to have something tangible for you to look at."

More tears formed in her eyes. "I've seen it and I hate it."

"Only because you haven't considered it."

"And I won't."

There was no time to answer, because the door swung open and Sharlene and Juan rushed into the room.

"Have you seen the girls?" Sharlene asked breathlessly. "I can't find them anywhere."

"They came to help me for a while," Juan added. "Then they said they had your permission to go riding on their own and have a picnic."

"What?" Zannah and Brady both whirled around. Zannah said, "I didn't give them permission."

"I saddled two horses for them and they took off." Juan glanced at his watch. "It's been about two hours since they left." He looked up, sick with dismay. "I'm so sorry. I should have checked with you."

"They came in here, too," Brady said. "It was a couple of hours ago. They were looking for something in the desk, but they wouldn't tell me what. They didn't find it, though, and left after a few minutes."

"Why didn't you tell me?" Zannah asked angrily.

He tried to sound reassuring and not defensive. "It didn't seem like anything out of the ordinary. They come in here just about every day."

Zannah shook her head as if she couldn't accept his explanation and looked at Sharlene and Juan.

"They've never wanted to go off on their own before," Sharlene said. "They like being here where all the action is."

"What did they take with them, Juan?" Brady asked.

"They each had a saddlebag. I assumed it was their lunches."

"Lunches, dinners, maps, whatever else they think they'll need to get up into the mountains and find their grandpa," Zannah said.

Brady could tell that she was trying to quell the sense of panic that threatened to choke her on top of the distress she was already experiencing from his news.

"I think you're right," Sharlene said. "They were showing me the map that Gus left behind. They've gone to find him."

"Against my specific orders," Zannah fumed.

"Yes, but we can deal with that when we get them back," Brady said. "Juan, put in a call to the sheriff's office. Tell them we've got missing kids. Again. But we'll begin looking for them right away. Ask them to be on alert if we need help, but we have a good idea where they went and we're going to follow them."

Juan swung around the desk and grabbed the phone.

"I'll call Dad," Zannah said, but when the call didn't go through, she shook her head. "He's probably out of range."

"What can I do?" Sharlene asked. "I mean besides think up a list of odious chores for them to do for the next week as punishment."

Zannah answered with a weak smile, appreciating her attempt at humor. "Keep your phone with you and make sure everything goes smoothly here. We'll get Phoebe to help us track them. Could you call her and ask her to meet us at the stables?"

Sharlene nodded and scooped her phone from her pocket, then looked up. "What about Casey and Vanessa?"

"Let's wait a little while," Zannah answered. "No need to panic them unnecessarily."

Brady appreciated that Zannah seemed to

be including him in the search party. "Should we take the quad?"

"No, the terrain is too rough." Zannah made the statement firmly, but then her voice broke. "Certainly too rough for a couple of inexperienced kids. I don't know what they were thinking. We'll have to follow them on horseback."

Juan hung up and said, "Deputy is on his way."

"I'll meet him," Sharlene said and hurried out the door.

"We have to get going," Zannah said. "The sheriff's office knows that Phoebe is the best tracker around. They'll trust us to start the search on our own and keep in contact with them."

Brady fought the urge to take her into his arms. This wasn't the time, and even if it was, she wouldn't welcome his comfort.

"Sounds good," he said. "Let's go."

ZANNAH RUSHED TOWARD the stables with Brady and Juan. Once there, they saddled three horses, including Phoebe's favorite, Winnie.

Having something to focus on, getting

ready, grabbing supplies and gear was a blessing, and in spite of her profound disappointment and upset at Brady's plan to carve up her land and sell it off, she was glad that he was going to help her find her nieces.

Phoebe arrived in record time, double-checked everything they had prepared, then examined the ground to find the girls' tracks.

"How do you know which ones to follow?" Brady asked.

"I know which horses they took. Luckily, one of them has a little nick on the bottom of the shoe on his right foreleg. Once we follow that track out of the corral, it should be easy to keep it in sight." She turned to Zannah. "Do you have any idea where they were going?"

"Dad said he's on Anvil Peak, and he told them where to find a map so they could see exactly where he is. But he also said he's going to check out Two Horse Canyon, so they could be headed to either place."

"Good grief," Phoebe said. "Do they even know how to read a map?"

"They must think they can." She shook her head. "I can just about guarantee you that this was Emma's idea."

After one final check of their gear, they mounted up and started toward the foothills.

The three of them rode in silence for several minutes, making sure to keep sight of the prints they were following. Once they were well away from the ranch and sure of their direction, they picked up speed.

When they reached the foothills and the trail leading up to Anvil Peak, Zannah paused to call her father and was finally able to get through.

She told him what was going on, then asked, "Where are you now? Still on the peak?"

"No. I'm about an hour from there, headed home."

"Already?" She glanced at Phoebe and Brady. "Did you find gold?"

"No," he said. "But I found what I needed to find. Listen, Zannie, I'll go back to where I was camped in case they actually find the place. I'd recommend keeping on the path you're on now."

"We will. We'll let you know if we find them, but you'll have to stay up where you can get cell service."

He agreed and hung up.

Immediately, Phoebe asked, "Did he find the treasure?"

Zannah shrugged. "He said he found what he needed to find."

"Don't know what that means, but we'll know soon," Phoebe said. "In the meantime, we've got two kids to find."

They went up the trail single file until it leveled out on a small mesa, where it split in two. They rested the horses for a few minutes while Phoebe crouched on one knee and studied the faint marks on the hard ground.

"I think they got a little mixed up here," she said. "Whatever map they had probably wouldn't have shown the way this splits off." She walked several yards each way and came back to them. "They went to the south, but, from what I can tell, Anvil Peak is north."

Zannah felt sick. "There's no telling where they are now, or where they might end up. Maybe they thought they were heading into Two Horse Canyon. They would have seen it on another one of their grandfather's maps."

"We've still got tracks to follow," Brady pointed out. "We'll find them."

"Absolutely," Phoebe agreed.

The two of them sounded so sure that Zannah couldn't doubt them. She smiled. "Then, let's go."

The going was slow, but they made steady progress.

At one point, Brady said, "I guess I don't know much about how kids think, but how did they expect this to turn out?"

"With them riding home triumphantly dragging a load of gold behind them. Don't forget who their grandfather is, the big treasure hunter. And they know we need money."

In spite of the urgency she felt, and worry about her nieces, Zannah's mind circled back to the soul-deep betrayal she felt over Brady's plan to carve up Eaglecrest into ranchettes. How could she be in love with someone who would do that?

"Ranchettes," she muttered. "What in the world is a ranchette?"

"Did you say something?" Phoebe asked, glancing around, then seemed taken aback by the grim look on her cousin's face. "Zannah, don't worry. We'll find them."

"I know," Zannah said, avoiding Brady's curious gaze. "I have faith in you."

Her belief in Phoebe was well-placed when they rounded a rough curve in the trail and found themselves in a small, dead-end box canyon where they spotted two horses and two crying little girls.

"Aunt Zee!" Joelle yelled when she spotted them. She jumped up and ran over to them. "Emma's leg is hurt. We need to call nine-one-one."

Zannah hopped down and caught the frantic child as she barreled into her, then hurried to Emma's side. "What happened?"

Brady and Phoebe were right behind her. All three adults gathered around Emma. She lay on her back with her left leg stretched out before her and her right leg crumpled at an unnatural angle.

"Whoo," Brady whistled softly through his teeth. "We're going to have to be really careful here."

"I'll get the first aid kit," Phoebe said.

Brady pulled out his phone as Phoebe went through the saddlebags. "I'll call emergency services and then call the ranch to let them know we found the girls."

Seeing the concerned adults caused Emma to begin crying hysterically. "Is it broken? Will they have to cut it off?"

"It's almost certainly broken," Zannah

answered in a no-nonsense tone. Now that the girls were found, she could stop imagining the worst and deal with reality. "But they won't have to cut it off. You're going to be fine. We have to figure out exactly what to do."

Phoebe returned with the kit, and the two women gently probed Emma's leg to see the extent of the injury.

"There's no blood," Phoebe said, opening the first aid kit and removing a roll of gauze. "But I'm sure it's broken in more than one place. We're going to need to splint it. I'll find something to use."

"That shouldn't be hard," Zannah said. "That big storm we had must have flooded here and washed in all of this debris." She pointed to a massive tangle of uprooted bushes, broken branches and rock. "We'll have to be careful, though. There are probably snakes in there."

Phoebe nodded and strode toward the tangle.

"Everyone has been notified and help is on the way. Sharlene is going to try to call Gus." Brady put his phone away and asked the girls, "How did this happen?"

Joelle wiped tears from her eyes as she answered, "We thought we were going to the right place to find Grandpa. We had a map and a compass and everything, but when we got here, Emma's horse fell, and she fell, too, and then it rolled on top of her when it got up."

Brady looked at the ground around them. "The horse must have stepped in this hole," he said, pointing to a deep depression in the ground. "Fortunately, they landed in soft sand or it could have been much worse."

"Is Pancho okay?" Emma asked.

"I think so. He and his buddy Belinda found some grass and they're busy having lunch, but I'll take a look at him."

Phoebe returned with two pieces of wood, which she placed on the ground, as Brady came back to report that Pancho was in good health.

Phoebe said gently, "We'll have to straighten out her leg to splint it."

"Will it hurt?" Emma asked, her voice shaking.

"Yes, it will," Brady answered. "We're not going to lie to you and let you think that it won't."

"So you'll have to be brave," Zannah added.

"No! I'm not brave," Emma wailed. "I knew we shouldn't go after Grandpa, but I talked Jo into it, and then I couldn't let her know I was scared."

"We'll talk about all of that later. Right now, you have to stay completely still while Phoebe bandages your leg. Do you think you can do that?"

"I...maybe."

The three adults exchanged a look. Brady nodded toward Emma's head and Zannah gave a nod of her own before she knelt beside the uninjured leg. Leaning over, she held her niece's hips in a firm grasp with one arm, leaving her other one free to help Phoebe.

Brady crouched beside the little girl's head and bent forward to cradle it and her shoulders firmly between his forearms.

"Here we go," Phoebe said. With Zannah's help, she gently lifted the broken leg and straightened it. Emma let out a shriek of pain and then went limp.

"Is she dead?" Joelle cried.

"No," Brady said. "She fainted, but she'll be all right as soon as we get her leg splinted."

He looked around. "This canyon is too

small for a helicopter to land here. We'll have to go back the way we came and carry her to the top of the mesa."

Within minutes, Phoebe had the leg splinted, and Emma began to come around.

Brady gave her some water while the two women found two much longer sticks. They made a stretcher using a large square of waterproof cloth from Phoebe's saddlebags.

Brady lifted Emma onto it and grasped the handles at one end while Zannah took the other. Phoebe placed Joelle on Belinda and handed her Pancho's reins, then gathered up the reins of the other horses and climbed into her own saddle. She gave the nod to start off.

Joelle sniffled. "This is the worst day ever."

"No, it isn't," Brady responded. "Five people and five horses are coming safely out of the canyon and heading home. I think this is a great day."

Zannah gave him a grateful smile.

CHAPTER FIFTEEN

"HER LEG IS broken in two places, but it's been set, and Emma's going to be fine," Casey said, entering the waiting room to speak to Zannah. "She was pretty excited about that helicopter ride, but she's asleep now," he added, sitting down and wiping his forehead, then laughing ruefully.

"So was I, for that matter. Never rode in a helicopter before," Zannah agreed.

"I'm sure the bill is going to be exciting, too."

"Well, if we have trouble paying it, maybe she and her sister can go treasure hunting again," Vanessa said, sitting down beside her husband. Shakily, she reached for his hand. "She'll be here for a couple of days, then we'll take her home. That's when the fun will start."

"Joelle will be waiting on her—"

"Yes, hand and broken leg," Zannah finished for her brother, who smiled.

"So, she'll be punished almost as much as Emma. Poor kid," Vanessa said.

Zannah looked at her carefully. Usually unflappable, her sister-in-law was pale and drawn. Her dark hair, always flawless, was lank and falling around her face. She and Casey had rushed south to Tucson from Phoenix, arriving not too long after Emma was wheeled into the emergency room. Zannah had stayed with Emma until her parents had arrived.

Brady, Phoebe and Joelle had taken the horses and returned to Eaglecrest. Phoebe called to say that they had arrived safely and Gus was expected home soon.

Now that it looked like things would be okay, she called Eaglecrest to arrange with Sharlene for someone to make the two-hour drive to Tucson to pick her up.

"It's nearly 8:00 p.m. We're going to get something to eat, Zannie," her brother said, standing up and stretching, then pulling his wife up beside him and drawing her close in a one-armed hug. "Do you want to join us?"

"I already ate, but I'll sit with you."

"I'm going to get soup," Vanessa said. "So I can have plenty of crackers to settle my stomach."

Casey laughed and regarded his wife with pride.

Zannah started to follow them, then stopped suddenly as images and hints lined up in her mind like dominoes.

"Vanessa," she cried. "Are you pregnant?"

Her sister-in-law laughed. "Yes. Since I'm thirty-eight, and I'm considered to be high-risk, we were waiting to tell everyone, but it's going to be hard to hide pretty soon."

Laughing, Zannah hugged them both. "We need to celebrate."

"Yes, with lemon-lime soda and crackers."

After lunch and checking on Emma once more, Zannah returned to the waiting room, read her messages, flipped listlessly through a couple of magazines that were older than Emma and then sat and tried to stay awake. Because she couldn't keep herself from it, she brooded over everything that had happened that day.

The worry about the girls, then dealing with Emma's injuries, had pushed everything else out of her mind, but sitting quietly now, the memory of Brady's shocking plan came flooding back.

She knew she should be fair, should consider it from all sides. The problem was that she didn't feel like being fair. She felt betrayed. He wanted to carve Eaglecrest into ranchettes. She hated that word.

"It's a carved-up piece of a ranch," she muttered.

She was barely five minutes into her brooding when Brady strolled into the room. A combination of joy and annoyance flooded through her. He spotted her immediately and hurried over.

"How's Emma? Are you okay?" He sat down beside her and studied her face. "You look tired." He reached out as if he was going to take her hand, then thought better of it.

"So do you. It's been a long, eventful day." She told him everything that was happening with Emma, then said, "How did you get here so fast?"

"I left as soon as I got home. Juan and Phoebe took care of the horses."

"Why are you here, though?"

He shrugged. "I knew you'd need a ride. Sharlene called to say you were ready, so here I am."

"What if I'd decided to stay overnight in a hotel, like Casey and Vanessa?"

He shrugged. "Then I would have rented a room and waited for you." His smile flickered. "I brought my toothbrush."

Something about that statement stopped her and had her studying his face. He'd had exactly the same kind of day she'd had, topped off by a two-hour drive to pick her up, followed by another two-hour drive to get her home.

Touched by his thoughtfulness, she said, "Thank you. That's really nice. About this morning, Brady—"

"No." He held up his hand. "We're not going to talk about that yet. I'm tired, you're exhausted and nothing will be resolved peacefully after the day we've had." A muscle in his jaw worked. "We're not going to resolve anything in anger. And, to tell you the truth, Zannah, I'm done. I don't know what it will take to change things, but I'm done."

His words sent tremors of alarm through her, but he looked so grim, she only nodded. She couldn't give either of them more stress and worry today. She didn't yet know what "I'm done" meant, but his whole demeanor had changed. He no longer had the sparkle that new ideas and plans always seemed to bring to his eyes. In fact, he looked guarded. But maybe that was because the idea of selling off part of Eaglecrest was much bigger and more critical than something like trust exercises or golf on horseback.

What did it mean that he was done? Was he leaving?

"Okay, Brady. Are you okay to drive?"

With a fleeting smile, he said, "Yeah. You can sleep."

They said goodbye to Emma, Casey and Vanessa, then began the long, mostly silent ride home. He had predicted it correctly, Zannah thought, settling into the cushy leather seat of his sporty car. She was going to fall asleep immediately.

BRADY PULLED INTO a fast-food drive-through and ordered a cup of coffee. While he waited for it, he reached behind the seat and pulled out a light jacket. He spread it over Zannah. The air-conditioning wasn't particularly cold, but he needed something to do, something to prove to himself that he was taking care of her.

After he got his coffee, he pulled onto the road and started toward Eaglecrest, dreading when he would have to pull off the smooth highway and onto the ranch road that would certainly jolt her awake. But that was two hours away, and she would sleep peacefully until then.

He shook his head. When had he ever worried about a woman being awakened by a rough road? Never. But then, he'd never been involved with one like her.

Involved. In love was more like it. He'd felt it coming on for days. Maybe that's where the word *lovesick* came from. It didn't hit him like a thunderbolt. Testy encounters followed happy ones, each building up, compromise on top of compromise, one after another, into a solid foundation of love for her.

He was done fighting with her, having one confrontation after another. They had to find a way to settle things more easily, and he was going to tell her that when they were rested up and willing to listen to each other.

He hoped that was soon.

GUS STOOD IN front of his mirror and did something he rarely did—took a good look at himself. He'd shaved that morning for the first time in days and had gone into Raymond for a haircut. Maybe he didn't look too bad for a man nearing seventy who'd had more broken bones than he cared to count due to sudden meet-ups with the ground. Yeah, his hair was gray, but it was still thick. Physically, he was in good shape, and he looked pretty good, except that now he was dressed up like a dog's dinner and felt like a damned fool.

He was wearing his only good suit with a white shirt and striped tie, which he thought would strangle him. He couldn't seem to get the knot right. He started to jerk it off when someone knocked on his door.

As soon as he said, "Come in," the door opened, and his daughter swept into the room.

"Are you okay? Why were you headed home before—" She stopped and stared at him. "Why are you in your suit? You haven't worn that since—"

"Your mother's funeral. Yeah, I know." He tugged at the tie once again. "This is a special occasion."

"You mean because Emma's being released from the hospital?"

"That, too, but that wouldn't need a suit and tie."

"I can't think of anything that would." Zannah frowned at him. "It's a Thursday. What's so special about it?"

"I'm going to propose to Sharlene." He threw the words out there and waited for a reaction.

"Sharlene? What—?" She rushed to him and placed a hand on his forehead. "Did you experience sunstroke?"

He batted her away, but he found himself enjoying the look of worry and shock on her face. "No, of course not. I wasn't up there long enough for that. I'm serious. I'm going to ask her to marry me."

"What on earth makes you think she'd say yes?"

"She told me she loves me. I realized I love her and I've been a damned fool, so I'm going to propose. If she says yes, I'll help her run her inn. Now that you and Brady have Eaglecrest, I won't be needed here."

Zannah opened and closed her mouth a couple of times. She obviously needed a minute to process this.

"Come here, Zannie," he said and guided her to the desk chair, where she sat down with a bump.

He grinned at her and went back to wrestling with his tie, but he positioned himself so he could keep an eye on her in the mirror.

After a minute, she drew in a deep breath and asked, "Are you serious?"

"Serious as a parolee trying to impress a judge. I had some time to think while I was up there on Anvil Peak, which, by the way, I still think is the location of the mine."

"But you didn't stay and look for it."

"Got something more important to do."

"Like propose to Sharlene."

"Damned straight." He told her about the conversation he and Sharlene had before he left. Finally satisfied with the look of his tie, he turned away from the mirror to face her. "I'll go back someday to look—maybe Sharlene will come with me. Doesn't matter. I plan to spend the rest of my life making her happy. If she was courageous enough to tell me she loves me, then I should be brave enough to do the same."

"I don't know what to say."

"I didn't, either, but once you told me that Realtor seemed to be getting cozy with her, things clarified in my mind. I've been lucky enough to have two wonderful women love me. That's more than a lot of men get, and I hope I'm smart enough not to waste it. I love her, too. Thought for a long time it was gratitude for her faithfulness to Esther, to my family, this ranch, but that's not all of it. I want to spend the rest of my life with her. Love isn't something that should be squandered."

"That's the most amazing thing I've ever heard you say." She stood, tears forming in her eyes, and came to hug him. "If it means anything, you've got my blessing."

"That means everything, honey." He gave her another hug, then stepped back. "So do I look okay?"

"You look wonderful—happy."

"I am." He looked around for his keys, spotted them on the dresser and scooped them up. "I heard Sharlene finished work early and has gone into town. Is that right?"

"Yes. She also gave Joelle a list of chores that will keep her busy until her next birthday."

"Good! I had a talk with that little lady early this morning. I know she's sorry for what she did, although I'm sure the idea started with Emma."

"It certainly did."

He jingled the keys in his hand. "I'm guessing Sharlene will be at the inn."

"I'm sure she will be. Good luck."

"Thanks, Zannie. I'm hoping I won't need it, that good looks and charm will carry the day. But I think I'll stop and buy some flowers, too."

He heard her chuckling as he hurried out the door.

Half an hour later, Gus pulled up in front of the old Mosely house hotel. He didn't give himself time to think but jumped out of his truck and marched up the front steps. He could already see improvements being made to the old place. The yard had been cleared of weeds, and stacks of lumber occupied the space, covered with blue tarps, ready for use inside the house.

There was a car he didn't recognize parked out front, but he didn't speculate about the owner. He opened the door and hurried in, a bundle of yellow roses cradled in his arms.

"Sharlene," he called out as soon as he walked inside. "Are you in here?"

"Gus? I'm in the kitchen." Her voice came from the back of the house, so he strode purposefully in that direction, stopping briefly to smooth his hair and his tie.

"What are you—?" she started when she saw him but then stopped to stare.

As he'd expected, Jeff Denton was with her, the two of them standing close together looking at blueprints spread out on a beat-up old table. He gave the other man a challenging look, staking his territory.

"I need to talk to you, Sharlene." To Denton, he said dismissively, "Will you excuse us, please?"

"Sure." Denton looked from one to the other of them, then scooted away. "I'll see you later, Sharlene. Let me know what you think about these. I've got to go. I promised my wife I'd take her to lunch today."

He had a wife? Good, Gus thought. That made things easier. He watched the other man leave, then looked back at Sharlene. Stepping forward, he handed the roses to her, trying not to appear awkward.

"These are for you."

Sharlene took the flowers, but her eyes never left him, traveling from the tips of the highly polished dress shoes he hadn't worn since the last time he'd had on this suit to his fresh haircut, then back again.

"Gus." She sounded stunned. "What are you doing? Why are you dressed up? Did something happen?"

"Yes. I realized I've been a complete idiot and I came to say I'm sorry and see if you'll forgive me, marry me and let me help you run this place." He held out his hands as he went on, "The change of clothes is to show there's been a change in me."

"Oh, thank goodness," she said, laying the roses on top of the blueprints and walking into his arms. "It's about darned time."

ZANNAH WALKED TOWARD the office slowly, knowing she would find Brady inside. She thought about her conversation with her father. It took courage for Sharlene to admit she loved Gus, and it wasn't something to be squandered. It was a precious gift, one to be both given and received. She hoped she had that kind of courage.

When she reached the office, she paused to catch her breath, then turned the knob and stepped in. Brady looked up and came quickly to his feet, hurrying around the desk.

"Good morning. Are you okay?" He eyed her with concern.

"I'm fine. Are you?"

"Yeah. A little saddlesore from all that riding yesterday."

They paused, suddenly awkward, then they both spoke at once.

"I'm giving up on the ranchette idea—"

"You're right about the ranchette thing—"

They stopped and looked at each other.

"What did you say?" he asked.

"What did *you* say?"

"I talked to my dad," Brady said. "He's willing to give us a loan to do the road repairs. He'll give us reasonable terms. After that, I'll be a silent partner in the ranch, or maybe I'll sell to someone you can work with."

"You'll lose the challenge," she blurted.

"Doesn't matter. I thought I could do this, help run this place, make it secure, but obviously I can't."

The defeat in his voice caught at her heart. "No. That won't be necessary. I've—I've thought it over, and you're right. The best way for us to secure our future, the future of Eaglecrest, is to sell part of it." She held up her hand. "Though not river access to Lucas Fordham."

"Agreed. But why did you change your mind?"

"I realized that I've been hanging on to the past so much that I couldn't move forward. Being gone from here for years was the worst thing I could have done. It made me rigid about the ranch, wanting to keep everything the way it had been. I thought you wanted to change simply for the sake of change, but that's not true."

"I always had what I thought was a sound business reason."

"I—I know." She looked out the window where the mountains loomed, solid and secure. "I finally realized that my resistance comes down to the fact that I couldn't save my mom."

"I doubt anyone expected you to. Why did you think it was up to you?"

"Because I was twenty years old and pretty much convinced that the fate of the world— or at least the fate of this ranch—depended on me."

"You still think that," Brady pointed out.

"I know, but I've learned something from you."

"How to fall on your keister, or fall on your face, or—?"

She shook her head. "How to keep getting up."

"What do you mean?"

She cleared her throat, took a deep breath and plunged in. "One of the best things about you is that you always look ahead, always have new ideas. I'm guessing you get that from your upbringing, the way your family moved around."

"I guess so." His dark eyes were thoughtful. "Never really thought about it."

"You don't live in the past, but I have. So have Dad and Sharlene. I think it partly comes from living in a place where we've been for four generations. The past is as ingrained as the present, and in a way, it pulls us back."

"That's why you don't like change, because change means you have to adjust how you feel about Eaglecrest."

Zannah released a whoosh of breath. "I really do sound rigid."

"No, only craving stability." He stepped

closer. "If you agree to sell off part of Eagle-crest, what will give you stability, Zannah?"

Her heart pounding in her throat, she met his gaze. "You, Brady. I love you."

"Thank God," he said, pulling her into his arms. "I love you, too."

Their lips met in a rush of tender heat that warmed her all the way through. His mouth tasted sweet and welcoming. After a moment, he pulled away and began placing kisses on her cheeks and forehead.

"What are you doing?" she asked shakily.

"Returning the favor," he answered. "You made my wounds all better. I'm hoping this will heal yours."

"You're doing a fine job, but my lips feel neglected."

With a laugh, he returned to kissing those, as well, then eased her away from him and said, "I know this is sudden, but I got a call from my mom. My parents are going to be in Phoenix next week. I was thinking maybe we can take Joelle home and then you can meet them."

She blinked. "You want me to meet your parents?"

"Well, it's kind of traditional. I mean, I

know your family. Probably be a good idea for you to meet mine before the wedding."

"Wedding? Who said anything about a wedding?"

"I did. Just now. You've really got to start listening to me, Zannah," he teased, then grew solemn. "Will you marry me? A life without you would be grim."

She looked up at him, at the still-healing scrapes on his face highlighted by a flush of pink—the sunburn he'd probably picked up yesterday on the long ride home.

"Yes," she said, standing on tiptoe to reach his lips. "Of course." She smiled. "Will I be meeting your brothers next week, too?"

"No! You might change your mind about marrying me."

"Won't you want them for groomsmen?"

"Maybe. If they can behave. Of course, we'll probably have to really limit their time with our kids. No telling what they might teach them."

"Our kids?" She laughed. "There you go again, making plans for me."

"Yeah," he agreed proudly. "I'm getting really good at it."

"Oh, that's about to change," she responded,

wrapping her arms around his neck and pulling his face down to her. "Marriage is all about compromise."

"I'm good at that, too." He kissed her again, and she realized that this was the kind of change she would enjoy.

"THIS BARN HAS never looked so good," Gus observed. "I'll bet it hasn't been this clean since the day it was built."

Zannah straightened the full skirt of her wedding dress, clutched her bouquet in nervous fingers and slipped her other hand into the crook of her father's elbow. "It's perfect for a double wedding. I'm so glad you and Sharlene decided to do this with us."

"It's our pleasure, honey," Sharlene said from behind them. When Gus started to turn around, she reached out and gave him a gentle shove as she said, "Uh-uh, forget it, mister. You're not seeing me until the wedding starts, and they haven't played the march yet. Chet, you might have to make him obey," she said to the man who was giving her away.

"I'm all over it, Sharlene," he answered with a laugh. "But after this, it's all on you."

"I know. I'm so lucky."

Gus laughed and tightened his grip on Zannah's arm. "I'm the lucky one, Sharlene," he said over his shoulder.

Zannah looked toward the front of the scrubbed and decorated barn. Phoebe and her mom, Stella, had outdone themselves with beautiful bouquets of flowers and meadow grasses placed in stands along the way.

Before her were her bridesmaids, Joelle and Emma—now in a walking cast. Both of them were looking beautiful in teal dresses and fairly vibrating with excitement. As expected, Brady's brothers, Finn and Miles, were his groomsmen. They treated her nieces as if they were a couple of princesses, and the girls reveled in the attention.

She looked to where Brady awaited her at the altar, his smile full of pride and anticipation, his eyes full of love. No moment in her life had ever filled her with this much joy and happiness.

"You ready, honey?" Gus asked as the wedding march began and the guests rose to their feet.

"Oh, yes. This is a change I can live with."

* * * * *

Get 4 FREE REWARDS!

We'll send you 2 FREE Books plus 2 FREE Mystery Gifts.

Love Inspired books feature uplifting stories where faith helps guide you through life's challenges and discover the promise of a new beginning.

FREE
Value Over
$20

ReaderService.com has a new look!

We have refreshed our website and we want to share our new look with you. Head over to ReaderService.com and check it out!

On ReaderService.com, you can:

- Try 2 free books from any series
- Access risk-free special offers
- View your account history & manage payments
- Browse the latest Bonus Bucks catalog

Don't miss out!

If you want to stay up-to-date on the latest at the Reader Service and enjoy more Harlequin content, make sure you've signed up for our monthly News & Notes email newsletter. Sign up online at ReaderService.com.

RS19

If he saves her ranch
Will she lose her dream?

Zannah Worth loves welcoming guests to beautiful Eaglecrest Ranch. Unexpected new partners, not so much. Maybe the struggling family business needs Brady Gallagher's cash, but she can't tolerate his bossiness or his big ideas. Brady intends to turn a fast profit and win a wager. Zannah's wishes—and her stubborn heart—shouldn't matter. Though they keep butting heads, Zannah wants them to move forward...together.

CATEGORY: **HOPE & INSPIRATION**

$7.25 U.S./$8.25 CAN.

ISBN-13: 978-1-335-88963-8

50725

EAN

Wholesome stories of love, compassion and belonging.

HARLEQUIN
HEARTWARMING

harlequin.com